# A Veil of Blood Hangs Over Africa

## The Birthplace of Slavery

*"Those who deny freedom to others
deserve it not for themselves."*
—ABRAHAM LINCOLN

# A Veil of Blood
# Hangs Over Africa
## The Birthplace of Slavery

## Lucia Mann

Grassroots Publishing Group

Grassroots Publishing Group™
9404 Southwick Dr.
Bakersfield, CA 93312

10 9 8 7 6 5 4 3 2

First Edition 2015

Printed in the United States of America

ISBN: 978-0-9794805-7-7

Library of Congress Control Number: 2015908088

Cover & book design by CenterPointe Media
www.CenterPointeMedia.com

# Dedication

I have personally heard the voices of the many broken hearts and crushed souls forced into servitude. This book is dedicated to all victims of slavery, past and present, who were and are being cruelly *murdered* by the unconscionable trade in human flesh. May their memories live on forever and change the world we live in.

With their voices forever stifled, I now lend them mine.

# Acknowledgments

It is not an easy thing to revisit the ugliness of slavery's past or the ongoing existence of modern day slavery, but I couldn't have written this book—or my other related books without many talented professionals to help me.

The author gratefully acknowledges Nesta Aharoni—my friend, publisher, and superb editor at Grassroots Publishing Group—for not only correcting my age-related grammar hiccups, but for strongly believing in me and supporting me.

*Many thank-yous to the many friends who
have supported me over the years:*

CenterPointe Media for bringing *life* to the covers and interiors of my books.

Simon Wallis for valuable research continuities.

Ruth Orcutt for her proofreading eyes, which never miss a misplaced or absent comma.

Gale Detta for being my ambassador and orator when my voice has faltered into tears.

Nicole Jeannot Picasso, the sister who I never knew existed, until now. I love you.

Maureen Kelleher, my film producer. Thank you for making my dreams come true.

For all my Facebook fans. I am humbled by your praises.

Last but not least, my husband, Hector, who has put up with my writer's tantrums for too many years to count.

# Table of Contents

**PART TWO**

**1927–1950**

# Table of Contents

# Introduction

*"If men and women are in chains anywhere in the world,
then freedom is endangered everywhere."*
—John F. Kennedy

The abominable *history* of slavery has not yet pricked the world's collective conscience ... because slavery *still* exists.

Modern day slavery is a larger problem than it was during the legalized slave trade from Africa to the Americas. According to the U.S. Justice Department, slavery has become the second fastest growing criminal industry worldwide, just behind drug trafficking.

Slavery is a $32 billion industry, and half of those enslaved are children. It is almost impossible to buy clothes or goods anymore without inadvertently supporting this reprehensible trade.

Global slavery, in all its forms, is predicated on the reprehensible exploitation of other often helpless or ignorant human beings for material and personal gain. Why, in a supposedly enlightened age, does slavery still exist? The practitioners of this inhuman trade lack a conscience and moral center. Would they enslave their own children for money? Probably. It speaks poorly of the human race that such predatory individuals are not more effectively curtailed and brought to justice.

# Preface

*"Every one of us should be ashamed to be
free while his brother is a slave."*
—FREDERICK DOUGLASS

---

### - HISTORICAL FACTS -

❖ In 1653 in the Dutch colony of Capetown, South Africa, Abraham van Batavia became the area's first slave. Slavery lasted there over 180 years, until 1834, when the practice was abolished in all British colonies.

❖ On August 1, 1834, all slaves in the British Empire were emancipated by the Slavery Abolition Bill passed by both the House of Commons and the House of Lords. In reality, though, they remained slaves—indentured to their former owners. The obscenity of one human owning another continues in the twenty-first century.

---

❖ The estimated number of slaves transported from African homes to European colonial possessions in the Americas ranges from 9- to 15 million people.

❖ In 1776 the American Declaration of Independence stated, "We hold these truths to be self-evident, that all men are created equal, that they are endowed by their Creator with certain unalienable Rights, that among these are Life, Liberty, and the pursuit of Happiness." In 1865, with the passage of the Thirteenth Amendment to the Constitution, Congress abolished slavery within the United States, but this amendment did not result in the equality of all men.

❖ According to the United Nations today, there are more than 27 million slaves worldwide. This is a far higher number than those enslaved over the 400 years of transatlantic human trafficking to the Americas.

# Prologue

*"The white man's happiness cannot be
purchased by the black man's misery."*
—FREDERICK DOUGLASS

It has been historically documented that certain transatlantic slaves did not shed a tear during or after capture. Instead, they sang full-throated, cheerful songs to soothe the sorrows of their hearts. "Only an aching heart is relieved by tears," one young Mandinka slave proclaimed. "My heart is not aching … it is grieving for the loss of a rightful life to walk freely on the land of my birth."

This profound statement of grief was brought to life in 1840 to a sobbing, pregnant eighteen-year-old captured from a remote Upper Volta village in West Africa six years after the abolishment of slavery in the British colonies.

Her West African name was Mabali. Her slave name, Maisie. Her daughter, Nobuntu, went by the slave name is Netty. This is their story.

Remember their names, for they will be immortalized for all time.

# Part One

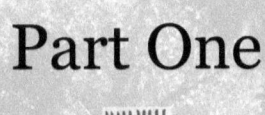

## 1784 - 1883

# CHAPTER ONE

# The Hallworthy Estate, South Africa
## -1840-

*"The travesty of slavery isn't just physical abuse,
but the moral abuse of looking at human
beings as if they are less than an animal."*
—ANONYMOUS

It was late November, a month into an African summer that guaranteed thunderstorms. On this starless evening in the British colony of South Africa, not even a restless spirit could have journeyed through the foreshadowing night. A darkness like no other descended over the Valley of a Thousand Hills, a scenic, hilly area west of the Port of Durban. One could *touch* the blackness of the midnight-quiet that swathed the vast Hallworthy estate like a burial garment.

A piercing howl shattered the ominous shroud. Was it an alpha wolf calling to the pack? No. It was the sound of raw, human fear: "*N deme!*" Mabali, age eighteen, howled in her native Mandinke tongue. "Help us! We have been captured by *toubabs* and are being caged like wild animals."

Part of her felt as if she was living a slow-motion nightmare.

The rest of her, as if she were suffering through an agonizing wakeup call. Her earsplitting cries for help continued incessantly until a small, shackled hand reached out for stillness. "Please stop, Amma. You are hurting my ears, and no one is out in the dark listening to you," a child said, her voice filled with pain.

Nobuntu, age five, was right. The baying sounds of her mother's anguish drifted mournfully into space. They went unheard beyond the thickly mortared walls of the abandoned brick-and-stone building set on mud flooring. The loathsome owner of the vast Hallworthy estate, Lord Nigel Hallworthy, had ordered the ten-by-ten-foot construction years back for his scent hounds, Rhodesian Ridgebacks and German attack dogs. The windowless structure, half a mile from the Lord's homestead, was deliberately positioned according to an entry in his journal:

*To convert a savage to the proper English way of life is impossible. Even the strongest of us cannot bear their odor. I cannot have savages, none of whom have decent hearts, living in proximity to my house and upsetting my guests. Africans are not entirely human. They are just a short step up the evolutionary ladder from apes.*

Would the denigrating, evil Lord be bothered by Mabali's cries, which were loud enough to shatter rock? Not in a million years! His newly acquired malodorous beast-apes might as well have been trapped on another planet. No one could hear them.

An eerie silence descended within the "doghouse," which was rank with the odor of vermin and human excrement.

Nothingness!

*Time stood still.*

Ultimately, the abysmal darkness of the thunderstorms transformed into a bright and sunny day.

Slumped on the mud floor, having been unable to sleep a wink, Mabali, barely five feet tall, rubbed her tired, puffy eyes. The crushing truth of her whereabouts tumbled in her head like a hamster on a running wheel. Her tribal life left her unsophisticated and ignorant about the rest of the world. She didn't *fully* grasp what was happening to her and her daughter or understand the depth of the unfolding tragedy. She focused on one thing only—*food!* Mabali and her young offspring had not eaten in three days. While the *essence of time* had played a familiar and important role in her West African village life, it did not exist here. Nor did the stark reality that roaming freely through the natural beauty of her village's surroundings no longer existed.

With great mental effort, Mabali detached from her helplessness and tried to make sense of what was happening. Reflecting with eyes as dry as a desert, it seemed unimaginable that she and her daughter, after weeping through the trauma of their capture and transport, would end up as prisoners in a strange, foreign place, tied up like animals for slaughter. It was a sad reality for two wretches who were alone, hungry, and scared.

Mabali became preoccupied with secret, consuming worries: Would she and her child ever taste the sweet smell of freedom again? Would she have the opportunity to accuse her captors of their crimes? Would the prophecy Agosi delivered on the slave ship—that the spirit of her dead son would return and avenge the wrong committed against his mother and sister—ever be fulfilled?

Ultimately, vengeance *would* come, but not from a disembodied entity.

Retaliation *would* come from a person Mabali could never have imagined.

Mabali's life had been stolen. Dreaming is what now occupied her time. Swallowing hard, she felt unable to stop the whimpering in her heart, or the cascade of salty tears flowing down her cracked, thirsty lips. She allowed her weary mind to return to *that* ill-fated day over a month ago, during the West African dry season … to the time of her capture when her adrenalin-charged inner voice shrieked at her to "*Run, run, run!*"

The cold moisture of the mud floor penetrated Mabali's bare buttocks and instantly returned her to the present. "*I could have chosen to flee—to save myself,*" she muttered.

Mabali's glum musings were interrupted by a sharp shudder passing through her body. Was it a jolt of guilt, shame, regret, or the weight of what *could* have happened to Nobuntu and the others who were left at the mercy of the slave traders? What had prevented Mabali's natural survival instinct from triggering her to run? She wasn't brave, but she was tenderhearted. Her next act would make up for her earlier failings.

Mabali shuffled her bottom over the packed mud to where Nobuntu was curled up in a ball on top of some moldy hay. The young mother stroked her precious daughter's feverish forehead and wondered, "How could I ever have contemplated running away?" Mabali could never have lived knowing that her running would have caused her daughter unspeakable harm. Mabali began sobbing like a baby until, once more, a hand reached out. "Amma, please don't cry. We have each other."

Mabali's tears blended with her daughter's. The young mother exhaled slowly. Her daughter's devotion was touching, and it filled Mabali's heart with pride. Nobuntu's support renewed Mabali's depleting strength.

With her legs spread apart, Mabali drew her daughter close. Embracing her child, she whispered, "I love you, daughter, more than life itself."

Nobuntu smiled and tenderly patted her mother's tear-strewn face. As if nothing else in the world mattered, she said in a sing-song, nursery rhyme voice, "Tell me a nice story, Amma, like you used to back home."

Mabali sighed heavily. It was a struggle to permit herself to feel a natural tendency to crease her face in a smile. She stroked her daughter's unwashed face and began:

"Two gray monkeys came down from the sacred tulip tree to help a little bird that had fallen out of its nest …"

Light snoring ended the fictional tale.

But there was no escaping their predicament: she and her daughter were powerless in their abductor's clutch. *Their* fate depended on *her* strength and protectiveness. She would give up her life to save her child's.

Mabali's oath to sacrifice herself for her daughter lingered in the waiting room of time to come.

What had brought this young African mother and child, classified as subhuman by traffickers, to this appalling hellhole on the Hallworthy estate was clear ... *money!*

What Mabali did not know was that earlier, in 1833, the Slavery Act had passed, abolishing slavery. Yet the blatant disregard for the law—the continued unconscionable trade in human flesh—continued to be as unstoppable then as it is now.

Mabali bore immense pain in her spellbinding, ebony eyes as she scooped a handful of reddish clay from the floor and squished it through fingers. Distressing thoughts trickled into her consciousness: "I am holding the lumpy mud of this wretched place. Will I ever again feel the soft earth and fine sand of my homeland? Will I once more feel the river clay squish playfully between my toes? Will I sense soothing sun rays on my back, or feel my husband's breath close to mine as we lay together at night?" Her husband was her everything ... her untapped strength ... soul mate ... the reason she breathed hope. His love sustained her. He called her his "precious treasure."

A big cause of Mabali's heartbreak lay in a question that had no answer: "Will I ever bear another child to replace the baby I lost on the ill-omened sea voyage?"

Mabali's tears flowed from a bottomless well. Her untroubled wilderness life had vanished, and she did not know for how long. Right now it felt as if her life would never be as it was. She had little choice but learn to survive in an insane world of greedy economics. The question was this: How deeply did she wish to survive?

Mabali *had* arrived at the journey's end—hell. In her traumatized mind, the dead captives who had accompanied her on the journey were better off in their disembodied states. On the verge of mental collapse, Mabali's tortured musings came to an end as the hand of Mercy gently caressed her eyes and closed the doors to her pain.

In dream sequences, Mabali returned to the life she had left behind.

# CHAPTER TWO

# Bobo Tribal Village, West Africa
## -1840-

*"The worst sin toward our fellow creatures is not to hate them, but to be indifferent to them: that's the essence of inhumanity."*
—GEORGE BERNARD SHAW

Sixty days before Mabali's imprisonment on the Hallworthy estate was a day like any other for the Bobo females of a remote West African oasis settlement—chores, chores, and more chores. But it was also the day that their monotony was replaced by terror. Daily village commitments would soon become the farthest things from their minds.

At the first streak of daylight on a fine summer morning, the world changed … in an instant. A massive *haboob*—dust storm— engulfed their village as it churned and howled with winds that felt strong enough to blow the feathers off a chicken.

The Mandinke-speaking dwellers of this leaderless, self-ruling community had never before witnessed such powerful winds. The villagers disappeared into their huts as if their lives depended on it. The angry dust storm lashed their compound, blacking out everything that stood in its destructive path. Miniature sand dunes piled up against the walls of their huts, and a thick layer of swirling dust coated their thatched roofs. The foliage of the succulents they lived among changed from green to the color of cement. The only things missing from the newly designed scenery were Lawrence of Arabia, Bedouins, camels, and scorpions.

The *haboob* abated as quickly as it began.

Mabali, whose name means "flower" in Mandinke, waited for the wind to stop howling before she stepped outside of the small, round, peak-roofed hut she shared with her husband, Kofi, and their daughter, Nobuntu. She spotted her elderly neighbor, with broom in hand, tackling a mountain of dirt.

"Good morning, Agosi," Mabali greeted. "It looks as though we have a lot of cleaning to do." Agosi, age fifty-eight, turned her eyes heavenward and commented. "God Wuro worked hard today. He sends his blessing by sweeping away evil forces with his strong breath."

Mabali heaved a long sigh. She was a little over five months pregnant, and she had waited so long for this second baby. She didn't have the luxury of stopping her work to wonder why she had not conceived before now—or whether the God Wuro had anything to do with what had just happened. *Time was of the essence.*

Behind her hut, she raised her ankle-length cotton dress above her waist and squatted to empty her near-bursting bladder. A smile creased her pretty face when her baby soccer-kicked within her five-foot frame. She massaged her belly to calm the child within, and laughed. Was the baby hyperactive because she had gorged herself on kola nuts, which contained high levels of caffeine?

Her chuckles mingled with the dust, until more serious thoughts took over. Her unborn child's antics and the earlier sandstorm were of little concern now. *Time was of the essence.* She had numerous responsibilities to accomplish: collect firewood (a forty-minute round-trip journey); fetch water from an oasis spring well; grind and make maize porridge; sweep the hut of ants, spiders, scorpions, and ticks.

Yet unknown to Mabali, a different type of invader—a nightmarish, two-legged creepy-crawler—would soon arrive that could not be casually swept away.

Mabali's head was filled with everything she had to accomplish. If time allowed, she would weave cloth on a handmade wooden loom, now that she had a new baby on the way. His or her clothing was a priority. *Time was of the essence.* All these domestic tasks had to be completed before Kofi, her eighteen-year-old hunter-gatherer husband, returned with the evening meal. He had departed well before sunrise with the purpose of gathering enough seasonal wild plants and bushmeat (feral mammals, reptiles, and birds) to feed five mouths: himself as well as his wife, daughter, and elderly grandparents. Mabali expected him home, as usual, by late afternoon.

During the five years since they were married, Kofi had arrived home late only once. On that hapless day, he had speared a charging feral boar that had sent him flying into the air. Kofi landed badly, but luckily, no bones were broken. He did sustain an injury to his right ankle, though, which swelled like a dead hippo. Unable to walk without excruciating pain, Kofi flushed with embarrassment as he was carried to the village on the back of a fellow tribesman. The accident definitely slowed down the hunters' return that day. Kofi did not hear the end of it. "Ah, children, wanting to be like us grown men!" one hunter laughed.

"They think they know all there is to hunting," another chuckled.

"Well, this is a lesson learned from stupidity."

"Don't you know that a wounded creature has the speed of a cheetah?"

"One must wait for the kill until the blood has left the animal's body."

As the sounds of village life returned—crickets chirped, birds sang, monkeys called, brooms swished, and chatter continued—Mabali rose from her squat. She was about to return to her hut when, for no apparent reason, she looked skyward. A deep frown creased her forehead. "What is happening?" she questioned.

It appeared as though what she saw was about to swallow her up. Hovering above her was a large, ink-black cloud. It began drifting downward and then froze, as if glued to its spot. Mabali could not believe her eyes. The formation appeared darker than a starless night. She had witnessed many other dark clouds drop buckets of rain, but this was the *dry* season! How could this be? Was Wuro in a happy mood? Maybe he *was* about to deliver some much-needed rain? Mabali hoped so because the children, especially Nobuntu, loved to dance open mouthed as they sucked in falling droplets.

Mabali was soon joined by other villagers who stood like

statues as they gazed upward. Everyone gasped when the anomaly unexpectedly displayed a veil of grotesque red. The sky appeared to be bleeding.

The talkative Agosi, with mouth agape and eyes wide, did not utter a word. And the other scared faces dared not speak, either, of the possible message from their God Wuro.

Agosi, who was the Bobo's elderly, revered prophet, finally spoke. "Something bad is going to happen. Why else would the sky bleed?"

Questions spewed from frightened mouths.

"What will happen, Agosi?"

"Are we going to die when the blood spills from the cloud?"

"Our men are gone," an anxious woman cried. "What will they do when they return and find us drowned in blood?"

The old woman wrung her hands and bemoaned, "If I had the answers, I would give them to you, but I do *not* feel this is Wuro's doing."

Agosi inhaled sharply before concluding, "It is a sign of something worse than death!"

Mabali watched her tribespeople lower their heads and slink away to their huts, just as they had during the sandstorm. Then she lost interest. She was not going to become transfixed in happenings that had no answers. She fluttered her lips percussively, determined not to spend another minute in contemplation. The sun was rising fast, and *time was of the essence.*

"Chores don't get done by themselves," she mused.

Should Mabali have given more thought to Agosi's prophecy? Was the red veil really a shroud of blood? Was it a bad omen, or was it *Kwere*, the God of destruction, simply toying with them?

Sadly, a mantle of death *would* descend before sunset, but it would not appear out of the strange cloud formation or from unseen beings.

In her childhood, Mabali had feared the God Kwere, who, according to Bobo belief, could punish those who broke strict tribal rules. Now grown, she was not convinced of the supposed consequences gods visited on miscreants. After all, she had broken more than one rule and had never been punished by an unseen hand. What's more, she had not always been the most obedient wife, and worse, she had had eyes for another young man in the village who was married and untouchable, as was she.

Mabali headed toward her child.

Inside the hut, fast asleep on a straw mat on a dirt floor, Nobuntu continued to snore. Mabali gently shook her shoulder. "Time to get up, girl child," she said in a firm, motherly voice.

"If we do not fetch wood for our fire," she continued, "and collect water from the oasis spring, we will not eat breakfast today."

The child's woven-hair blanket rolled as Nobuntu turned over. She opened her big brown eyes and yawned so broadly she nearly locked her jaw. She then mumbled, "Yes, Amma. I will hurry."

Nobuntu threw off the bed covering and rubbed her doe eyes, still heavy with sleep. She headed for the urination area and, like her mother, hoisted the long dress she wore both day and night up to her waist. Her mother had weaved two dresses for her. This one, adorned with a plant-dyed crocodile print, was her favorite. In days to come, this distinctive dress would leave a permanent imprint on her father's heart.

Nobuntu straightened her dress and returned inside. With a beaming "I'm-ready" smile, she said to her mother, "Let's go."

Mabali could not help but beam with pride. Her sweet daughter was adorable. She had been an easy newborn: slept through the nights, never cried excessively, and had no teething troubles or illnesses. Mabali sighed. Nobuntu was growing up too fast for her liking. Her new baby once more kicked her insides. Soon, she thought, another child would bring her comparable joy. Although her love for her firstborn could never be replaced, it could be equalized.

The day Mabali had announced her pregnancy, Nobuntu had responded, "When my sister comes into this world, I will take good care of her, and she will become my best friend."

Mabali smiled. "What if it's a boy child?"

Nobuntu made an "ugh" face. "Then I won't have anything to do with him! Boys are *nasty!* They always pull my hair and stick out their legs to make me stumble and fall."

Mabali's laughter bounced off the mud walls. Funny, she had felt the same way about boys at that age.

Mabali loved being a mother and wife. Nobuntu and her husband were the loves of her life. As she thought about sharing her love with another tiny soul, Mabali shivered with excitement. She hoped it was a boy. However, deep down, she didn't care about gender. A child was a child—to love and protect unconditionally.

Her motherly instincts would be tested before the day was out. Her happiness was to be short lived.

With the sun warming their dark-brown faces, Mabali and Nobuntu headed away from the settlement. It proved to be the start of a beautiful day. The strange cloud formation had vanished and been forgotten. The air was filled with full-throated singing that matched the marching beat of twenty bare feet—all females, both young and not so young. Two newborn babies were strapped to their mothers' bosoms. No one in this cheerful group could have suspected another dark cloud would appear—one that would not vanish so easily.

After a twenty-minute trek uphill, the firewood gatherers reached the wide-ranging semi-deciduous forest, which was teaming with chattering gray monkeys. These primates were revered—never to end up on a meal plate. They were the guardians of the dead who were buried in this forest. This magical place also held the guardian of them all—a sixty-foot tulip tree. Exclusive to this area, the mystical tulip tree produced magnificent clusters of bright orange-yellow flowers year round.

Because the Bobo believed tulip trees housed the spirits of their ancestors, these trees were venerated. They acted as focal points for tribal ceremonies and offered places for the tribespeople to commune with their dead. The sacred tree's health was tied to that of newborn children. If the tree declined, the mother concerned was obliged to seek medical attention for her child. In the past, Mabali had spent time there, begging the sacred tree to speak on her behalf to the fertility spirits. She asked for the right to bear another child, as none of the herbal medicines had helped.

With a broad smile adorning her pretty face, Mabali stroked the trunk of the sacred tree and whispered: "Thank you. I am with child."

*Time was of the essence,* so Mabali set about the work she had come to the forest to undertake—foraging for twigs and branches. Busy as she was, she had a bad feeling in the pit of her stomach.

A couple of hours later, with her firewood bundled and balanced on her head, she and the others began heading out of the forest. Before they reached the open clearing, though, their normal day came crashing down …

A deafening sound, like none they had ever heard, halted the women and children in their tracks. Mabali, in the lead, turned around and motioned her followers to silence by clamping her hand over her mouth. Intuitively, Nobuntu sensed her mother's fear and scrambled beneath her long dress, wrapping her arms in a vice grip around one of her mother's legs. Most of the other young children followed suit with *their* mothers.

Mabali was so scared she did not feel Nobuntu's fingernails stab into her bare flesh. The eighteen-year-old stood still with the other villagers. They were quiet as mice as their eyes darted nervously from side to side.

*Boom! Boom! Boom!*

Hysteria swept over the females as repetitive, thunderous rumbles followed by the *whss* of bullets sent most of them dropping like rocks to their knees. Terror gripped them. The children's knees knocked as they remained hidden under their mothers' dresses. Mabali was the only person standing upright. Why, she didn't know because she also felt her knees were about to give way. Paralyzed with fright, Mabali stood rooted like a tree. She had never heard gunfire before. "*Run, run, run,*" her inner voice screamed. "Run back into the forest, and the sacred tree will protect you ..." It was now or never.

Mabali's survival instinct was halted by the sound of a choked scream, much louder than the gunshots. She turned to see if she could make sense of the cry. The other women also turned toward the shrieking girl. Even though the hidden children thought they were invisible—their ears were keen! Their cries joined the orchestra of panic.

From out of nowhere, several ghostly, dead-eyed men flanked the horrified Bobo females and raised their weapons to fire. To Mabali and the other primitive souls who dared look at the men, the scene would have been intriguing if not for the dire circumstances they were in.

The men were attired in single-breasted frock coats with three buttons, white drill collar vests, and drab trousers. Their stylish straw fedoras, which normally decorated the heads of politicians and others with social status, seemed inappropriate.

Though unsure of what was happening, Mabali sized up the intruders. Undoubtedly, they were *toubabs,* those pasty-faced white men the storytellers had spoken to her of when she was an impressionable child. She remembered how some of the ghastly tales had caused her fretful, sleepless nights. Today, those toubab nightmares seemed surreal. But Mabali still had no idea how wicked the white race could be.

Afraid for her life and the lives of the others, Mabali's insides trembled as she imagined the mortal bite of a black scorpion. A tsunami of uncertainties surged within her: "Where did the *toubabs* come from? Did they fall from the sky? Were they hiding under the dark cloud? What are they doing here? What do they want? If they did not fall from the cloud, how did they get here?" Only camel traders from the north had traversed the treacherous rocky trails that lead to their remote Bobo settlement, and those traders had ceased coming long ago.

Mabali's wandering mind rushed back to the present when a pudgy man, his shirt bursting with rolls of fatty tissue and his backside large and unsightly, waddled forward, raised his weapon, and aimed it at Mabali. Standing inches from the scared mother-to-be, the overweight man said in a menacing voice, "Don't make me kill you. If you give us any trouble, you *will* die. Is that clear?"

Mabali squinted. She hadn't a clue what the man was saying. Nor did the other females understand his foreign tongue. All of their stomachs were knotted in fright. The kneeling women, with shoulders drooping and heads lowered submissively, began mumbling miserably—sending help-prayers to their god Wuro.

Mabali did not join them in their prayers, even though fear coursed through her veins. Instead, she thought, "Don't give the fear power over you. Be strong."

In an instant, as if she had swallowed a magical warrior potion, Mabali's fear vanished. Her mental paralysis also washed away. She clenched her fists until her knuckles whitened, straightened her back, and became the giant she had always wanted to be. Her eyes flashed ember red as they made contact with the "lard man" who had delivered the foreign-tongued order. She replied, "I do not understand your language, unhealthy-looking man. Who are you? What do you want? Why do you scare us, appearing as ghosts with iron rods of thunder?"

The lard man, with his shifty glare locked on Mabali, suddenly turned his head as if he were searching for someone. Laying his eyes on one of the men in his party, the lard man ordered him to "Come here!"

Behind the four encircling white men was a man Mabali hadn't noticed before. A deep frown furrowed her brow. She weighed him up as if she were buying a prize bull. This man was different from the others. He was tall with a humped, muscular frame. He had long arms that seemed to stretch past his knees. His skin tone and deep-set eyes were as black as coal, and he was wearing a full-length, desert traders' robe embroidered with bright colors. A Turkish Kufi cap rested on his head. The outsider coolly sidled up to the fat man, whose glare of repulsion reverted back to the brazen Mabali. He spat out words to the interpreter. "What did the whore *midget* say?"

"Big Boss, I think that *I*," he emphasized, "should communicate with them. They cannot possibly understand your language." He spoke in a falsetto voice unlike any other Mabali had ever heard. It sounded neither male nor female. His bizarre tone and misshaped body could have belonged to an ancient culture. A reliable eunuch, perhaps, who fiercely guarded his master's harem at the risk of his own life?

"Go ahead, *darkie!*" snapped the lard man. "Isn't that why I'm paying you?"

The Arabian-looking man, a camel trader, bent his body in half towards tiny Mabali's right ear. In a genderless voice, he cautioned, "Listen carefully, girl. You are now prisoners of the all-mighty *toubabs*, and you are coming with us. Don't give them any trouble, or they will shoot you dead."

Mabali yanked her head away from the foul-smelling, cat-litter mouth that had delivered the ultimatum.

"*Coming with us!*" she spat. "What do you mean by that? Who are you? You speak our language, but why do you accompany these pasty-faced men and give orders to women not of your tribe?"

The spokesman released a throaty, evil chortle that sent chills down Mabali's spine. Before she could ask another question, he disclosed a bone-chilling fact: "You healthy women, girls, and children are going to make me a very rich man."

"What …?"

Suddenly something happened.

Pandemonium broke loose when unexpected trickery ensnared the prisoners. A heavy, knotted rope-net descended on them like a cloudburst. None of the women had spotted the preset trap when they had entered the forest. Now the sheer weight of the heavy ropes buckled Mabali's knees, sending her body crashing to the ground. Squished under her rotund mother, Nobuntu cried out, "Amma, you're hurting me!"

With difficulty, Mabali shifted her pregnant body off her distressed child and muttered, "Sorry, beloved child. Amma did not mean to hurt you."

Nobuntu's pleading eyes searched her mother's face. "Can we go home now?"

Mabali found herself in a vacuum of uncertainty. How could she answer her daughter when she wasn't sure herself? But there was no doubt in her mind that they *were* in terrible danger. So she murmured a warning in her daughter's ear. "I don't *really* know what's to become of us, but do as you're told, sweet girl, and you won't be harmed."

"Amma ..."

Mabali placed a finger to her daughter's lips to silence further questioning.

But *her* mouth was not going to be silenced. Her eyes sought the harem man's and locked on to him like a deer in rutting season. "*Traitor!*" she raged. "You are nothing but animal dung beneath my feet!"

The man's chest shook with laughter—the same mocking amusement that had sent chills down her spine earlier. This time, the sound did not ruffle her feathers. Her mind focused on survival. How and when depended on opportunity.

But for now, imprisoned by the net, thoughts of escape evaporated.

Within forty minutes, the tethered females were yoked with wood restraints designed to harness plow animals. Each captive, including the children, was shackled in iron chains to the left foot of the person to her right. They were herded out of the forest like bovine plodding to auction.

As they neared their homestead, the elderly people who had stayed behind stood still and stared, their arms folded. Their disbelieving eyes were glued to the slave coffle being led past the compound wall.

Although the group had been trapped like poor creatures, Mabali was not going to be muzzled. Before they passed out of sight of her village, she bellowed, "Old women, tell our men when they return that we have been kidnapped! We're being taken away to who-knows-where by these ugly *toubabs* ..."

The next sound to escape her mouth was a bone-chilling howl.

The braided rope-and-birch whip looked like a horse whip, but thicker. It was intended to tear flesh and draw blood at every stroke. The whip cut deep into Mabali's left shoulder blade. Within seconds opportunist flies began to suck her raw, bleeding flesh, making the pain even more unbearable.

"Make her see sense!" screamed her attacker, the lard man, to the black man.

The slave trader's long fingers dug deep into Mabali's injury. She let out a deafening howl of pain. He released his grip and brought his diabolical face close as he gave her a cautionary warning: "*Silence,* woman!" he hissed. "Not another sound or I'm going to kill you right here, right now. *Or* maybe I will kill the child that clings to your clothing. Is she your daughter?"

His chilling remark made the hairs on the back of her neck rise like porcupine quills. Her reaction was rage. With fire in her stomach, she retorted with glaring, murderous intent, "You will *never* silence me, traitorous black man ... servant of the pasty, white people! If you touch a hair on my child's head, I'll gut you like the animal you are."

There was a momentary silence. Then chuckling rained down

like poisonous gas, as did the weapon of admonishment—the bull whip.

Mabali felt pain shoot through her shoulder and back. Her agony swept silently up to the heavens. As did the high-pitched, alarmed cry of her daughter, who wore her mother's hurt like a precious necklace. "Mother, did that bad man hurt you? When I grow up, I'm going to kill him, like Father does the forest creatures."

Nobuntu's revenge did not escape Mabali, whose pride surged for her caring, protective daughter.

Emotionally overwhelmed, Mabali cautioned her daughter, "Hush, child. Do not give these evil *toubabs* an excuse to bring the strap of pain to you."

"Yes, Mother. I will listen to you," Nobuntu responded respectfully.

Unable to cover a torn, bare breast, Mabali wept softly. Her bust had never before been exposed outside the marital hut. Her confidence and brazenness were vanquished by excruciating pain. As she numbly shuffled onward, her sad-eyed child gripped the back of her dress. It appeared that the happy world they had once shared was disappearing.

While this impression was close to true, their ordeal was far from over.

A distance away, Mabali imagined she heard the shrill cries of the old Bobo women who were powerless to prevent the *toubabs* from taking their loved ones.

Within the village compound, wails of despair swirled, but they were silenced by the matriarch, who turned her head in the direction of the sacred forest. "I am going to the forest of dead souls to ask our ancestors what we must do to bring our loved ones back."

While most cheered in acceptance, one person did not.

"Your old legs are long dead, Sister. You will not make it back alive. I'm younger than you and will take your place under the sacred tulip tree. I will beseech our ancestors for help."

Many eyelids stretched with incredulity.

The two sisters, almost blind, were only a year apart, and neither was fit to walk anywhere or see anything!

A few hours before sundown, in preparation for the evening meal, the menfolk returned with dead creatures and sacks of edible plants draped on their backs. Mabali's teenage husband, Kofi, was the first to learn of the abduction.

"They are all gone," wailed the matriarch, whose old legs could not have carried her anywhere.

Kofi threw his hands in the air in disbelief. Nothing like this had ever before shattered the village's peaceful existence. With his mind in hazed confusion, Kofi turned to Jata, his grandfather, who was as blind as the sisters, and whose legs were also troublesome.

"Old man," Kofi said, "with your knowledge extending beyond this earth, tell me who did this and why."

Kofi did not like the reply. He gasped, "*Toubabs!* Are you sure?"

Kofi repeated the dreaded word many times before reality sunk in.

"*Time is of the essence,*" he proclaimed to the hunter-gathers.

"We will find them. I am confident."

How naïve!

Without further ado, the frantic men set out on a hunt—this time to rescue their loved ones. They wasted no time in tracking the women's footprints to the Volta river estuary just as the sun was sinking.

During their hurried, arduous trek, the men were barely aware of the screeching buzzards circling overhead. Their minds were focused. They paid no heed. Had they looked up, they would have seen scarlet, blood-stained feathers, and beaks dripping with muscle sinew that had been plucked from the dead. At the edge of the riverbank, the tribesmen noted muddy depressions similar to those left by slithering crocodiles. Though the phenomenon puzzled them, their loved ones were nowhere to be seen.

Their women and children had inexplicably disappeared.

One of the tribesmen, who had wandered off alone, spotted something and yelled, "Over here … come over here!"

Kofi raced to the spot. There, grappling with mixed emotions of hope and fear, his body stiffened as he stared down at the disturbed mud. He hoped it was a hallucination, or maybe laundry left at the riverside by an unknown tribe.

But there was no doubt.

The clothing, piled like the shredded skins of molting snakes, belonged to their Bobo women and children. Shock turned to anger and then to sadness as Kofi rummaged through the clothing. The fresh blood stains on his wife's apparel chilled his spine. He examined the sticky patches on the torn dress and lifted the garment to his nose. "It can't be," he thought. Yet, he recognized her unmistakable scent. The perfume she made from the crushed flowers of the tulip tree wafted up to his nose. Normally, Kofi was a passive man who seldom showed emotion, but this day his heart broke into a million pieces, and he wept unashamedly.

No one had ever seen Kofi sob before. Today was different. As Kofi clutched the crocodile dress his daughter loved so much, his despair became unbearable and his tears continued to flow.

Suddenly, Kofi's body braced. He had been taught from childhood that crying was a weakness. Surreptitiously, he glanced around him to see if the other men had noticed his sobbing, but none of the other men scoffed at the tear-streaked husband and father. They, too, were sorting through the pile for identifiable clothing. They, too, shed tears. But as quickly as their emotions surfaced, their faces set with resolve.

*Time was of the essence.*

After continuing their search through the moonlit hours and into morning sunrise, the men became overcome with exhaustion. Plagued by fatigue and mental strain, they had no choice but to return home.

Upon arriving at the village, none of them wanted food or any other comfort, not even homemade alcohol. They wished only to be left alone with their thoughts. Following a short period of stunned silence, a panicked flurry of questions spewed forth:

"Nothing makes sense," said one man, warming his cold, sore feet over the fire pit.

"Our women do not swim like we do," another chipped in.

"How could they vanish in the water? They couldn't all have drowned!"

Kofi threw his arms up in frustration. "How is this possible, that the *toubabs* arrived at our *unreachable* settlement? Not even desert traders or marauders find their way here anymore. The shifting desert sands have seen to that. Besides, if they had been walking this land, we would have encountered them during our hunt!" Drained of reasoning, Kofi postulated, "If the *toubabs have* taken them ..." He paused and felt some doubt before he continued, "... where to? If the women *were* taken through the desert, we would have seen their footprints heading out of the village."

"They couldn't have *walked* on river water," said another hunter-gatherer.

"They must have been taken in a boat, but to where I do not know," another piped up.

While it was natural for other tribes living near rivers to travel by boat, it was not natural for the Bobo. They had no reason to travel that way. Their drinking water was from a spring in their backyard.

One of the most burning questions in the men's minds was, "Why are our women defiled by nakedness?" Silence was the only response.

Too many whys and what-ifs boggled the minds of the tormented men. Would they ever see their loved ones again?

The menfolk, with bowed heads and numb minds, did not notice the woman whose legs could not carry her approach. She gently tapped Kofi's shoulder. "I will cast a spell. Your wife and child *will* return to us."

Kofi did not respond. He couldn't think straight, and he felt tears building at the back of his eyes threatening to embarrass him again. His sigh was heavy with helplessness. Throughout the remainder of this ghastly day, the disappearance and fate of their loved ones weighed heavily on the tribal members. That is, until Kofi could no longer cope with the heartache.

The Bobo have lived a nomadic, hermit-like existence in West Africa since 800 A.D. This particular settlement was challenging to reach because of the miles of desert terrain and rocky hillsides one had to cross to get there. Narrow game paths provided barely enough room for a camel to pass. The Bobo had heard from a camel trader who had conquered the obstacles many years ago of big boats waiting at the Ivory Coast to transport African men, women, and children to parts unknown, as slaves for the *toubabs*. This seemed unbelievable to a tribe of uneducated innocents. None of them had ever seen a canoe, rowboat, ocean, or seafaring vessel.

Kofi's grandfather's explanation was steeped in superstitious rites dominated by evil spirits and witches. No one suspected the truth except old Jata, who believed the tale of the slave ships.

With his shoulders hunched and arms folded tight, Jata let out a long, croaky sigh before bluntly stating, "Forget about your women now. They are *toubab* slaves. They are servants of the white race. You will never get them back."

Gasps shot like stars racing across the heavens, from all except Kofi.

At Jata's revelation, Kofi's head pounded with denial. He stood up and stamped his feet in anger. Jutting his neck muscles forward like an angry puff adder, Kofi vowed, "I will hunt down the people who have taken our women. I will gut them open like the carrion they are." He inhaled deeply and exclaimed for all to hear, "I love her. I won't stop until I find her."

To all who knew him, Kofi was a spirited young man whom Jata had declared blessed by Wuro, their creator God. Hadn't Kofi proven over and over again that he had received Wuro's gift?

As a toddler, Kofi's life had been saved from fire. At ten, he had rescued his three-year-old cousin from a male baboon's clenched mouth by poking out the creature's eyes with a sharp stick. At eleven, he had saved the village from a raging brush fire by getting everyone to dig a trench outside the compound wall and fill it with water from cooking pots. He even insisted the villagers urinate in the ditch to raise the water levels. At twelve, he had been mauled by an antelope, and had walked home with flesh hanging from his legs, insisting it was nothing. He had the strength of Samson and could lift weighty objects without buckling at the knees. At thirteen, he had picked his own wife, contrary to tribal customs. Only elders had the right to select couples, but that rule hadn't fazed the head-strong orphan boy.

Kofi's parents had died tragically when he was ten months old. Embers from a cooking fire outside their hut had ignited the strands of braided straw that acted as a door. The flames had quickly risen to the overhang of the grass-thatched roof. Inside the windowless home, unable to escape the fire, Kofi's parents had perished from smoke inhalation before the flames could be doused. Baby Kofi was spared. How was that possible?

Depressions dug into the earthen floor were a common

practice of the tribe, designed to keep babies cool in the blazing summer temperatures. This custom spared baby Kofi, even though he had been entombed by the flames that had swept over the cured hides of his cover. At the time, Jata had offered an explanation as to why Kofi had not perished. "Wuro has saved this child for a divine purpose."

From ancient times, Bobo men, women, and children of age were taught to believe in spiritual forces. Wuro, the first man created by their God, was a hunter-gatherer who had asked for a companion. Thus it was that their tribe was born. Subsequently, Wuro withdrew, leaving behind his three sons: Dwo, the helper of humankind; Soxo, the spirit of untamed Nature and the bush; and Kwere, the dispenser of such punishment as sunless days, dark clouds, and lightning—but never fire! If further angered, Kwere could send visible evil spirits—malevolent deceased humans—hell-bent on making Bobo lives miserable until the day they died.

This fear of evil forces was always in the minds of the Bobo.

The tribe lived in a region of Africa where life depended on rainfall. Generations before the Islamic doctrine swept through Africa, the Bobo had exercised a series of purification rituals that helped them bond with Nature. They saw Nature as basically good, a sharp contrast to the ambivalence with which other tribes viewed Her. By building shrines and fashioning wood and fiber masks resembling the creatures of their land—warthogs, buffaloes, hornbills, black birds, fish, antelope, and serpents—the Bobo endeavored to erase evil and reinstate balance between sun, earth, and rain.

On the day of the abduction, Kofi did not join the others at the sacred shrine of their favorite god, Wuro, to pray for the safe return of their loved ones. Silently, Kofi cursed Wuro. The tortured young man no longer accepted the divine being as a good, protective deity. Instead, he saw Wuro as an inhumane, cruel god, like his brother Kwere, who relished pain and suffering.

As hunter-gatherers, Bobo males were the breadwinners of their tribe. But the women worked equally hard to survive the daily challenge of the intense, ever-changing, African climate. Droughts were common as a result of 120-degree heat waves. Locust plagues were frequent—devouring all life-sustaining plants—and an ever-present danger. Although the short wet season produced torrents of rainfall, it wasn't enough for long-term cooking and washing needs. A daily three-hour trek to the river was the alternative. The tribe lived on the edge of survival. Not collecting enough edible plants in one meager season could result in a year of hunger, despair, and death.

Kofi had grown up with Mabali, an orphan who had lost her parents to a parasitic disease. He had no doubt *she* was the one for him. At the tender age of seven, when the pair was sitting in the shade of the thatched roof of his grandparents' home, Kofi grabbed Mabali's hand, much to her horror. Squeezing it tightly, he declared his love and his intention to marry her one day. Mabali hurriedly withdrew her hand, laughed, and looked at him as if he had two heads. "Why would I marry someone shorter than I am and who is as ugly as a boar's backside," she teased meanly.

Mabali thought of the other village girls, most of whom had one thing primarily on their minds: *marriage*. But that was not Mabali. She was the exception, hoping to one day leave the village for good. She dreamed of finding a "better" village where back-breaking work and near starvation were not daily occurrences.

Today, as a captive, Mabali did leave her birthplace, but not of her own free will.

By age thirteen Kofi's height was a fraction over five feet, and the likelihood of his growing taller was slim. The village's diminutive, pint-sized tribespeople were the result of inbreeding. No one in the village was tall, and the limited gene pool made Mabali and Kofi close blood kin.

Knowing they were of small stature would not have made an impression on these bushpeople, who thought they were as tall as trees.

On that "proposal" day under his grandparents' roof, Mabali's hurtful words had stung Kofi's male pride. Nevertheless, he wasn't going to be defeated by his size.

"Yes, I am short, Mabali, but I am as strong as any grown man here. You will need a strong man to hunt and take care of you."

Mabali flashed an "I don't care" face and then spitefully pointed out that she would be much in demand for marriage and had already received compliments that she was the most beautiful of all the girls.

And she was.

Mabali's petite facial features *were* captivating: a small, flattened nose; oval face; eyes the color of black pearls; tiny ears; and a flawless, dusky complexion. Her head of undisciplined hair was her only resemblance to the rest of the villagers. It stood straight out, as if she had stuck her finger into an electric socket. Nothing could tame it—not even the warthog fat commonly used by the village women to manage unruly, knotty curls.

In the end, Kofi got his wish to marry his sweetheart.

Mabali didn't have much choice. She couldn't say "no" because Kofi's grandparents, her adoptive parents, had the last say in the matter. It was their "right" according to tribal custom to hand her over to whomever they thought fit. They had the right to hand her in marriage to their grandson. Her adoptive parents wanted nothing more than to see these two wed before they departed the earth.

Mabali and Kofi were married in a ceremonial forest gathering. They were both thirteen—the coming of age. There was little doubt to those who knew them that Kofi loved the girl-child he had grown up with. Hadn't he sat patiently outside his grandparents' hut while she underwent the mandatory twenty-one-day purification rite? Other boys in his age group typically ran away until it was over.

*All* Bobo females followed and obeyed the rules of purification, a sacred ritual that was taken seriously. Women who did not follow the principles of this rite were regarded as unclean and, therefore, unfit for marriage. When a girl came of age, she was mercifully spared genital circumcision, a practice rampant among other tribes. Instead, with the onset of her first menstruation, she began a twenty-one-day purification.

In preparation for the ritual, the tribeswomen collected small, yellow, scaly flowers from the rubia cordifolia shrub, a bitter flowering plant of the cocoa family that was native to the region. They prepared a porridge-like, foul-tasting concoction that the girl ate for seven days. The young woman was directed to stay in her hut accompanied only by her mother. If her mother was deceased, another woman of the family (Kofi's grandmother for Mabali) would attend to her. "Purification" girls were not allowed to be seen by anyone else, although sometimes they were allowed to have one girlfriend with them for support.

Prior to her purification, a Bobo female did not have to perform any village tasks for a period of time. When she came out of confinement considered clean and renewed, the tribe limited the number of days she could interact with men.

The Bobo believed that menstruation is a process of cleansing the body and that females should be left alone by men for seven days. Afterward, the woman is considered fit, once again, for sexual intercourse.

While boys did not undergo any specific ritual, they had to prove themselves from the age of eight onward. They were put through grueling tests: running for three hours to strengthen their leg muscles, sitting quietly for hours in the boughs of trees, outswimming the many crocodiles that frequented the river. All this demonstrated they were strong enough for the daily hunt.

On the morning of their wedding, twenty-eight days after Mabali's purification, a deep carpet of green velvet grass swayed in the morning breeze. Kofi, the "prophet," and Mabali, the "princess," were dressed in elaborate woven outfits and colorful head wraps. Wearing traditional face masks, the couple entered the forest while the other villagers trailed behind. Later, standing under the canopy of the massive banyan fig tree, Kofi adjusted his banyan-wood mask sculpted to resemble the male buffalo. His bride-to-be concealed her pretty face with a carved hornbill mask covered in the aromatic, delicate, orange-and-white flowers of the sacred tulip tree. Beneath her ornate mask, Mabali hid a secret. Her lips were curled in a disgruntled snarl, and her black pearl eyes were dull with unhappiness.

Marriage was supposed to be the most significant event in a woman's life, yet Mabali was livid at being *forced* to marry an ugly boy she did not love—or intend to respect and obey, as the Bobo culture decreed. Mabali had made up her mind that, sure as there were evil spirits, that she was not going to subordinate herself to her husband despite the tribal rules that bestowed Bobo men a higher status—even higher than older women. Regardless of a young boy's age, the women were required to respect him.

While the couple stood under the sacred tulip tree, not a word was uttered between them. Silence was respectfully maintained during the ceremony, which was followed by feasting, dancing, animal sacrifice, and a blessing to ensure the couple's prosperity.

Mabali tuned the festivities out. Her mind took her, instead, to a quiet inner place of relief. Eventually, she *would* have a change of heart.

Almost a year later, their daughter, Nobuntu, was born. Mabali became an attentive, doting mum. There wasn't a moment she didn't proclaim, "You are the best thing that has ever happened to me, girl child. I will protect you with my life."

Her absolute love for her firstborn eventually extended to Kofi. Her roving eye had long been stilled. Kofi became the love of her life. She showered him daily with tender smiles and genuine affection. Even though she had not yet given him a son, he could not have been happier … until now.

Following the kidnapping, the sullen, grief-stricken, "widowed" men realized they had to resume hunting if they were to prevent the remaining tribe members from starving.

And so their lives continued.

Kofi had no interest in the hunting activities he once enjoyed. His wretchedness pushed his emotions out of control. He hid the depth of his despair in homemade alcohol. His resulting mental fragility caused him to become irritable and anxious, with mood swings and sleep deprivation. Long hours of wakefulness brought Kofi to a breaking point. Life without his family was meaningless. His world grew darker and darker.

A concerned friend told Kofi, "It will get better. You will take another in marriage, like I will soon. Then life will go on once more."

Kofi struggled with his feelings every minute of every day. He couldn't move forward. He couldn't live as if nothing had happened. The loss was too much for him to bear. He had known Mabali all his life, and her disappearance left him inconsolable—a tortured soul full of blame. He felt he had failed to keep his wedding vows—to protect Mabali and his future children from harm. It was impossible for him to continue living.

Would Kofi recover from his emptiness and depression?

No.

Another tragedy would soon strike a cruel blow on the "recovering" Bobo tribe.

Two days later, well before sunrise, Kofi crept into the forest. He was determined to get relief from the torture of remembrance. He didn't notice the large, jet-black cloud that hovered over the forested area, the same type of cloud Mabali saw the day of her abduction. If he had looked up, would he have hesitated? Would he have changed his mind?

No.

Familiar with his surroundings, Kofi located a creeping, exotic plant called the calaba bean, known locally as the "doomsday plant." A poison made from its seeds was often used in village trials to challenge the innocence of an accused. Those who survived the plant's toxin were proven innocent—an extremely rare event.

With a handful of crushed seeds clenched in his fist, Kofi approached the banyan tree of his wedding ceremony. There, he lay down on a carpet of leaves. With his eyes pointed heavenward, he swallowed the poison and ended his life.

"A swift death is better than the prolonged agony of not knowing," he thought.

As he lay dying, Kofi whispered his final words, "I can't live without you, my darling wife. I will always be with you. We will be joined once more."

Was Wuro watching over his prodigy?

Would the Bobo deity intervene and protect Kofi from the poison he ingested?

Clearly, he did not!

Kofi's lifeless body, with a bloated belly and arms clutching his wife's and his daughter's clothing, was found that same evening. A look of peace rested on his cold face. His corpse was surrounded by a gathering of gray monkeys that snapped up insects daring to feed off Kofi's decomposing flesh. In the highest branches of the banyan tree, another troop of monkeys was keeping the vultures at bay with loud *oo-hoo-hooh ah-ah-ah* screeches.

Village members wore fearsome tribal masks to chase away evil energy that might be lingering at Kofi's death site. Then, the ceremony of the passing of the dead into the underworld was performed. Once the tribe was satisfied that no malevolent spirit would steal Kofi's soul, they buried the broken-hearted boy under the wedding tree where he had begun his married life.

If only he had known that the god whom he had turned his back on *did* intervene—not for him, but for Mabali.

*She* would be the *rare event,* a survivor of a different kind of poison—racial hatred. That is, until she joined millions of other souls in the veil of blood.

# CHAPTER THREE

# The Infamous Outbuilding, November
## -1840-

*"Death is better than slavery."*
—HARRIET ANN JACOBS

Inside the hellhole, shortly before midday, Mabali opened her eyes and surveyed her surroundings. "Where am I? Why am I tied up in this strange building?" The present collided with the past. She and her daughter were prisoners, objects of profit, human trade goods driven by the darkest forces of humanity. No words could express how she felt being trafficked for greed.

As Mabali faced the unknown, she never could have imagined the future that lay before her and her daughter. She did, however, suspect the worst—death.

"I want to die on my own terms," she said to herself, rocking from side to side. "It is the only thing left of my miserable life in a cage."

Mabali had no idea that her and her daughter's fate was going to be worse than death.

She glanced at Nobuntu, who was touching the collar that restrained her bloodied and bruised neck. The girl reached for her mother's hand and gripped hard. "Amma, why does this new necklace hurt like crocodile teeth? I want my other one, the one you made from sparkling stones."

A solitary tear rolled down Mabali's dirt-encrusted face as her fingers wiped away the blood that trickled down the nape of her firstborn's neck. "—Nobuntu' means *human kindness*," she thought, "yet no kindness or compassion has been shown to my child, from the moment of our capture to our imprisonment in this dank building that invites rodents to run freely over our feet." Despite the cruelty they had endured, they could at least draw comfort from each other. However, Mabali had lost the ability to protect her child. She had not been able to combat the evil that had captured them, and she could no longer clothe their bodies. Her mind cried out, "Breathe … breathe … bring calm for your child."

Unlike other African females, Bobo females, regardless of age, always covered their arms and legs with suitable attire: dresses woven from mud-cloth—a cotton fabric dyed with fermented mud and decorated with intricate patterns of animals, such as lizards, tortoises, and crocodiles. They also wore head wraps made of long pieces of fabric draped over their hair. Their dress communicated respect for their menfolk.

Now dehumanized, Mabali and Nobuntu wore the ultimate shame—nudity. To their owners they were just naked bodies without names.

"I'm not no one … I am *Mabali*," her head screamed. "And my daughter's name is *Nobuntu*."

Looking into her child's sad eyes, Mabali whispered, "Hush now, girl child. As soon as we get back to our village, I'm going to make you the most beautiful sparkling necklace ever."

For the first time since their capture, Nobuntu grinned. But the grin was quickly replaced by a drooping lower lip. "Amma, I'm thirsty and my belly is grumbling for food."

"We'll get something to eat and drink soon," Mabali lied.

Nobuntu fell silent.

Not having had a drop of water or a bite of food for some time, Mabali prayed for the heavens to open and shower rainwater through the building's broken rafters. But rain was a tall order. The rainy season had long passed in this part of the world. This was the time thunderstorms delivered forks of light—nothing more. Not one morsel of foreign food had passed over their tongues since they were brought here. Mabali closed her eyes and imagined the Bobo cooking pot sitting above the fire, bubbling with the day's critter catch. Her nose wrinkled. She could smell the meat stew.

For no perceptible reason, Mabali's body suddenly stiffened like a corpse. She couldn't move a muscle. Terror invaded her being. She was so scared she could hear herself breathing. It felt as if a spirit had entered her body and instructed her to close her eyes for the last time—to die and join someone in the afterworld.

"Who could it be?" she asked herself. People died all the time in the village. Mabali gasped disbelievingly. In her mind's eye, she envisioned the deadly bean associated with suicides. "No … no … no," she cried. She knew it was Kofi who had invaded her physical being.

She wept for the man she loved and would never see again.

But she wept also for herself. How had she arrived at this journey's end—this gateway to evil?

# Chapter Four

# Diaspora

*"I call heaven and earth to witness against you this day."*
—Deuteronomy

The enforced walk was much harder than anything the captives had ever known. It was an agonizing march. Their legs weakened and their children stumbled. They were not strangers to long treks. They routinely walked long distances to collect spring water and firewood. But back home they had had the freedom to stop when tired. Now, with straining, painful calf muscles, Mabali thought the trudge would never end. This lengthy route had been circumnavigated to the Bobo village and now from it by their kidnappers, but *they* wore comfortable walking shoes and carried open umbrellas.

Through tearful eyes, Nobuntu walked alongside her mother, whimpering. Her blistered feet were smarting, and her mouth was dry. Not a drop of water had passed through their parched lips since their forest capture hours ago. The woozy child tugged her mother's dress. "Amma, I'm thirsty. Give me water, please," she said between sobs.

Mabali's first reaction was to invent an excuse, but instead she said honestly, "I don't have any at the moment, child. Be patient."

Mabali, too, was feeling woozy, but it was the blood-sucking mosquitoes feasting on her open wounds that drove her most crazy. She tried to take her mind off her discomfort by reflecting on the life she had left behind, like the daily trips she took carrying a large gourd filled with fresh river water balanced on her head. She could smell the water. She could hear the villagers singing. She saw her daughter, a sweet girl who loved everyone, playing joyfully in the village confines with other children …

Her memory of happier times ended. Now all she could smell was her fear and helplessness. The reservoir of her memory had run dry, just like the pool of freedom that used to quench her thirst.

Back in the *now*, shrieking sounds from above brought Mabali's anguished mind and dehydrated body back to earth. Like large black flies, opportunistic vultures circled overhead, biding their time. Already, the hot sun had claimed the lives of two parched older women and three babies. The babies' bodies were tossed into passing shrubbery, as if they were discarded fruit pits. The winged scavengers were going to feast on this tragic day.

Mabali envied the independence of the birds. Maybe they could teach her how to fly and return home for help!

They were now down to *fifteen* live wretched souls.

Mabali cried silently for the dead. There would be no funeral ceremony for them, no kind words inviting the departed souls to return and watch over the living. But her melancholy for the dead vanished when she heard lapping water. The sight of river water brought shrieks of delight from the remaining tribe members. They hurriedly shuffled toward the elixir of life. But it was impossible for them to bend down in unison.

In the coffle's lead, Mabali was the first to slip and fall, which brought the rest of the group down with her in a domino effect. Like human crocodiles, the captives slithered to the water's edge and filled their bellies to bursting. The action was too much for one fifty-year-old woman. For her, the life-saving water was a deadly elixir. She began to heave violently, finally choking to death on her vomit.

*Fourteen* wretched souls.

Sadistic peals of laughter rang from the slave traders, followed by hissing whips. The prisoners' former delight at the sight of water turned quickly into hysterical wailing. The lard man stopped the mayhem by screaming above the din, "Take off your clothes. You will be boarding this rowboat." With meaty hands, he pointed toward them, then mocked, "As naked as the day you were born."

His black cohort translated. Faces turned pale with shock. Mabali felt fierce anger. Hatred consumed her. "*Toubab*," she spat. "You have taken us away from our families and homes. You are not going to take away our dignity as proud Bobo women. We will *not* remove our clothing."

An intimidating voice punctured the air. "We will see about that!"

*Boom … boom …*

Two teenage girls lay dead. Their bloody, gaping bullet wounds sent the head slaver into a fiery rage. "Are you crazy!" he screamed. "You have just lost me twenty-eight English pounds. That's on top of the money I lost on those who have already croaked!"

The impulsive shooter smirked. "We still have *that one*." He pointed to Mabali. "She has a baby in her belly ... so, two for the price of one!"

The lard man threw the shooter the evil eye. "You take another shot without my permission, and I will shoot you myself."

The shooter quietly scoffed, "If I don't get you first, you son-of-a-bitch!"

There was no love lost between these two men. From the moment they had learned they would be working together, their character differences sparked verbal whiplash.

*Twelve* wretched souls.

After the murders, there wasn't a captive standing at the river's edge whose insides weren't knotted with fear. Mabali's heart hurt with guilt. What had she done? If she hadn't protested, the poor girls would still be alive.

"Was modesty worth it?" Mabali asked herself.

She glanced at her daughter. "Oh, no!" her insides screamed. "Nobuntu could be this madman's next victim."

With her heart beating like a drum, Mabali tried to help her daughter. "Please, toubab, take me, but let my daughter go free. She is only a child and not well in the head," she lied, hoping the false affliction would stir compassion. "Let her go back to our village unharmed."

The answer was not what she expected.

Weapons aimed at both their heads buckled Mabali's knees. Fear overpowered her outspoken ways. Her tongue became glued to the roof of her mouth ... for now.

Parted from their clothing, the last remnant of their tribal identification, the naked females lowered their heads submissively to their bare chests and boarded a rowing craft, a seventeen-foot dory.

"Let's get a move on, the lard man ordered the rowers. If we miss the damn boat, there will be no wages."

*Time was of the essence*—to make good rowing time, sail upwind, to their intended midnight rendezvous.

Back at the water's edge, the smiling camel trader, clutching a cloth bag stuffed with coins, waved to everyone as if he were seeing them off on a summer vacation. Mabali wanted to kill him with her bare hands. "Traitor!" she hissed under her breath. She silently cursed, "You are going to get what's coming to you one day. You are tainted with the blood of innocents. I pray that the evil spirits hear me and end your life before the cock crows."

Her wish was granted.

Walking back to the secluded area where he had tied up his camel, the wicked trader of human flesh was stung by a deadly scorpion. He died a slow, painful, paralyzing death.

The scavengers in the air took advantage of *another* easy meal.

As the last of the day's sun beat down mercilessly on the bare women, sweat poured into their eyes. The rowboat began its journey along the south coast of the African bulge to their destination, Abidjan, a small fishing town that would eventually become a major port. Awaiting their arrival was a seafaring vessel, an astonishing sight to the captured women. With sails billowing, it looked like a gigantic hornbill bird with huge white pupils. To Mabali's primitive mind, it looked as though an evil wind god had taken a bird's form. She tried not to let fright overcome her, but her insides did not comply. She, like the rest of the weary travelers, shook uncontrollably with trepidation. Whimpers and whispers followed:

"What is this huge bird?"

"Why are we being led into its mouth?"

"Are we being scarificed to the *toubabs*' god?"

But the main question on all minds was this: "Where was *their* tribal god, Wuro?"

Mabali worried, "Has our tribal god forsaken us? Wuro had not rejected Kofi when he was a boy. Kofi was a proud member of the god's flock." The image of her husband triggered her to shed cascading tears that coalesced with her worrisome thoughts. Life as she knew it was over. At that moment, Mabali was clueless as to her fate ... but intuition nudged her.

Her future would not be good.

The assaulting smell of brackish air and salted fish were new scents to the prisoners waiting to board Lord Hallworthy's brigantine. The new odors drifting from the dock were somewhat refreshing to the bedraggled slaves, but that would soon change.

At the quay, fishermen going about their business did not bat a curious eye when the dark souls lined up in front of the sailing vessel. It wouldn't be the first time that *brown* people were brought to this tiny fishing inlet to head for parts unknown. The fishermen carried on with their activities as if the bodies were a mirage. They had seen it all before.

The sorry group of naked Bobo continued to stare fearfully at the unfamiliar object bobbing on the ocean. Lit with numerous lanterns, the privately owned brigantine was a small vessel decked with oars and sails. The ship was the most common type of sailing craft of its day, with two masts. These ships were popular in trades that required windward ability such as slaving and piracy. Brigantines were capable of speeds up to 11 knots.

On the forward deck, with the ship's lantern at his back, Captain "Red" Rory Wallace presented a memorable sight. Though he had left the British Royal Navy ten years earlier, after being transferred to the British Colony of South Africa, he still retained an expensive and personalized naval uniform. A fine wool frock coat with gold-laced buttons and white facings adorned his barrel chest. Golden braided epaulettes denoting a captain status added an impressive touch to each shoulder. A frilled white shirt, immaculate white trousers, shining calf-length black leather boots, and a dashing captain's hat completed his costume. Unfortunately, this elegant attire failed to disguise his short stature, marked paunch, and unruly red hair, which matched his temperament. His once neatly trimmed beard and moustache were now somewhat overgrown and ragged. A prow-like, pocked nose and ruddy complexion stood testament to the march of time and, no doubt, to liberal consumption of dark navy rum.

During his commissioned days he had run a tight ship as he carried slaves to a life of forced labor.

> *In the 100 years ending in 1810, British vessels carried about three million slaves to a life of forced labor abroad. How many were brought to the Port of Durban before and after abolishment is not documented.*

There was a reason they called him "Red" Rory. In his day, he had been a martinet in the finest tradition of the Royal Navy. The sixty-year-old captain was still a commanding presence as he cast an anxious glance toward the promenade. He exhaled so loudly his lips quivered. "Where are they?" His surreptitious human cargo was well overdue. He cracked his knuckles with impatience. *Time was of the essence.* He *had* to set sail before he aroused unwanted attention. His crusty annoyance soon turned to relief. "At last, they are here."

At dusk he spotted the naked figures who were about to board his pristine ship. He wasn't expecting *females*! And from what he could see, females who scarcely reached five feet tall. His orders had been to bring back twenty healthy, strong *bucks*.

The knuckles of his clenched hands turned bloodless as Red Rory yelled down the gangplank, "Not another step, mister!"

The captain's menacing command stopped the lard-man *herder* in his tracks. "They are clearly *pigmy women*! Where are the young *men*?"

Before the herder could reply, the captain turned his back and ordered a sailor, "Bring a stronger lamp. I want to see more clearly."

With the lantern high, Captain Wallace was momentarily speechless. When he found his voice, he said, "I will not allow these stinking *savages* to come on board my ship." A spray of angry saliva hit the salty air as he continued to rant. "What were you thinking?"

"Look here, sir," the lard man responded, evading the last part of the captain's question. "Have you any idea how far we've come and under what conditions? I was ordered to bring slaves to you, and that's what I'm doing! And I'm sorry we are late, but it took us longer to find their village, and we didn't see one man or boy!"

"Damn, damn, damn!" the seething captain swore. His head would be on the chopping block if he didn't bring *something* back. Sailing empty-handed was out of the question. The vessel's owner, who had ordered male slaves, was an insanely evil man, and Wallace didn't want that monkey on his back.

"Wait there," Rory commanded.

He addressed the members of his crew, whose mouths were open as wide as the ocean inlet. "Pump water into buckets and get these filthy creatures washed. Snap to it."

Thirty minutes later, salty ocean water stung Mabali's wounds, but it was a relief from the itching she'd endured from the many insects that had invaded her torn flesh. Nobuntu thought the water was a new game. She cupped her chubby hands and brought the droplets to her mouth. Immediately, she gagged. "Amma, the water is bad! I want good water. I'm thirsty."

Mabali remained silent. She had promised more than once that drinking water would come. Her excuses had long dried up.

There would be no pity for these human beings who were looked upon as *apes*, not humans.

Icy-cold seawater continued to rain down on the captives until all the buckets were empty. Captain Wallace ordered the soaked women below deck, but not before counting heads: "*Twelve!*" he screeched. "The order was for twenty slaves, not twelve!"

In the lantern's glow, the fat man looked sheepish as he mumbled his reply. "We did capture twenty, Captain, but some died along the way. Ten guineas a head is what we agreed upon. So I'll take my pay and be on my way."

Wallace shook his head thinking, "Oh boy! My employer is not going to be happy about this!"

Slavery wasn't a perfect business, and this *order* for slaves had been bumbled. Wallace was still puzzled by why they had to travel as far as West Africa. Before this disastrous trip, they had simply crossed from Natal into neighboring Zululand and captured *young men*, according to the slave owner's shopping list. The owner of the new batch of wretches being forcibly transported across seas was a wealthy English lord—Nigel Hallworthy.

"Well, sir, there is nothing I can do about it," the slaver said, interrupting the captain's musings. "Like I said, some died."

The problem of explaining this turn of events at the Port of Durban was in the back of Captain Wallace's mind. Naturally, he would blame the blundering, idiotic hired men. As to why *he* had let the women on board, he had a simple answer. In his opinion, females could run just as fast as males—the conclusion being that

Hallworthy's sport had no gender!

Money wasn't the captain's biggest prize. The thrill of the hunt was. And not for traditional wildlife prey. Wallace enjoyed being part of a two-legged manhunt!

"The females will have to do!" the captain mumbled under his breath. What choice did he have?

The kidnappers set off after counting their money, leaving Rory to wonder how he was going to explain the sparse cargo ... and its gender!

Rory had had many dealings with Lord Nigel over the years, and he was painfully aware that this relative of Queen Victoria was an arrogant sociopath whose mood could change from happy to foul in an instant. Hallworthy was indifferent to the rules of law-abiding citizens; he was a criminal who got away with breaking laws. In a perfect world, the Lord would have been prosecuted for his deeds, but Lord Nigel Hallworthy was the richest man in Natal. He flaunted the law—thought nothing of handing out bribes to those who might or might not inform on him. But then, who would *dare* inform on a member of the royal family?

Even though the Lord was a soulless man who led a parasitical existence, Rory felt him to be a kindred spirit. Lord Hallworthy had no empathy for black human beings, whom he referred to as savages and *apes*. Nothing showed in his eyes but darkness.

# CHAPTER FIVE

# Lord Nigel Hallworthy

*"The Prince of Darkness is a gentleman."*
—SHAKESPEARE, KING LEER

In the late 1700s in Germany, Nigel was born Frederick Otto Wettin. At age twenty, he sported his newly inherited title, Lord Nigel Hallworthy. He was over six feet, slim, with a full head of golden hair. His blond mane was always smartly parted on the side, and his matching moustache was neatly trimmed. His intoxicating, Germanic, cobalt-blue eyes were his most attractive feature. And he was a ladies' man. Clicking his heels at women came naturally to him. He often attracted furtive peeks, not only from unattached females, but from married ladies alike. Little did these infatuated women know that Nigel was a shell of a man without compassion, heart, or soul. Money, a princely sum, enticed ladies into the eligible thirty-year-old widower's life—not his insincere charm. He inherited considerable wealth, including a stately home in Yorkshire, England, and vast lands in South Africa and Germany.

The young Lord of the Manor steered clear of the many gold diggers who were attracted to him, and he frequently fobbed off introductions to the daughters of his wealthy friends, whether they were beautiful or unattractive. He wasn't going to forfeit his bachelor freedom for a roll in the hay. He paid courtesans for that favor.

Nigel was no stranger to death. As a matter of fact, death intrigued him. Murder was an obsession. Before he turned forty, he would commit unspeakable horrors—crimes against human-ity—that were surreptitiously swept under his ancestral, wealthy rug.

Nigel's *untitled* mother had died in childbirth. And three months later, his *untitled* father went out of his way to seduce and eventually marry an extremely wealthy English widow, Duchess Gertrude Hallworthy, ten years his senior. She was besotted. He was not!

Throughout their seventeen years of marriage, the long-suffering Duchess turned a blind eye to her husband's sexual liaisons with many of the female servants who lived in the quarters below. And thanks to her blind eye, his scandalous and adulterous behavior never reached the ears of the many upper-class guests who visited their home. The day after their eighteenth wedding anniversary, the couple was traveling to a celebration for a close relative. On the way, they met their demise in a freak accident. The carriage overturned, crushing them both to death.

Nigel immediately inherited the Hallworthy fortune—and the Hallworthy title.

The *new* Lord Hallworthy was economically savvy and, like his deceased father, went about enjoying his inheritance and the finer things in life. He dressed only in the most fashionable clothing: loose-fitting frock coats with wide lapels, expensive pocket watches, low-cut waistcoats, checkered trousers, white silk shirts, the best top hats, and the finest men's jewelry. Nigel enjoyed imported culinary delicacies as well as premium wines and champagnes. But his deepest desire was to have a mansion befitting the royal status he acquired from his stepmother, Duchess Gertrude Hallworthy, who had adopted Nigel when he was three months old.

Following the fashion of nineteenth century noblemen, Nigel, acting as the architect, ordered the building of Hallworthy Manor. The work was carried out by slaves and Italian stonemasons. The inspiration to build the three-story stone residence came to Nigel after he had visited a wealthy plantation in Mississippi. Nigel's grand manor was a monumental structure. Greek columns, eight feet in circumference, fronted a massive arched oak doorway. The entryway was accented by a series of wide, white Italian marble stairwells tastefully adorned with pale pink and emerald swirls. Spacious balconies set around the perimeter walls afforded unrestricted views of the extensive gardens and landscape beyond. Towering chimney stacks penetrated the blue slate roofing, like sentinels guarding the property from high.

The interior appointments were no less grand, affording a splendor that is only accessible to the very wealthy: rich oak and marble flooring, twenty-foot cathedral ceilings of intricately adorned plasterwork and friezes, massive bronze chandeliers and candelabras, marble fireplaces and mantles, and the finest furniture from around the world. Nothing but the best and most exclusive would satisfy the resident Lord.

For all its splendor, Hallworthy Manor looked hauntingly unloved.

And it was—because love cannot survive in a house of evil.

Nigel took up permanent residence at Hallworthy Manor following the death of his wife, the Duchess of Dorchester, whom he had married when he was thirty. During the construction of the manor, the duchess, then age forty-one, succumbed to consumption in England. Nigel's son, Peter, aged nine, did not join his father in South Africa after his mother's death. He remained in England in the care of his maternal grandparents until Nigel died and left the Hallworthy estate to him when he was in his twenties.

In England, Peter followed in his father's footsteps. He was a troubled boy who committed acts of violence against animals, a rehearsal to the human killing he would eventually commit in South Africa. Being constantly humiliated by his grandmother for persistent bed-wetting, Peter drew upon his father's genes to cruelly vent his frustration and gain control.

In due course, Peter Hallworthy would spawn the last Hallworthy fiend, his only son, Alan.

*An apple doesn't fall far from the tree.*

Nigel's nineteenth-century, sixteen-bedroom, sixteen-bathroom *hotel* was built on a rugged rise. Its mountain scenery was the backdrop of the Valley of a Thousand Hills. Magnificent landscaped gardens surrounded the residence. The air hung thick with the perfumes of croton pseudopulchellus, a small shrub with delicate lemon flowers; pelargonium; arum lilies; daises; impatiens; and the giant protea—South Africa's national emblem—that bordered the stately home's semicircular driveway and environs.

Concerned that he had overspent for the costly construction, Nigel put into motion a shrewd business plan that he believed would recoup the building costs.

Being fluent in German, Russian, French, and Dutch, Nigel *privately* offered his residence to titled Europeans, other trusted royals, the fraternal organization of Freemasons, and the crème de la crème of society who came to Africa on hunting expeditions. He invited them to *enjoy* a different sport. He did not say what kind of *sport* it was, but his offer intrigued the bored, wealthy patrons who had more money than they could spend in a lifetime.

*Lies are complicated ... the truth even more so.*

It didn't take long for word-of-mouth advertising to reel in bloodthirsty, upper-class sadists. The grounds of Lord Hallworthy's grand estate would eventually witness more killings than the Tower of London had ever seen.

The Lord's malevolent deeds would haunt the majestic Hallworthy manor for generations to come.

*Darkness has no limits.*

The Devil was not complaining!

# CHAPTER SIX

# The Fishing Town of Abidjan
## -1840-

*"I wish no living thing to suffer pain."*
—P. B. SHELLEY

eep in the bowels of Lord Hallworthy's sailing vessel, unsanded planks saturated with sea water awaited the remaining twelve wretched souls. Mabali, her heart pounding, could not see a thing in the cold, damp, dungeon that would be their *home* during a journey of unknown length. Life as she had known it vanished the moment the hatch was sealed. No fresh air. No light. It could be daytime. It could be night. For the time being, their quarters were the closest to hell a person could get.

In the compact belly of this sailing vessel, the human cargo was packed head to tail, like sardines. It didn't take long for the little bit of clean air in the hold to become putrid. Most of the captured had lost control of their bodily functions, and the vile odors penetrated Mabali's nostrils and seeped into her skin like a flesh-eating disease. The conditions seemed to be devouring her sanity.

How could any of them remain sane among such brutality?

How could they survive without fresh air? The ghastly conditions compelled Mabali to speak up: "We are worse off than animals. We are all going to die." She tried to see her child, who was lying behind her, but the iron restraints pinned her down. So she shouted to her daughter, fighting to be heard above the din of footsteps trampling on the deck above them: "Nobuntu, are you all right?"

"No, Amma," returned the girl's feeble, tearful voice. "I'm scared and sick in my stomach, and I have wet myself. When can we go home?"

Mabali's heart broke. She eluded Nobuntu's latest question because she knew their former lives were lost forever and they would continue to suffer further humiliations. Yet Mabali also understood that if she didn't find a way to cling to the dream of returning home, she and her daughter would be lost forever.

Mabali's pensive, contradictory deliberations were interrupted by a touch to her right thigh. Agosi said hoarsely, "I don't think I'm going to live much longer, but before I die I want to tell you that I've had a vision."

Agosi sputtered a hacking, pneumonia-like cough after each pause.

"Save your breath, sick Bobo sister," Mabali returned with concern.

But there was no quieting the spiritual woman.

"The God Wuro wants you to live, Mabali. He has plans for you, your daughter, and your unborn child. Wuro says the soul-spirit of your son will one day avenge the wrong done to us."

Agosi's prediction was a false prophecy.

The avenger would be someone no one would have suspected!

"Hush, woman," Mabali said. "I don't want to hear another word about a god that has forsaken the proud women of Bobo. As far as I'm concerned, he doesn't exist."

"You are incorrect, wife of Kofi," Agosi argued. "Wuro has not forgotten us. He told me so. He also told me that your son grows *anxious* to be born."

Mabali let out an exasperated sigh. "Save your strength, Agosi. Get some rest if you can because I can hear your lungs rattling to breathe."

Following the onset of rapid chest movements and the inability to swallow, Agosi died.

Haunted by the last rasping sound escaping Agosi's mouth, Mabali's mind spiraled into indifference. No tears fell. She was emotionally spent. She simply touched the dead tribeswoman and said, "Go in peace to the god you believe in, dear Bobo sister."

"*N Demi!*" she screamed with all her might. "There is a dead woman here!"

*Eleven* wretched souls.

Being extremely agitated, Mabali could not process the diabolical happenings. There would be no decent burial for Agosi or for any of the other people who had died at the hands of the slavers. Refusing to pray or cry, Mabali instead began to sing a lively tune about an abundance of food and good weather. Soon the others joined in, and their uplifting voices were heard above. Surpassing the sounds of the waves and the din of the sailors going about their tasks, the *choir* increased its volume and climaxed with a series of high-pitched, penetrating screams.

Puzzled, the sailors stopped what they were doing and looked toward their boss for an explanation. The captain's red-enraged, puffed cheeks gave them their answer.

Agosi's naked body was unceremoniously tossed overboard. Instantly, the loud splash brought sea creatures to the surface. A school of sharks that had been accompanying the vessel hoping for an easy meal thrashed in a feeding frenzy. Agosi's emaciated, disease-ridden body satisfied them for the time being. The remaining victims onboard the death ship lay numbed. It didn't take long for them to lose all sense of time, a concept which carried no importance in the ship's hold.

*The essence of time* was ebbing fast.

Though Mabali had entered this death ship as a young woman, she now felt very old.

# CHAPTER SEVEN

# The Ill-fated Sea Voyage

*"Death hath so many doors to let out life."*
—JOHN FLETCHER

Just after midnight, the vessel weighed anchor to commence sailing four thousand nautical miles to the Port of Durban on the east coast of South Africa. Captain Wallace had calculated that the passage would take no longer than thirty-three-odd days. How wrong he was!

During the last leg of the voyage, Rory swung the *Lady Elizabeth* around the Cape of Good Hope, a rocky headland on the southern tip of Africa. The Cape was a treacherous passage feared by sailors. Many had shipwrecked and died in the originally named *Cape of Storms*. The King of Portugal didn't like the initial name given the Cape because he wanted to encourage more traders to come to South Africa. Fearing that they would be repelled by the *Cape of Storms*, he renamed the promontory the *Cape of Good Hope*.

The captain, to his alarm, found himself right smack in the middle of a notorious Cape storm. Rampant category two hurricane winds pitched the boat into swells of gigantic height. In addition, the powerful Agulhas current from the Indian Ocean tossed the vessel like a summer salad. Although the captain had travelled these seas several times before, this storm was the worst he had encountered. His knuckles were white from gripping the helm so tightly. To complicate his fight to keep control of the *Elizabeth*, the heavens bucketed rain onto the ship and its surroundings. The wind howled and struck the vessel with awesome fury. Lightning charges danced into the raging ocean. Was Poseidon, the God of the Seas, about to strike, as well? The wretched souls could have benefitted from Archimedes' giant mirror. According to legend, Archimedes constructed an enormous mirror that could focus the sun's rays and set enemy ships on fire.

"Lower the sails," Captain Wallace bellowed to his deck crew. "We are going to shipwreck if we don't slow down in a hurry."

"We are all going to perish!" a shy sixteen-year-old boy named James hollered in terror. It was his first voyage, and he silently vowed it would be his last. If he survived the storm, could he live with what he had seen and heard aboard ship? Having taken an oath of silence before signing on, James Smith had little choice but to keep his mouth shut. His silence and a sailor's wage were going to help him support his out-of-work father, his sickly mother, and seven younger siblings.

A violent storm was also raging below deck. Severe seasickness took its toll on the passengers. Acidic stomachs emptied their contents of stale rice mixed with insect parts. The two remaining children—Mabali's daughter, Nobuntu, and a three-year-old boy—wailed in distress as they tried not to breathe in the stench. But Mabali howled the loudest. Her baby was no longer moving. He hadn't kicked since he was sandwiched with his mother on the plank bed. With her free hand, Mabali balled her fist and pressed hard against her womb. She felt no retaliatory movement from the baby. She punched harder. There was still no don't-you-dare-do-this to-me whiplash from her unborn child. Suddenly, she felt something! The whoosh of vaginal bleeding; the tightening of pelvic cramping; and the acute pain of abdominal spasms sent her into wolf-like howling. There was no doubt in her mind that she was in labor. Rocking, Mabali clutched her stomach and cried out, "No … no … no …!"

Nobuntu, her face and body covered in vile stomach discharges, bolted upright, causing her iron ankle restraint to cut deeply into her flesh. She hollered, "Amma, what is it?"

"I think I'm losing the baby."

"What does that mean?" asked the innocent child.

Alarmed by Mabali's statement, the adults spoke:

"You are more than five moons with child."

"No, your baby is not going to abort!"

"It's the bad conditions that cause the fear."

"Call out for help."

"The *toubabs* are not going to help her …"

The last woman's words were cut short as the *Lady Elizabeth* lurched violently to one side, crashing the captives onto a floor that was quickly filling with ice-cold seawater.

Were they all going to drown?

Finally, the angry seas calmed, but there was no pacifying the death toll below deck.

Mabali clung to the lifeless, blue body of her premature son. Her cries of grief bounced off the wood-encased dungeon like cement Ping-Pong balls. White splotches of pain danced before her eyes. She could no longer function mentally ... a huge piece of her was gone. She felt as if a large bucket pierced with holes was draining the tears intended for her eyes.

Not so for her companions.

There wasn't a dry eye below in this vessel of death. But there *was* thunder.

The loud clanking of metal chains, fists pounding on wood, and voices screaming were heard above ... the din was worse than the crescendo of the earlier songs.

Captain Wallace scowled. To the sailor standing closest by, he ordered, "Go and see what the hell is going on." Rory handed him a solid brass padlock key. "And lock up when you are done."

James Smith went below—his first time—and wished he hadn't.

It was a horrendous scene.

He pinched his nostrils shut. The overbearing stench made the bile rise in his stomach. He stood frozen, staring at the feces-soiled humans huddled on planks.

"Jesus weeps," he muttered, making the sign of the cross. His face was filled with pity. Yes, he knew what the cargo of this vessel was, but he never thought it would be this barbaric.

"God help you, poor things," he ended with sincere compassion in his voice.

James was a good-natured lad and a good soul. His conscience would no longer allow him to remain silent. He shot up the stairway as if his life depended on fresh air and rushed over to Rory, who was facing the bow, smoking his pipe. With tears in his eyes, James admitted, "Captain, I'm just a country boy, not sophisticated like you. But I must speak my mind. This is not moral. You can't keep them locked down there. It is inhumane. Please let them come up on deck."

Rory gave him a death stare. Then he threatened, "You had better keep your mouth shut, or you're out of a job."

James returned defiantly, "I don't care. What you're doing is the Devil's work. I'm going to report you when we land! You'll go to jail, and I hope they throw away the key!"

The poor boy didn't see it coming.

Like the two unfortunate girls at the riverbank, a gaping hole told the tale of his insubordination.

Captain Wallace lowered his weapon and casually looked around. The crew's eyes were wide with shock as they witnessed this unprovoked killing. Like a crybaby in a schoolyard, the captain announced without remorse, "You *all* saw what happened, didn't you? The whippersnapper tried to strike me, and as captain of this ship, I had the right to defend myself."

Not a word or sound escaped the mouths of *Lady Elizabeth's* crew. Fearful of meeting the same fate, they turned their backs and went about their business as if nothing had happened. But silent, provoking questions hung in the air.

How could this murder on international waters be explained away? As hardened as many of the crew members were, could they turn a blind eye to the demise of one of their own? Could blackmail and secrecy bring a larger paycheck? What was the captain going to do with the dead body? Would it simply lie there until they docked?

Rory stared down at the dead boy, who wore a stare of his

own: glassy eyes fixed straight up. Forcing himself to think things through, Rory pictured himself standing in front of James's parents, fabricating false condolences: "My deepest regret for the loss of your son, Mr. and Mrs. Smith. James was a sterling lad, well liked by me and the men. One evening we encountered a major storm at sea; the ship lurched from side to side, while waves lashed the deck. The first mate reported that James was struck by a large wave and thrown against the ship's rail, rendering him unconscious. With a violent tilt of the ship, he was washed overboard. I'm convinced he never felt a thing."

Unseen by Captain Wallace, the muscles in James's eyelids twitched. Was his restless spirit reacting to the captain's contemptuous intention to explain away his death? Or was the convulsion simply rigor mortis setting in?

The boy's murderer wanted to detach himself from James Smith, but he couldn't. The vivid memory of their meeting took him to another time and place.

A month and a half ago, Rory Wallace strolled through the Durban dockyards toward his favorite drinking haunt. The weather was mild and the air fresh with a salty breeze. Several ships of various types were moored along the dockside. Sailors and officers were busily working their end-of-the-day tasks. A chorus of voices, some cheerful, some not, filled the evening air. Ahead of the captain loomed the Mariner's Rest, a quaint, rambling stone structure with a brown-tiled roof. A welcoming yellow glow illuminated the leaded diamond panes of the arched, wood-framed windows.

The heavy oak door with massive wrought iron hinges stood ajar, issuing forth a babble of noise from the patrons within. Above the lintel, swinging gently on rusted chains, hung a wooden sign depicting the tavern's name. Painted on it was the upper body of a jolly Jack Tar hoisting a tankard to his waiting lips in anticipation of forthcoming revelries.

Next to one of the ornate doorposts squatted the gaunt, ragged figure of a young man wearing a miserable expression. A battered gray cap at his feet held a few tarnished coins—farthings and halfpennies. The captain observed the lad. Despite the boy's grimy appearance, he had a sturdy frame, possibly from farming stock. "Now here's a likely lad!" he thought to himself.

"What ho, young man," Rory addressed the stranger. "You look as if you've seen better days. Do you care to join me for a drop of liquid warmth and a bite to eat from the kitchen?"

The young man looked up at the imposing figure standing before him. "Why not," he thought. "I'm starving." Hunger was his enemy, but this man appeared to be a friend.

"Thank you, kind sir. My name is James Smith, and I have fallen on hard times." He extended his arm. Rory, smiled benevolently and shook the outstretched hand. "You may call me Captain."

Rory draped a friendly arm around the lad's broad shoulders as they entered the inn.

It would be the last time this lad would see the inside of a pub. But one had to wonder: Would the happenings on this voyage end up being be just another sailor's sea tale?

Time would be the judge and jury of this ill-omened voyage.

On the last leg of the sailing, Captain Wallace became increasingly hostile. The remaining five crew members kept their distance, despite the limited space, until an order was given. "You and you," Rory gesticulated to the nearest sailors, "go and check the savages."

The crew members unchained the departed from the living dead. Minutes later, seven more bodies, including Mabali's aborted son and James Smith, were tossed overboard to feed the trailing white sharks. Like the bone-pickers of Africa, these scavengers of the seas seemed to sense a free meal was coming.

An artist's palette of vibrant scarlet swirling in aquamarine decorated the ocean. The colors were all that remained of human beings whose only crime was being in the wrong place at the wrong time.

*Four of Lord Nigel's apes were left.*

# CHAPTER EIGHT

# In the Bowels of Hell

*"There is a special place in Hell for slavers."*
—ANONYMOUS

The sea was getting rougher as a ubiquitous fog shrouded the vessel. No Divine hand emerged to calm the raging sea, like it did for the biblical Jonah. Even though many human sacrifices had been thrown overboard, no whale came to swallow them. The sharks accomplished that *divine* deed.

Below deck an invisible predator was devouring Mabali. She was in post-traumatic amnesic shock. She could recall nothing of her life. Her last memory had been of holding her dead baby and envying his death. She needed to find herself, but she could not. Mabali was as dead as the infant who was so cruelly tossed overboard to the thrashing sharks. A piece of her vanished. She was no longer whole. It was as if she had been amputated from reality.

Worse was the fact that her daughter, Nobuntu, was barely alive. She was growing increasingly weak by the hour. Their small daily ration consisted of a piece of stale bread and some stale rice containing smaller and smaller amounts of *crunchy* bits. Their three hundred or fewer calories a day was a death sentence. Having lacked nourishing food and clean drinking water for so long, an emaciated Nobuntu was reduced to stick-thin legs and protruding ribs. She had been unable to keep much food down during the journey. She was starving to death. Her dark, doe eyes were dull, her cheeks sunken, and her infected ankle sores oozing with pus. Her high fever alternated with periods of plummeting chills.

Nobuntu was the only surviving child. Just three women and she remained.

Four *apes* left.

A part of Nobuntu wanted to die … to get it over with quickly … but the developing *adult* within her knew that she had to be strong for another—for her grief-stricken mother.

"Amma," Nobuntu whispered weakly with an ashen face. "Wuro has taken my brother, but he has left *me* for you. I'm still here … your daughter."

When Mabali did not respond, the other survivors did their best to reawaken the lost young mother and encourage her to respond to her daughter.

"Sister, snap out of it!" an older woman cried. "We have all lost loved ones, and maybe none of us are going to make it, but please, listen to your daughter. She needs you …"

The woman's words were interrupted by the creaking sound of a hatch opening. Two sailors entered the putrid den, one jangling a ring of keys in his hand. They set about following their captain's orders.

The clinking of metal chains being removed ought to have been music to the women's ears, but instead, it brought a cacophony of distress, moaning, and groaning. Too weak to stand, the prisoners remained prone, their nervous eyes glued to their jailors.

The younger of the two men shook his head. "It looks as if we are going to have to carry them above one at a time."

This did not sit well with the older, seasoned sailor, a watch guard on the vessel. "Not for all the money in the world am I going to touch those filthy, disgusting heathens. That's *your* job!"

"I can't do it myself, and I can tell the captain why. If I do, then you will find yourself chained with these beasts … or worse!"

The watch guard, his expression livid, draped the hollow-cheeked Nobuntu over his shoulders like a lamb carcass and grouched his discord all the way up the stairs and onto the main deck. Then, he came back for Mabali. He had no choice. While his fellow sailor was carrying up the remaining two, he darted away to his cabin, where he swigged down half a bottle of rum.

Huddled on deck, the oldest tribeswoman cried out, "God Dwo, who helps man or woman, save us."

Mabali looked at the woman as if she had gone mad.

Released from the inhuman conditions below, Mabali forced her bloodshot eyes heavenward and implored, not to Dwo but to the Sun god, "Take me … take me … let your fiery breath end this misery… because I'm already dead with shame. I'm dead with the loss of my baby son. Take me. That is what I wish now."

While he was unable to understand Mabali's ramblings, a twenty-year-old sailor with a decent heart looked at Mabali and sensed that she had willed death to come for her. He had a sister her age. He wondered what he could do to alleviate her suffering. He tried to help her to stand. As he was bending to lift Mabali upright, a loud bellow reached his ears. "Don't you dare touch that savage, unless you have a death wish, young fellow!"

To the soulless captain, his cargo was unreal ... a mirage ... a trick of sun and sea.

"Get them cleaned up," Rory ordered. "We will be docking in less than an hour, and I can't have them stinking to high heaven."

With bandanas covering their nostrils and mouths, the crew once more threw buckets of cold, salty seawater over the cargo. When the dried excrement refused to budge from the bottoms and inner thighs of the females, Rory was furious.

"Use the deck mops if you have to. I don't want to see shit! And feed them everything that is left in the galley ... even the pig fat used for cooking."

With an expression of disgust creasing his seafaring face, Rory turned and headed for his quarters below deck.

Little Nobuntu stared at the retreating figure. She mustered up what little strength was left in a larynx numbed from retching. In a booming voice that quelled the roar of ocean waves, she shouted, "Why do you keep us chained like animals? Let us go home."

Captain Wallace stopped dead in his tracks, turned, and gave the child a condescending glare. "I can't understand a word, but be my guest ... dive into the sea and swim home. I really don't care if you *apes* live or die!"

His gloating chuckle and cruel thoughts accompanied him to his cabin. He wished he had never accepted this assignment, but it was too late. He had sealed his fate.

The compassionate sailor, whose duty it was to keep the deck clean, shuddered in disbelief, then spoke a truth to anyone who would listen. His angry voice rose higher than the waves. "If the rotten bastard had allowed them to come up more often, they would not be in this pitiful condition. Filling them with fatty food now is surely going to finish them off." The sailor looked heavenward. "If you are listening, God, please help them. After all, they are *your* people too, just like us white folk."

Would his heartfelt plea be heard in the heavens? No. Whoever was in charge above was on leave!

Like James Smith, this would be the last trip for the sailor who had dared to speak up. He vowed to never again work on board any vessel that Wallace commanded. But he wasn't going to spill the beans and end up floating in the sea with James Smith. Instead, he went about his duties wishing the boat had already docked.

An hour later, Captain Wallace emerged from his rest and took the helm. Standing at the wheel, he stared into the ocean as if hypnotized. The last thing on his mind was his wretched cargo. His primary focus was on saving his own hide. He had to come up with something viable that would answer some lingering questions: Would someone on board his vessel turn him in to the authorities for his role in the murder of their shipmate? Would one of his crew divulge the *real* reason for the *Lady Elizabeth's* voyage? Would blackmail become the order of the day?

From the beginning of his covert travels, Rory had not dared to risk being spotted by other seafarers, many of whom were staunch abolitionists. Lord Nigel could get away with anything, but not a lowly Scottish captain. The murdered James Smith had spoken the truth. The captain could end up in some dank underground prison cell with the key thrown away, or worse.

Captain Wallace was eager to dock the vessel, hand over what was left of the original shipment, receive his payoff, and hastily return home to Scotland, where his wife and three daughters were waiting. He thought about his talented teenage girls, who would play the piano, sing, and dance for him upon his return. He gave no thought to the inferior black girls … the victims of his and others' diabolical greed.

As the saying goes, payback is a bitch.

Captain Wallace wouldn't live long enough to enjoy the fruits of his ill-gotten labor. A week after the *Lady Elizabeth* docked in Durban, he was arrested.

The formerly proud seafaring captain languished in a dingy jail cell (with wall shackles and restraints provided for difficult prisoners) until his date with the court six weeks later. Rory's defense counsel, William Rathbone, reminded his client that the testimony of his crew was damaging but would not sway a jury without corroborating testimony from the owner of the vessel. Rory was falsely optimistic that the man who had hired him would speak up in his defense and deny the allegation of human trafficking. No such luck.

Lord Hallworthy was a no-show at the captain's trial. However, Nigel's spokesperson, Lord Frederick Guilford (the best legal representative money could buy) *was* present. Guilford adamantly argued on Hallworthy's behalf that his client knew nothing about a cargo of slaves, that he had commissioned the ship to bring spices and other commodities for his personal use. Using dramatic gestures and facial expressions as convincingly as any crook, Guilford went on to praise Lord Hallworthy for his generous donation to the upkeep of the forty-bed jail Captain Wallace was inhabiting. The most hypocritical statement, not amusing to the captain, was Guildford's ending speech:

"Your Honor, my client is a staunch abolitionist."

Guilford opened his briefcase and removed a notebook.

"Your Honor, I'd like to read a note that Sir Nigel Hallworthy handed to me before I appeared in this courtroom."

The wigged judge nodded his approval.

The representative adjusted his reading glasses. "Your Honor and jury members, I quote from Lord Nigel Hallworthy's own handwriting:

*"If we ignore slavery crimes, we are just as guilty; we become accomplices. In my opinion, the captain I once trusted is now untrustworthy and guilty of this crime. May God rest his dark soul."*

Rory felt faint. However, he did not speak in his own defense. He could have defended himself, but at what cost! It was his word against a nobleman who was an ancestor of Queen Victoria, a man who, in Rory's thinking, was as morally diseased as he was. There was no room for the captain to prove his innocence. He had willingly participated in the transport of slaves to the coast, and he had participated in their disposal overboard.

The judge ordered the jury to select a foreman. Surprise! The man was one of Nigel's lodge buddies.

In less than twenty minutes, the twelve-man jury returned a verdict of guilty in the first degree for the death of James Smith, and a recommendation for mercy for Captain Wallace—no date with the hangman.

On sentencing him to life (which literally meant dying in jail), the judge described Captain Wallace as a man of "a most diabolical nature" who had caused the brutal death of a young sailor. The judge also admonished the prisoner for having the audacity to blame a nobleman, Lord Nigel, for his own scurrilous crime. The judge directed his next question to Wallace. "What happened to the surviving slaves?"

Rory's defense counsel answered glibly, "They all died on the journey, your Honor. God have mercy on their poor souls."

Wallace bowed his head, not in remorse, but in regret. He had had a sixth sense about the undertaking of this sea voyage, only he had chosen to ignore the inner warnings.

Red Rory Wallace accepted his fate. There would be no appeals for him. He didn't want to face endless years of appeals. Even though his loss of freedom was the worst kind of punishment, he was not prepared to languish in jail for the rest of his life. He wanted to spare his family … to hang … to die … to get it over with, but that was denied him.

While the judge rambled on about his scurrilous deeds and retribution for the crimes committed, Rory was thinking about the gallows snapping his neck like a twig. Could he get his wish if he strangled one of his jailors? His macabre thoughts were interrupted by the judge's final address, primarily to the solicitors.

"This case doesn't just stink. It reeks of untruths. However, I have little choice but to accept the evidence presented and the decision of the jury; therefore, my sentencing stands. Captain Wallace, the only way you will ever get out of prison is in a pine box."

With his head lowered to his chest, the former decorated captain of the seas was led from the courtroom, his ankle shackles resonating on the tile floor in a tune of despair. Captain Wallace was now history. Rory Wallace was a convict.

The cell door clanked shut. A metallic click of the lock secured Rory in his dingy cell. The sounds sealed his reality. They were like no other sound he had ever heard. Rory took a deep breath. Suddenly, his confinement registered. "God help me," he whispered as he looked upward. His only contact with the outside world was a tiny window fitted with stout metal bars. They cast a dim light on the contents of Wallace's new world. A thin mattress on the floor was his bed, a coarse thin sheet his covering, an earthenware bowl his source of water, a battered metal pail his toilet facility. The floor was comprised of damp stone slabs and raw earth seeping up between uneven joints. White-washed stone walls, on which previous tenants had scribbled messages, surrounded the cell.

Rory glanced up. The discolored plaster ceiling had peeled away in several places, one directly above his bed. The opening revealed exposed wood beams. His cell was a far cry from the luxury of his captain's cabin. At least the prison authorities had allowed him to keep his pocket watch. It was a cruel reminder of a past in which *time* mattered.

*Time* was now his crucifier.

Finally, heaving a deep, remorseful sigh, Rory, clothed in ill-fitting prison grays, sat down on his thin mattress. How had it come to this—a man who had roamed the seven seas being confined to a human cage?

As days drifted by infinitely, the former seafaring captain slowly became familiar with his dull new routine: a meager breakfast of lumpy porridge at 7 A.M.; an hour of outdoor exercise in the prison yard; and supper, no better than he served his human cargo, at 5 P.M. The food served was barely sufficient to keep him together. His jailors made three daily patrols, the last at 10 P.M. when the inmates were expected to be asleep in their beds. Other than these few diversions, he was left confined and alone. He wasn't allowed visitations, not that his family had requested any, and no letters had arrived for him. He had been abandoned—shunned by all who had once held him in awe.

As time rolled on, Rory steadily became more despondent. Although it felt to him as if he had been incarcerated for years, in reality it had only been a few months.

Late one evening he caught a brief glimpse of a full moon hanging like a luminous pearl against the black velvet night. Shortly, it would become obscured by a bank of lazily drifting clouds. A nocturnal verreaux—a giant eagle-owl—called haunt-ingly through the night as if bringing additional bad tidings to the soulless captain. Prisoner number 492 hit an all-time low.

The next day, Rory woke with an uneasy feeling, as if he were not alone and he was being watched. Alarmed, he thought, "No one else is here, dear chap, but you." Then he spotted something perplexing: bright red stains dotting his gray prison garb. He gasped when he discovered the deep, claw scratches on his arms and legs. These unexplained injuries sent a cold shiver down his spine. A thick iciness blanketed his cell like Arctic sea ice. He exhaled winter's breath. An unpleasant odor similar to rotting flesh sent additional quakes down his spine.

The sounds rapping on the window, the footsteps on the floor, and the whispering all around him sent him over the edge. The captain slunk into a corner, sat on the cold floor, and cradled his head in his arms. Then they came ... *one by one* ...the shadowy figures. The dead souls from the *Lady Elizabeth* were accompanied by the brave young sailor, James Smith. He was holding Mabali's baby son in his arms. James shepherded the earthbound souls toward their murderer.

Rory Wallace prayed for madness, not forgiveness. He responded as he had lived, remorselessly.

With shaky hands, Rory twisted his rough sheet into a crude rope and fashioned a slip noose at one end. Using the wooden crate that was resting on his bed, he climbed up and secured the other end around an exposed beam. He finally uttered a prayer for forgiveness and then, placing his head through the noose, kicked aside the crate. His body jerked downward, swinging wildly, as the crude rope constricted his neck. Irregular flashes of colored light paraded before his mind's eye. They were accompanied by a high-pitched buzzing in his ears.

The last sounds he heard were the pitiful cries of the slaves. Scenes from his life passed before him, becoming fainter as the noose's grip grew tighter. The final image he perceived was of the rolling heather-covered hills of Scotland cloaked in the pale blue haze of an early dawn. A fugitive ray of golden light from the rising sun danced across the waters of a nearby lock as he sank into death's dark embrace. No white light was present to greet Rory.

At five o'clock in the morning, the jailor made his first check of the day. Peering through the small aperture in the cell door, he noted that all was quiet. But what was that awful smell? Curious, he unlocked the door and entered the space. He was confronted with the sight of the prisoner's body hanging at the end of a makeshift rope. Wallace's ashen face seemed placid, in stark contrast to his bulging eyes and his extended tongue, which lolled down one side of his blue-lipped mouth. His arms hung limply by his sides, but his hands were tightly clenched, nails biting deeply into the palms. His gray prison trousers were stained with bodily fluids, the smell of which permeated the cell walls.

The seasoned jailor had seen it all before. He drew a long knife from his belt and slashed the rope. Wallace's body hit the floor with a dull thud, never more to tread the gentle hills of his native Scotland.

The caring souls of James Smith and the other victims of Captain Wallace were smiling down from Heaven. Justice had been served. *Or had it?*

Would Lord Nigel Hallworthy ever pay for his participation in crimes against humanity?

*What goes around comes around.*

# CHAPTER NINE

# Before Wallace's Demise

*"Let them hate so long as they fear."*
—Accius

Waiting dockside at the Port of Durban, a horse-drawn carriage with unlit coach lanterns blended in with the darkness of a stormy night. Inside the carriage, a well-dressed man wore a tightly tailored coat and trousers over a gentleman's white linen shirt. A broad, high-brimmed hat covered his thinning, dyed hair—peroxide blond to cover the gray.

With an eyeglass resting on the bridge of his pointed nose, Nigel, age fifty-five, anxiously checked his pocket watch. It was past one thirty in the morning.

"Where the hell is he?" Nigel fumed, tapping his foot. Captain Wallace had never been this late before. Nigel had been assured they would arrive around midnight tonight.

Two hours later there was still no sign of his vessel. As a fidgety Nigel clenched a cigarette holder in his mouth, he decided not to risk being spotted near the dock during daylight hours. He rapped his brass-handled walking cane on the outside of the carriage door and shouted to the coachman, "Take me home, Skinny Tom, and don't spare the horses. I'm bloody tired and very angry."

"Yes, Master. Immediately," the coach driver subserviently replied. With a sharp tap of his horsewhip, Tom, age sixty-eight, set the two powerfully muscled carriage horses into a fast trot and then a gallop. Full black manes and thick tails danced in rhythm to the turning of the hickory-wood wheels. Tom was concerned that *his* horses would be *knackered* if they were not given a break on the four-hour trip back to Hallworthy Manor. He hated the place and had utter loathing for its owner, who forced him to do unspeakable things. There would be no green pastures for Skinny Tom when his time came.

The aging coachman and stable hand reckoned his body was worn out from so many years of slavery. But his mind remained active, as sharp as the bristles of a hedgehog. He was able to recall the details of his capture when he was four years old from a Bophuthatswana kraal in the northwestern region of South Africa. And how could he ever forget … the promenade of unimaginable horrors he witnessed growing up on the Hallworthy estate? He felt lucky and thankful, though, to have escaped Nigel's annual manhunt. Because of a spinal-curvature, he wasn't *fit* to run for his life—to be hunted like a wild animal. That was the fate that awaited whoever alighted the brigantine. In a way, he was happy the boat hadn't arrived. In fact, he hoped it had sunk! But he knew that was wishful thinking. Tom was still unaware that slavery had been abolished.

Tom's reflections were blasted away by a powerful, gusting wind that appeared out of nowhere. Birds clung to tree branches and Tom gripped his hat. As the fierce wind continued to rage, a volley of twigs and crusty leaves pelted Tom's face. The thunderous sounds were accompanied by the hard rapping of a cane. Nigel gingerly poked his head out of the carriage window and yelled, "I'm being bowled over in here. Steady the damn horses, ape, or you'll be in for a *whipping!*"

The last word out of Nigel's mouth sent Tom's mind lurching back to yesterday.

# CHAPTER TEN

# The Shongweni Girl

*"Life lasts a single day because tomorrow
you might not awake."*
—ANONYMOUS

Ten years ago, a slim, ten-year-old Shongweni girl was picking wild summer mulberries from the abundance that grew in this region—the Valley of a Thousand Hills. She had her baby brother strapped to her back in a tightly woven blanket. Two-month-old Umfunti was sound asleep. The girl's caretaking role was not unusual in this part of the world. Children as young as seven often took on motherly duties while their parents were otherwise engaged.

A couple of hours later, with her cotton bag filled to the brim, Kholika stretched her arm back and patted Umfunti's behind. She said, "Time to go home, brother, to show mother what delights we have found."

At a brisk pace, she began retracing her steps back to the Shongweni settlement, a few hours' walking distance from the Hallworthy property line. Along the way, she dipped her hand into the bag and munched on some of the day's spoils. She was eager to return home and share the berries with her family and friends. Happily chatting to her sleeping brother, she was totally unaware that her happiness and her eagerness to share her spoils were about to sour.

From the moment the girl was seen, everything went wrong.

Kholika had hardly walked a hundred yards when a sound like no other caused her to turn. Her mind couldn't process what she was seeing, so her body shook as fear consumed her. Wild-eyed, she gaped. Racing toward her were two enormous black beasts. Her throat constricted, her stomach churned, and her hands flew to her mouth in terror. She bolted in a zigzag fashion, as if she were trying to fool the beasts that she was sure were going to devour her.

*"Run like the wind. Don't look back. Don't stop!"* an inner voice commanded.

She was running fast, like she was chasing a shadow, but she was no match for the lightning speed of the Arabian stallions. The beasts were upon her in a flick of a finger, flanking the out-of-breath girl. She was so scared she wet herself. In frozen silence, she looked up at one of the fiery dragons spewing hot breath from wide nostrils, and then at the rider.

"What are these beasts?"

She had only seen cattle before. These things were unimaginable. But it was the man who wore high leather boots polished to perfection and flicked a whip to and fro who scared her the most. She had never seen a white man, let alone the likes of the huge black beast he sat atop.

"What do you want?" she asked shakily in her language.

"What are you doing here? The man returned coldly. "This is my property. You have no right to be here, *black ape!*"

She became confused. She didn't understand his language, let alone the degrading insult.

In a flash, Lord Nigel leaned to the side of his saddle, lowered his riding crop, and hit Kholika square in the back, which resulted in a deep tear in her skin above her tailbone.

"Girl, you are trespassing," Nigel yelled down to the girl with a callous indifference. "And you have stolen *my* fruit!"

Kholika's heart thumped against her chest in a loud drum beat.

Nigel's companion was the slave Skinny Tom, whose gray hair was the texture of wool. Barefoot and wearing a frayed shirt and pants, he remained deathly silent while the scene unfolded. But his horse would not be silenced. It began to whinny loudly. Was it in commiseration for the beaten, prone girl? Or was it responding to the sound of the booming, air-splitting *thwack* coming from Nigel's riding crop? Nigel was known to punch, beat, and whip his horses when they didn't heed instruction.

Kholika managed to turn over and sit upright. She could now look directly into the cobalt blue eyes of the man who had violently abused her with no regard for the baby strapped to her back. Not a whimper had come from the child since his sister was accosted. It was as if an invisible hand closed his tiny mouth to prevent further harm befalling them. Wishful thinking!

But a *hand* would appear and smash into her reality. It definitely was not divine!

Sitting on the arid soil with sweat glistening on her dark, flat face, Kholika felt something inside her telling her not to be afraid, to speak her mind even though there was a language barrier. "I didn't know that this land, my *land,* belonged to the *white* people!"

With that said, she picked up the sack, held it high, and ended, "Here, take the fruit if it truly is *yours!*"

*Crack!*

Nigel's whip missed its intended target and severed the berry bag in two. The crimson contents spilled onto the ground mingling with the blood that had seeped from Kholika's wound.

Nigel's face was red with rage. "Insolent pig!" he spat. "How dare you talk to me in this manner? I have a mind to beat you to death," he said threateningly, shifting his weight in the saddle—unsure whether to dismount or remain on his horse.

He dismounted, walked up to Kholika, and slapped her hard across the face, sending her reeling backwards onto the dirt again. This time, the baby howled. The girl tried to soothe the child, but she became silent when she saw Nigel standing over her foaming at the mouth. Before Kholika could unscramble the scene, it took an unexpected turn. Nigel discharged a sinister directive. "Rope her behind your horse," he ordered his companion. "I'm going to teach her a lesson she will never forget!"

Skinny Tom winced. He was chilled by Nigel's heinous order, but why should this come as a surprise? Nigel's evil should not have astonished him. Tom felt a sense of rage. There wasn't a servant on the estate who hadn't suffered from Lord Nigel's brutality. He himself had been locked in the notorious slave building for days, without food or water, as punishment for not feeding the Master's horses at precisely at six o'clock in the morning. That was the one time Tom had slept in a few minutes. He vowed never to allow it to happen again. An extra ten minutes of shut-eye was not worth being locked up in the vermin-invested outbuilding.

Today Skinny Tom had been freed from the hellhole, the infamous outbuilding, and ordered to accompany Nigel after he finished his groom duties. They were to check the animal traps (mainly wild boar, a delicacy offered to Hallworthy Manor guests) that had been set the day before. Now, Skinny Tom felt uncomfortable and powerless as he watched Nigel's senseless confrontation with a girl whose only motive for being on the land was to find food. Tom's compassionate heart ached for the Shongweni girl. Should he dare speak up? Would he use the wrong words? Would he suffer consequences if he protested?

Tom soon discovered the futility of having a soft heart. An overwhelming feeling of pity engulfed him as he responded in shock. "Master, I just can't. I just can't! She is only a child, and she has a baby on her back!"

Nigel fired back in a denigrating, hostile voice. "I don't give a damn if this darkie has ten babies on her back. Do as you're told or you will regret it! Mark my words, *Negro*, you *will* regret it!"

Tears welled in Tom's eyes as he silently obeyed the devil and roped the girl's wrists. She searched Tom's face. He was the same color she was. "Why are you doing this?" she cried as terror overtook her. "I have done no wrong. Please let me go. I have to get my brother back to our mother, and I promise never to come back here again."

What happened next was the girl's worst nightmare.

Skinny Tom squeezed his eyes shut, but he couldn't close his ears to the screaming. "Dear girl, I don't know how to save you … or me."

The girl's agonized cries filled Tom with murderous rage. He wanted to choke Lord Nigel, bury him where he would never be found! But that was out of the question. He was the last person seen with the lord, and he would be blamed, with or without a body.

The Shongweni girl did not survive the savagery of this madman. Nigel's sickly practice of hunting humans was well known to Skinny Tom and the other slaves who had been captured by this master of life and death. This murder was not his first.

As a result of being forced to run with the speed of a horse, Kholika's courage and grit finally caved. Her heart muscle over-exerted and the light disappeared from her pretty brown eyes. Her limp, lifeless, body was dragged along solid ground for over a mile.

Riding the animal that was pulling the girl, Nigel sprang into action and hissed, "Get up, you insolent shit! I'm not finished with you!"

Skinny Tom, in a fog of rage and sadness, did not realize the girl was dead until Nigel screamed at him. "Get her up on her feet, *now!*"

Did Tom have a choice against this sadistic killer?

With unsteady fingers, Tom closed the dead girl's pain-frozen eyes. He did not look at his master when he confirmed, "She is dead, Master."

"Are you sure?" Nigel returned.

Tom's head nodded involuntarily.

Nigel held a stoic expression as he prodded lifeless Kholika with the flattened end of his riding crop. "What a pity!" he remarked callously. "My fun is ruined." He then poked the hump strapped to her back. The baby, who had not uttered a sound since his sister's race with death, let out a deafening howl.

Nigel's blue eyes were as cold as steel, as was his command. "Get the kid out and check if it's a boy."

Tom did what he was told. He untied the blanket knot and lifted the naked, soiled baby to chest level. He then replied in a choked voice, "Yes, Master. It is a boy child." Tom acknowledged the boy's stark reality. "He's now a motherless boy whose life will turn out to be as miserable as mine."

"Then all is not lost," came Nigel's sinister words. "He will make a fine runner when he grows up!"

The unconscionable slave owner never batted an eye when it came to unspeakable, vile behavior. For Nigel's *apes,* freedom was *not* a universal right!

Skinny Tom's head hung low. Although he had witnessed many heinous deeds on Hallworthy land, Kholika's senseless death would be imprinted on his heart forever. Tom would never be able to break his silence.

Tom took his secrets to the grave in 1840, the day he died of blunt force trauma to his skull by an unseen hand. That was the day two other pitiful girls landed on Hallworthy's unhallowed soil.

There was little doubt among the Hallworthy servants who had killed Skinny Tom. A gardener working nearby saw Nigel enter the stable carrying a brass metal rod and exit with the instrument of death covered in blood.

# CHAPTER ELEVEN

# Stanley, Aka Umfunti
## -1844-

*"For some slaves, the first step out of bondage
is to learn to see their lives with new eyes."*
—KEVIN BALES

I n a dank cellar, Stanley, age five, was rudely awakened in the pre-dawn hours by John Broome, the master sweep of Durban. A metal chimney rod prodded the boy, who was still asleep on a black sack that was used to collect soot during the day and cover him at night. "Wakey, wakey, Stanley. Time to go to work," the sweep said in a gravelly voice.

When the boy didn't stir, John prodded once more, but this time harder. "Get a bloody move on. *Time is of the essence.* The lord wants all of the chimneys cleaned today."

Broome grinned when the lad jumped to his feet saying, "Right away, sir."

The master sweep was more than pleased with the new worker he had purchased from Nigel for a measly few shillings two months ago. From that day on, the boy had been made to work mercilessly, from pre-dawn hours until late at night, with no time off.

Stanley was living through a terrible chapter in the history of human chimney sweeps. They were, in essence, slaves. They received no wages, little food, and existed in deplorable living conditions. The lives of these little ones, who were forced to climb chimneys without safety clothing or respirators, were the stuff of nightmares. Children who worked as chimney sweeps rarely lived past middle age. The abyss they inhabited had no bottom.

The practice of sending children, mostly small boys, up and down chimneys to ensure they were cleaned of harmful creosote deposits was the norm throughout the colonies. The use of child chimney sweeps—usually homeless orphans from the streets or purchases from slave owners—became widespread after the Great Fire of London in September 1666.

Stanley clambered up chimneys daily using a hand-held brush to remove hard tar deposits left by wood and coal fire smoke. He wasn't finished until his head poked out the chimney top. Because most chimneys were extremely narrow (eighteen inches or less), Stanley was often reluctant to wriggle into them. However, plenty of encouragement was provided. More than once Broome poked his bare feet with sharp pins to force him to the top.

Stanley never forgot the other little black boy he had worked with in the early days of his enforced labor. That boy had died of asphyxiation after Broome lit straw under the boy's feet to spur him on. Instead of crying out or climbing higher, the boy panicked and died at the spot his body was stuck. Under the cloak of night, his rigid body, stuffed into a coal bag, was tossed into the Indian Ocean—not a lot of pickings for the great white sharks that patrolled these warm waters.

At 8:30 A.M., using back, elbows, and knees that had been scrubbed raw by Broome to harden them into calluses, Stanley began vigorously brushing the chimney located in Nigel's study. Piles of soot fell down over him, blackening even the whites of his eyes. The boy's lungs were near to bursting. His coughing only brought the worst out of Broome, who was supervising the work detail. "I don't care if you swallow the whole bloody lot. Just get a move on," he barked at the tiny boy.

The working conditions were harsh and cruel, but Stanley knew no better. He was nothing more than an *ape!* He had learned this word while being raised as a toddler by a maid on Hallworthy Manor. He knew nothing of his past—how he had arrived in hell or that he actually belonged to the ancient Shongweni tribe. Who was *left* to fill in the gaps? Skinny Tom's secrets were buried with him in his grave. All Stanley knew from the time he entered the gates of hell was a life of drudgery.

Today would be a day Stanley would never forget.

High in the chimney, his knees gave way. Unable to cling to the sides, he plummeted down, down, and down, landing on the iron hearth grate. A new maid named Daisy (her Xhosa tribal name was Deliwe) had soft features and a gentle face. She was dusting bookcases in Lord Nigel's study when the boy fell. She let out an ear-splitting shriek, dropped the duster, and rushed to the boy's aid. "Are you all right?" she cried. When he didn't answer, another louder cry for help penetrated the walls.

In an adjoining room, Broome heard the commotion and went to investigate.

Standing over the fallen boy, he ordered, "Get up, you lazy bastard!"

Stanley was unresponsive.

Broome gave the boy a kick in the backside, shouting, "Get up, you!" He stopped applying further brutality when Nigel entered the room. In an irritated "how-dare-you-disturb-me" voice, Nigel demanded, "What's going on in here?"

With a shaky hand Daisy pointed to the fallen boy, whose body was obscured by a large oak desk. "Over there, Master."

Nigel, wearing an expression no one had ever seen on him before—genuine concern—bent down and touched the boy's forehead. It felt stone cold. Nigel stood up, removed a plaid throw from the back of an easy chair, draped it over the boy, and turned to Daisy.

He ordered, "Run as fast as you can to the stables and find Edward. Tell him to go to Alderbury House and tell Dr. Flynn he is urgently needed. He will arrive faster than my usual doctor from Durban."

Daisy seemed to be in a hypnotic stance. She stared into space. Nigel grabbed her roughly by the shoulder, shouting, "Go *now*, idiot girl!"

Lord Nigel's favorite horse, a black stallion named Diablo, was being ridden by Skinny Tom's replacement, Edward. Nigel's new groom was speeding toward Dr. Flynn's property, a good hour's ride away.

Two hours later, the tall, gray-haired doctor, Liam, entered the study. With a pronounced limp, the retired doctor strode across the room. His tight grip on his medical bag revealed his displeasure. He had gleaned from the young groom (who had sworn the doctor to secrecy) that little lads—black children—were used to clean chimneys.

On examination, the unconscious, naked boy who lay covered in coal tar soot had high-impact trauma below the knee, a fractured shinbone that did not require surgery. However, on further examination, Liam noticed a far more concerning medical problem. The skin on the boy's scrotum was swollen with inflammatory eruptions. Could it be chimney sweep's cancer caused by constant irritation of coal tar?

Stanley's shallow breathing and weak pulse were also concerns. For a moment Liam struggled with whether he should save this abused boy, or *not!* His Hippocratic Oath nudged him when he considered ending this boy's miserable life. But it was the nudge to his shoulder and the chilling question that followed that made Liam rethink.

"Can you save him, Doctor?" Broome asked. "You see, the boy hasn't worked off his debt."

Liam stiffened at the man's callous statement, but he did not respond. He thought, "I would like to silence this despicable human being who has selfishly used innocent children to satisfy greed.

The doctor, too, had chimneys in his home—lots of them—but

he had come up with the practical idea of using tree branches tied to a wooden pole to sweep them. Of course, it was long, arduous and messy work for his *paid* East Indian manservant. Liam would never have thought of sending a *child* up his chimneys. It was out of the question.

Chimney sweeping was a dangerous and filthy job for small children who were often maimed or killed from falls or burns. Other health effects of doing this work proved to be fatal in the end. The children's growth was often stunted and their bodies disfigured because of the unnatural position they were forced to work in before their bones fully developed. Cancer of the lungs and scrotum could strike them in adolescence. These poor children were pronounced a death sentence at an early age. Would Stanley become another statistic of this barbarism? Liam thought, "He would die at an early age, no doubt."

An overpowering desire to pick up the injured child and run away with him to his home entered the doctor's mind. He had once been in this boy's shoes, suffering horrors the human mind could scarcely conceive. But with the help of a stranger, he had escaped the death shroud that awaited *this* exploited boy.

Back in the day, a twist of fate had saved the doctor's dissolute soul.

# CHAPTER TWELVE

# The Workhouse, London, England
## -1784-

*"Troubles overcome are good to tell."*
—YIDDISH SAYING

L iam Flynn, age fifteen and half, had long, wavy red hair and a face dusted in freckles. He was the oldest of eight children, four of whom died in infancy.

Liam was born in County Mayo, Ireland, in 1769 to dirt-poor parents, tenant farmers known as cottiers. Their livelihood depended on farming as well as on spinning and knitting by Liam's mother, Eileen. Although the Flynn family had somewhat recuperated from the devastating potato blight that had killed so many people, they were not out the woods.

The winter of 1784 began with a blizzard. A freezing, frostbite wind from the north mercilessly attacked noses and fingertips. For the occupants of the dilapidated, 200-year-old farm cottage owned by an Anglo-Irish landlord, there would be no waking up to hot chocolate and cookies.

As dawn broke, snowflakes danced by the cottage's single window. Their landlord had refused to give Liam's father, Patrick, compensation for renovations and even threatened to raise their rent if another window was installed.

The stone dwelling they called home sat in stark contrast to the majestic mansions owned by the landlords. Their modest abode consisted of a single room separated into two halves by a narrow wall almost the height of an average five-foot-seven individual. Crowded behind this partition, Liam and four of his brothers—Aedan, aged ten; Bradan, seven; Cabhan, five; and Malachi, three—slept on rag-filled mattresses. In the front half, which served as the living room and kitchen, his parents slept with Liam's youngest sibling, six-month-old Patrick, Jr. The only furniture they owned was a rickety, unsanded table and bench.

The old plank door, which had invited folk in for 200 years, creaked with age each time it was opened or closed. Today it moaned and groaned to the tune of the whistling winds that threatened to blow it off its ancient, rusted hinges. The thatched roof was also taking a beating, even though it had been weighed down with stones as a precautionary measure.

Around the cottage dense silver birch trees, now stark bare, blocked seasonal sunlight and air from entering the home. The constant shade hastened the rot in the thatching. The old roof, repaired many times, fared no better than the ancient front door.

On this dreary morning, the Flynn family, who had slept in their only set of warm clothes, huddled around a small fireplace. In the center, an iron kettle with legs rested over a bed of glowing cow dung. With no money to buy peat, the family relied on a neighbor's cow for life-sustaining fuel. Fire was their main source of light and heat. Gone was the animal warmth of the past. The large pig that had once shared the home with them had been butchered ages ago. Nevertheless, many a night had been spent in front of the hearth with Patrick telling stories about fairy folk, banshees, and witches. On this night, there would be an untold story.

On this morning, as usual, the fire's smoke escaped through a hole in the thatched roof. Under the soot-darkened ceiling, the children eagerly awaited their breakfast—hot water sprinkled with a handful of cooked oat meal.

Eileen Flynn's head throbbed with anxiety as she ladled out the meager meal into small bowls, leaving very little to be dished out for herself. Knowing that this was the last of the oats, she cried inside. How was she going to feed her family? The small potato crop grown at the rear of the house had been eaten. The harvested vegetables, cabbages and turnips were dwindling to nothing more than parings. Her worries seemed to spin out of control as she joined her family at the table. They were living with insecurity. There was always a looming probability that they could be thrown off the plot—evicted at short notice by the landlord or his agent. They could not pay the 2£ per year rent. The poor working family was at the edge of destitution.

On winter days before 5 A.M., thirty-five-year-old Patrick and his three oldest boys—Liam, Aedan, and Bradan—set out in search of work, any menial job that could help them buy flour for bread. But they always came home late at night dejected and forlorn. Sometimes, they had to resort to begging. Eileen's spinning and knitting orders had long ago dried up, as had her breast milk.

She worried about her baby, who had pale, hollow cheeks, sunken eyes, a pinched nose, and no voice. Withering like the blackened stems of the potato crop, the baby no longer sucked on the rag soaked in sugar water. Their sugar supply was now down to a few grains.

With hunger rumbling in her belly, Eileen stared numbly at the whitewashed walls that now matched the color of her hair.

Eileen was only thirty-five, but the lack of protein had caused *marasmus*—premature aging. She looked frail, but she always had a twinkle in her blue eyes when someone needed comforting. She wondered why life was so cruel to good folk like them. They attended church every Sunday, until now. Eileen had reasons to stop attending: first, they didn't have a penny to put onto the collection plate; second, Eileen believed that God was angry with this land and his Irish people. She believed God had sent the potato blight.

At the last mass they had attended, Father O'Connell made it *real* for her: "Good heavens, can it be possible that man, who is created in the image of God, is forced to live on weeds?"

Eileen and her husband were relatively young and able to bear hardships, but not the younger children. Their bodies were becoming emaciated. The happy expressions of normal childhood had long fled their home.

A loud rapping on the old plank door made Eileen nearly jump out of her skin. It was the knock she had been dreading for many months. She scurried to her husband's side. Grabbing his hand in a fierce grip she begged, "Don't open the door."

"It's all right, my heart," he said with endearment. "I must see who it is." In the back of his mind, he had no doubt.

Standing beneath the rotted lintel that threatened to give way under the heavy snow, a stranger with a woolen cap pulled low greeted Patrick in Gaelic, "Mora na maidine dhuit."

"And top of the morning to you," Patrick returned politely. "How can I be of help?"

"It is two pounds I will be wanting from you for the year's rent," said the Earl of Lucan's agent.

Patrick tried to turn away from the man's probing eyes, but he couldn't. He had to face the problem.

Their inability to pay the debt had kept him in perpetual bondage and in a continual state of anxiety. That fear was real now.

"We have no money, sir. We are starving."

"Then I have no choice but to hand you this," the rent collector said, passing Patrick a folded paper.

"I can't read, sir. What does it say?"

The Earl of Lucan's representative was not surprised. Most of the tenant farmers could not read or write.

"It's an eviction notice, Mr. Flynn. You and your family must vacate this property immediately."

Patrick held back the tears that threatened to embarrass and humiliate him. Being poverty stricken was a terrible thing, but being homeless was unthinkable.

"Sir, I beg you. I have a wife and children. We have nowhere to go."

"Then it is the workhouse for all of you," he replied dispassionately. The agent had a job to do, and he had no doubt that if he showed weakness, he would find himself in the same boat as these poor people. He turned his back and headed for the horse and carriage that awaited him on the snow-covered ground.

The following morning, a mocking, radiant sun cast rays on what was left of the grass as Patrick closed the plank door for the last time. Having sold what little they had in the way of furniture and other household items, the Flynn family, with only the clothes on their backs, a few personal possessions, and the sales proceeds, set out on a long journey to their final destination—a workhouse in London. Patrick was told by the neighbor with the cow that workhouses across Ireland were already full. But her son had told him about an institution in London that never turned away Irish folk.

The iron gates at the entrance of the workhouse separated the facility and its inmates from the rest of society. People entered the workhouse unwillingly for a variety of reasons—but unemployment and famine were the primary ones. The workhouse also provided a safe haven for unmarried pregnant girls, married women whose husbands had deserted them, and orphaned children whose relatives were too old or too poor to care for them. The workhouse was the last resort for the destitute Flynn family—the lowest level to which a human being could sink.

After entering the workhouse, which was flanked by high stone walls on all sides, the Flynns were met by a stone-faced man of about forty. He introduced himself in cockney lilt. "My name is George Smith. I'm the administration officer. Sign here," he said, placing a blue ledger in front of Patrick.

"Sir, I can't read."

"Then mark a cross where I point."

Aware that many other good folk were dying by the thousands in Ireland, Patrick took the pencil and placed his cross.

The administrator closed the ledger and flatly said, "Your possessions, including the clothes you are wearing, will be put in storage until you leave." His cynical thought was, "If you ever leave here."

"Over there." He gestured to a table behind them on which folded bundles of clothing rested. "Put on the uniforms and report back to me."

The baby excluded, they were given standard-issue uniforms made of rough material that emphasized durability rather than comfort and fit.

Behind dividers, the Flynn family silently removed their familiar clothing. A few moments later Eileen emerged wearing an ankle-length, shapeless, waistless, blue-and-white dress. Draped across her shoulders was a threadbare wool shawl. A bonnet covered her straggly white hair, and hobnail boots one size too large covered her thick, black, wool stockings. Patrick, Liam, and his brothers—wearing rough jackets, trousers, striped cotton shirts, cloth caps, and boots—joined Eileen at the desk. The cheerless administrator's next directive was a shocker, to say the least.

Eileen had not expected what he said next, a living nightmare. But reality hit home. She dropped to her knees and started to pray, "Mother of God, have mercy."

"Under the Poor Law Act, your family will be kept apart, both day and night, with separate yards and work duties. Breaking this rule or disobeying the staff here will bring immediate expulsion.

You will be thrown out onto the road in the rags you came in with."

Patrick's and Eileen's eyes met.

When her husband failed to respond in words or actions, Eileen's adrenalin-infused heart spoke for the head of the family. "That's not right!" she screeched at the administrator. "It is cruel and heartless to be separated from my husband and children, especially my baby. He is sick and he needs me."

"Mrs. Flynn, the nursing staff will take good care of your baby," he said matter-of-factly.

The workhouse staff consisted primarily of the master, who dealt with admittances and general affairs, and the matron, who was responsible for women inmates. Other personnel included chaplains of various denominations, a teacher, a laundry maid, and a single medical doctor.

Finally, Patrick spoke up. "Sir, I know we have fallen on hard times. Like my wife said, this is wrong! Separating us is criminal and against biblical teachings!"

The master shrugged. He was merely a tool of the government dictators. He had no emotion in his voice when he spoke. "These are the rules, Mr. Flynn. If you don't like them, then take your family and go somewhere else. Go to your own families and ask for *their* help."

Patrick wanted to reach out and grab the surly man by the throat, but instead he meekly said, "My parents are dead, sir, as well as my in-laws. When will I be able to see my wife and baby son?"

"That depends," he said. "Work hard and you *may* get privileges."

Without further ado, the master rang a bell. A helper appeared at his side in seconds. "Yes, sir," the young man said.

"This is Mr. Flynn ..." the master introduced, "... and his sons. They are to be taken to the west wing."

The young man, who looked to be Liam's age, nodded.

"Say your good-byes," the master ordered.

The four younger children, their eyes large with fright, rushed to their mother. They cried in unison, "Don't let them take us, Mammy."

With tears flowing and feeling utter despair, Eileen wrapped her arms protectively around her boys. Lifting her head, she searched the face of the youngster waiting to take her brood away. "Please give me more time with my children so I can help them understand."

"Five minutes," came the soft reply.

It was Liam who finally disengaged the little hands clenching Eileen's shift.

"It's going to be all right boys," Liam said glibly. "You will see Mammy tomorrow."

Eileen grabbed her eldest son's wrist. "Liam, promise me that you will take care of your brothers."

She looked at her husband's forlorn face. "I love you, husband. May God watch over you and our sons. May He bring us together as a family once more."

Unknown to Eileen, this would be the last time she would see her husband. He would die four months later in a rock quarry accident while breaking stones.

In the months and years that followed, all of Eileen's children passed away, except Liam.

Behind a closed door, Eileen's wailing echoed down the empty hallway. Mercifully, Patrick and his sons were spared her piercing banshee cries.

The workhouse nurse removed the baby from Eileen's arms.

Every year since she was a child, Eileen had prayed to God. No more. How could He let this happen? In her current frame of mind, there was no just God.

With unbearable sadness in her heart, Eileen mounted the stairs and followed the matron to an attic dormitory filled with living skeletons, young and old. There were twenty-eight boys, seventeen girls, eleven men, and eleven women in this house of horror.

Her bed consisted of a tattered straw mattress resting on the bare floor. She had old rags for sheets. The beds were cramped together, barely one foot apart.

Left alone in the attic dormitory, Eileen spent the rest of the day curled up in a fetal position crying into her smelly mattress. She didn't even notice the stalks of straw poking into her withered flesh.

The next day, the workhouse bell woke her at 6 A.M. After the 6:30 roll call, Eileen followed the rest of the females to breakfast—

the cheapest porridge or grain and buttermilk, which was cheaper than normal milk. Then she was off to work—sewing duty. For twelve hours a day, she mended and tailored clothing that was delivered to the workhouse by the upper class.

Lunch was a pint of buttermilk and a piece of black bread.

Dinner was always the same: turnip soup. Fruit was only given at Christmas and Easter, usually a gift from the workhouse master, George Smith, who never shared the donations of meat and other produce donated by the rich.

Candlelight was extinguished at eight o'clock each evening.

Loneliness devoured Eileen. She would have lost her mind, as so many had, if it wasn't for the faint hope of reuniting with her family one day, especially her baby. That hope was crushed when Eileen learned that her baby had been "boarded out"—taken from the workhouse and given to an upper class woman whose clothes she had tailored. In a way, it was small consolation to know that at least one of her children would enjoy a better life.

But this was not to be.

Baby Patrick died from scarlet fever before he reached the age of one.

After Eileen was informed of Patrick's death, she lost track of time. For her, time was no longer of the essence. Having no reason to live, she longed to die. Eileen would soon get her wish—the Shroud of Death was nearby, waiting to enfold her in his icy cloak. She might have had a change of heart if she had known that her oldest son still lived.

Over time, more wretches were admitted to the workhouse. Clothing was in short supply. Garments of deceased inmates were reissued without first being washed or decontaminated.

The living conditions became severely overcrowded and increasingly unhealthy. Scarlet fever, typhus, and dysentery were rife. Inevitably, Eileen became a victim and died like her baby from scarlet fever. She was buried within the workhouse grounds in an unmarked pauper's grave.

Liam, now sixteen, was the only remaining member of his family. He found himself in the workhouse infirmary where his mother had died. His foot had been crushed in the rock quarry by a falling boulder. Covered in dust, with his eyes bloodshot and his throat tight, he held back the tears of throbbing pain. Sweat mingled with blood as he lay on a cot awaiting treatment.

An hour later, in walked a short, heavyset, ruddy-faced man with salt-and-pepper-hair and a warm smile. His white doctor's coat had seen better days; it was as gray as the painted walls. After an examination that caused Liam to cry out in pain, the doctor said, with a recognizable Irish lilt, "Well, lad, you are lucky."

"Thank God," returned Liam.

"No amputation for you," he added with a twinkle in his large blue eyes. "You have a couple of broken toes that will eventually heal. But you won't be able to put any weight on your foot, so no dancing with the girls for you," he laughed.

"How long does the swelling and bruising last?" queried Liam. "At least I have *some* of my twenty-six bones intact."

Dr. O'Brien's eyes widened. "How did you know there are twenty-six bones in a foot?"

"I read it in that book over there ..." Liam pointed. "...while waiting for you."

On the table was a set of books on human anatomy. The doctor was delighted. "The boy could *read!* And *understand* the complexity of medical knowledge." Unbelievable!

The doctor made eye contact with Liam and answered his question. "I'm not sure how long the swelling and bruising will last," he answered honestly. "Maybe six weeks, if you don't abuse it by putting too much weight on it," he concluded.

There was a sense of panic in Liam's voice. "But I *have to* work or I won't get fed."

Dr. O'Brien sighed. He had taken this low-paying position when the 1941 famine closed hospital doors to patients who could no longer pay. He was well acquainted with workhouse rules: You don't work—you don't eat.

"I will speak to your quarry manager myself," Dr. O'Brien offered. "You *cannot* work for six weeks, at least."

Liam smiled. "Thank you, Dr. O'Brien. When I was little, my mammy asked me what I wanted to be when I grew up. I told her I wanted to be a doctor, to help sick people. But my dream will never come true because I will never get out of this prison for the poor. So a rock breaker is what I will be."

The kindly doctor declared, "Dreams do come true, lad. I will have you transferred to this infirmary. You will be my assistant. I would like to teach you everything I know."

Liam, now age twenty, registered at a prestigious medical college on the outskirts of London. Dr. O'Brien had kept his word, and more. The widower had legally adopted Liam and, confident of the young man's vocation, paid in advance for his training. Much to the doctor's delight, Liam learned quickly. Medicine was second nature to him, and he progressed rapidly as he absorbed the complexities of medical science. Finally, Liam's dream came true. He graduated with an M.D. from the Faculty of Medicine. He was over the moon.

Liam's kindhearted benefactor, the "father" who had always believed in him, attended the ceremony proudly. Later, over a few pints of ale, they celebrated at a local tavern.

But it was to be a bittersweet occasion.

When Liam woke the next morning with a hangover, all was quiet. This was unusual because Dr. O'Brien always woke up earlier than he did. Thinking no more of it, Liam started to prepare breakfast. As the bacon sizzled, he felt an icy shiver as he remembered his home in County Mayo and his poorhouse days, when breakfast could hardly sustain a mouse.

Minutes later, their meal was ready, but Dr. O'Brien was a no-show.

Liam made his way upstairs to the doctor's bedroom. He gently tapped on the door and announced, "Breakfast is ready."

No response.

Liam repeated his announcement.

Again, no response. He pushed open the door and noticed there was no movement in the double bed. All he could see was a form hidden beneath bedding. Dread gripped Liam's heart as he pulled away the coverings. There, cold as ice and stiff to the touch was the extraordinary man who had saved his life.

Although he was fresh out of medical college, Liam, with steady hands, examined the body and noted that rigor mortis had set in. Dr. O'Brien had passed away during the night. Liam couldn't prove a cause of death, but heart failure was his first diagnosis. With tears flowing, he held his father's cold hand. So this was to be his first patient, the man who had set his feet on a medical path. The irony did not escape him. Though devastated, Liam set his grief aside and acted professionally.

Within a week preparations were made, and Dr. O'Brien was laid to rest alongside his wife, who had died giving birth to a still-born son. They laid side by side in a small cemetery in Dublin, Ireland, where the doctor was born.

Later, during the reading of the will, Liam was taken aback when he learned that his dear father had left him all his worldly possessions, which included a residence in the British Colony of South Africa.

After forty-five years of practicing medicine at Dublin Hospital, Liam decided it was time to retire. He left the land of his birth and its haunting memories to sail the seas to his new home in South Africa.

A decision he would come to regret!

# CHAPTER THIRTEEN

# Present Day, South Africa
## -1844-

*"Nobody should go through trauma alone."*
—ANONYMOUS

D r. Liam Flynn, now seventy-five, looked much younger. He had a gentle, boyish spirit and a twinkle in the sparkling blue eyes he inherited from his mother. He ate healthy foods and—come rain or come shine—took long walks daily. He was a fit and muscular man for his age. However, at this moment he felt as old as Methuselah.

Still kneeling beside the injured boy in Nigel's study, Liam's thoughts troubled him. Haunted by his own childhood, he struggled to come up with a plan for the injured boy. He knew the only way this child's ghastly slave life could end was for him to have a benefactor. He knew he was that man. But he was not a mind reader! He had to think quickly. A predatory approach seemed best, like a bird of prey diving down and surprising its prey.

Liam looked over to where Broome, the master sweep, was fingering his black handlebar moustache and regarding the doctor with a calculating gaze. Liam was not ruffled by the narrow stare.

To him, Broome looked like a person who would sell his mother for a pint of ale. The doctor made eye contact, and sounding as if it were an everyday question, blurted, "How much do you want for this child?"

Broome's face turned fiery red. Caustically, he roared at Liam, "The boy is not for *sale*, Doctor."

Disgust creased Broome's brow as he continued, "Whatever possessed you, a man worthy of respect, to come out with such a ludicrous request?"

"I'm new to this country and don't have any slaves of my own," Liam answered boldly and glibly.

He did have servants, though, a Hindu manservant and a female Hindu housekeeper, both of whom were paid well for their services. They lived on the doctor's premises in a small cottage.

Liam continued speaking with the artistry of an actor. "When he is healed, having my own chimney sweep would be a considerable advantage."

Nigel and Broome glared at Liam with surprise.

"My dear fellow," said Nigel in a chilly voice, his fist clenched behind his back, "You and I both know that slavery is abolished. This boy is *not* a slave. He is an *indentured* servant. Quite legal. And for your information, the boy is paid good money to work. His wages are deposited in the bank. He will have access to them when he is older. This orphaned boy would have died on the streets if Mr. Broome had not found him. Isn't that so, Mr. Broome?"

Broome nodded his agreement.

*Liar, liar, pants on fire!*

Liam wanted to expose these men for the liars they were, but he held back. He had never met either of them until today, but on the long horse ride to the estate, Edward, Nigel's groom, had divulged some of the Lord's other scurrilous practices.

Liam later learned that there had been no emancipation for Nigel's slaves when slavery was abolished. He had also been told by his loose-lipped bookkeeper that Nigel had received a generous reparation payment of £20,511 (worth millions today), a sum that was dwarfed by settlements made to other slave owners who received far more. Not a penny of this money went to the "freed" ex-slaves.

Liam didn't know much about the master sweep but guessed he hid under the same evil cloak as Nigel. It was well known among the elite that Nigel belonged to a secret society, the Freemasons. Liam wondered if Nigel's association could bring harm to him if he stepped out of line.

Liam hurriedly put plan B into action.

"It is now or never," he thought.

*Time was of the essence.*

"Then, may I suggest, Mr. Broome," Liam said in his most professional voice, "that I take the boy to my home to convalesce and heal completely before returning him to you."

Broome scratched his head with indecision before responding, "That's fine with me, Doctor, but no longer than a month."

"Oh, he will need more than a month to heal, Mr. Broome."

"Fine then," Broome agreed after a long sigh. "You can send for me when he's ready to be collected."

Liam smiled, but his acting was not quite over. He faced Nigel with an ace up his sleeve. "Lord Hallworthy, I live alone," he said shallowly, "and will need an assistant to help me take care of the boy. Maybe you can be of help?"

Nigel's stony expression relaxed, taking on a glad-that's-over look. He then played directly into Liam's hands.

"Of course, Doctor. I can *loan* you a helper," he emphasized. "I've just the person in mind. She will be brought to your home shortly." Nigel's sardonic laughter gave away how he truly felt: "Try to heal *that* one, you fool!"

"I am much obliged, Lord Hallworthy," was Liam's parting comment.

Nigel's parting words were sinister. "I don't suffer fools gladly, pompous fellow! So I sincerely hope you are a man of your word!"

Liam sensed that he had now joined ranks with a slew of Nigel's other mortal enemies.

After the doctor and his patient departed in the manor's carriage, Nigel remained in his study, his eyes fixed on the ceiling. He was in a foul mood as he turned over in his mind the events that had enraged him. He needed a stiff brandy, so he rang for his butler, the senior male "indentured" black servant who was still, in reality, a victim of slavery. The butler received *no* wages, yet his responsibilities were numerous: tending to the Lord's every whim, overseeing the domestic staff, taking care of the wine and silverware, and receiving guests.

When the study door opened, a slim black man walked in.

"Yes, Lord Hallworthy," said Moses dutifully.

"Bring me a bottle of brandy from the cold cellar, and after that, I want you to go to the outbuilding, you know the one I mean, and bring the wench—without her child—to the kitchen. When she gets there, have the seamstress find her suitable clothes to wear. She is going to work for Dr. Flynn at Alderbury House until further notice. When this is done, report back to me, Moses."

Moses made an affirmative nod. What choice did he have but to obey, or he would end up where the poor mother and daughter were being held.

With his guts as tight as a spring, Moses headed down three stairwells, a time-consuming walk he undertook five to six times a day to do his master's bidding. But this one was an order he was reluctant to undertake.

His thoughts were leaden. Not in a million years did he wish to return to *that* infamous building. The memory of pitiful cries and horrible images was fixed in his mind … imprinted like no other … impossible to expunge.

The nightmare of his visit to the outbuilding happened four years ago.

"Don't be scared," Moses had said softly that day. "I've brought you something to eat."

He spoke in English. His native tongue was long gone, along with the memory of his West African tribal roots.

The sight of the two chained wretches, a mother and daughter, drove his mind back to his own capture.

At the age of ten, Moses, along with his mother and father, had been abducted from the very same Bobo village as Mabali, but thirty years earlier. He was separated from his parents, who were shipped off to Grange Sugar Estate in Jamaica. Sometime later, he was bought by a wealthy, aristocratic family in Durbanville and was trained as their manservant. At a dinner party Nigel attended, he had been so impressed with Moses that he implored his hosts to sell the servant to him.

"No. It is out the question, my dear fellow," returned the Earl. "Moses can never be replaced."

Nigel leaned close and whispered something in this notorious womanizer's ear. Blackmail that would expose the man's adulterous affairs with his black servants did the trick.

The next day Moses, holding a small suitcase, entered Hallworthy Manor.

One early morning in the summer of 1840, sixty-year-old Moses and Daisy, in her twenties, were ordered by Nigel to go to the infamous building to take food to the two inmates. At first sight, Moses' heart sank. He assumed they were children because they were so small in stature.

However, Mabali's full breasts told him otherwise. With fearful, hungry eyes, Mabali and Nobuntu stared at the slim black man dressed in butler's garb and then at Daisy, who was wearing a crisp blue-and-white maid's outfit.

Moses gestured—rubbed his stomach—then raised his fingers to his mouth.

"Cook has made a rabbit stew for you," he said, "It is delicious. Please eat."

There was no verbal or physical response.

Mabali and Nobuntu remained still until the stale, putrid air in the building filled with the tempting aroma of food. Nobuntu's nose was the first to wrinkle.

"It smells sooo good, Amma," she said.

As weak as she was, Nobuntu mustered the strength to not only drag her body but also her mother's toward the large bowl placed in the center of the building. Hastily, Nobuntu dropped her head in the dish as if she was going to wash her hair, then let out a wild animal howl: "The food hurts, Amma."

The piping hot meal had scalded her tongue, but she told her mother it was worth the burns. "It's the most delicious meal I've tasted in a long while."

Mabali forced a smile. She waited, as would any caring mother, for her ravenous child to have her fill. Then she finished what little remained.

Moses' sigh was heavy with hurt as he observed the mother and daughter lap drinking water like animals. He had built a wall around his heart, vowing to never again show softness, but the sight of these two wretched humans crumbled his barrier. In a different world, he would have liked to know more about the pretty young woman with the unique, black pearl irises.

At this time, Moses had no idea that Mabali was a Bobo tribeswoman. He did not recognize her tongue because his Mandinke days were long gone, so he did his best to communicate in gestures.

In all his years of slavery, little had shocked him, but these females—thin as shadows, displaying bruises, whip marks, bloodied necks and wrists, and unhealed sores caused by metal chains—turned his stomach. His heart ached for the girls, who were undoubtedly destined for a living hell. Compared to them, he had been fortunate. His life had been filled with hardship, but it was a cakewalk compared to theirs. Moses' musings reminded him of the countless other people, mainly males, who had previously been incarcerated in the shack and were later hunted for private sport … and their broken dead bodies, gaping with gunshot wounds, unceremoniously disposed of throughout the Hallworthy grounds.

His head spun. "*Oh, no,*" he thought. "*Surely not!*"

Would these helpless girls also end up as trophies for Nigel or for his bloodthirsty hunter guests? Moses could not know at this point that neither girl would meet *that* ghastly end. Nor could he know that one of these Bobo girls would become the wife of a Zulu king.

Moses and Daisy walked in silence toward the manor house.

They had seen it all. Or so they thought!

Four years had passed since that encounter with the Bobo girls.

Mabali, now age twenty-two, and Nobuntu, age nine, had languished in those inhumane conditions for what seemed like forever. Of course, the passing of these merciless years had not changed Nigel in the slightest. As he heartlessly told his closest friends, he was furious at having paid good money for two useless, diminutive females. When his cargo of two had finally arrived at the estate back in November 1840, Nigel was more than livid, which created a perfect storm!

Nigel later learned from a sailor who had crewed on the *Lady Elizabeth* that there were *four* captives for delivery, but a girl and her aunt had flung themselves overboard shortly before the ship docked at Durban Harbor. Their bodies never turned up.

"These two should have drowned like the other two apes," Nigel had informed the sailor.

It seemed as if Nigel lived in perpetual rage. He kept the two survivors of the sea voyage imprisoned for so long—without ever a compassionate thought, until now. A vile notion had crossed the lord's mind back then: It was more economical to kill them than feed them.

One of the prisoners, Mabali, had a purpose. She was to become the doctor's aid, during which time he wouldn't have to spend a penny on food for her. What was to become of the other, he had not yet decided.

Throughout the long, cruel years they were held in captivity, laughter had kept Mabali and her daughter sane. From memory, Mabali would tell Nobuntu hilarious stories, especially the one about Koki and the king boar. Both had practically laughed their heads off. The mother and daughter had survived the hellhole this long because they shared love and devotion.

At 10:30 A.M., after Liam and Stanley's departure, Daisy carried a shabby, hand-me-down garment draped over one of her arms. Clenched in Moses' hand was a key.

The smell of the outbuilding seized their throats. What a stench! The hole dug in the earth had reached its capacity. But the visitors showed no disgust.

Neither inmate shied away when Moses and Daisy entered. They had become accustomed to the daily routine of receiving water and food. Eyes were fixed on what the visitors carried in their hands. Nobuntu, now taller than her mother, spoke up. "Amma, they bring no food or water."

"I see that," Mabali replied.

Moses could only guess at the conversation that was transpiring, but his hands were tied. "No food. No water." were Nigel's orders. Only after Moses carried out his instructions—removing the mother—was the other to be given something to eat and drink.

Moses humbly lowered his head as he reflected on Nigel's cold-heartedness. Moses' conscience felt as if it had been stung by a bee. But if he did not carry out Nigel's orders to a "t," he would be the child's next companion.

Moses unlocked Mabali's chains. She thanked him. Intuitively, Moses smiled.

Finally, free of her brutal restraints, Mabali rubbed her scarred neck and wrists as she looked at the clothing Daisy handed her. "At last," she thought, "I will be decent. I will no longer have to live naked, exposed for all to see." As she inspected the dress, though, Mabali was saddened to see that it was sleeveless. It looked as though her previous Bobo code of cultural decency would be a thing of the past.

Nobuntu wasn't thinking of Bobo dresses. She reached for Daisy's hand. "Where's mine? I want a dress like my mother."

When Daisy did not respond, she turned to Moses. "I want clothes like my mother, and I want you to undo *my* bad necklace, as well!"

Moses sighed. The language barrier hindered communication.

Before Nobuntu knew what was happening, a weeping Mabali touched her daughter's face as if it were the last time. And it was!

As Moses helped Mabali from the dark, oppressive building and locked the door behind him, Nobuntu's hysterical, frantic, rapid-fire screams punctured the walls. A grieving, sobbing voice pleaded, "Where are you taking my mother? I'll be good. Please, bring her back."

Moses shoulders slumped like leaden rock. The anguish of their separation caused Mabali to scream, "Where are you taking me without my daughter?"

Keeping a tight grip on Mabali's arm to prevent her from running back, Moses tried to soothe the weeping mother.

"Don't fret," he said. "You'll be back in no time to reunite with your daughter."

Truthfully, he didn't know if Mabali would ever see her daughter again. Her fate was now in Nigel's hands, as was the fate of the child left behind.

"Only *you* are to be taken to be a helper," Moses said.

Mabali squinted. She tried to communicate with words she had picked up in the four years she had been fed by English-speaking servants. "Where I go?"

Moses was done talking. His heart lingered on the child left behind.

Piercing sunshine hit Mabali like a blow to the face. Her hands shot upward to shield her sun-blinded eyes. Her heart and thoughts weighed on her heavily, but she was at the mercy of whatever awaited her.

Mabali, attired in an unbleached slip made from coarsely woven upholstery fabric and a white cloth head cover, walked alongside her minders in silence.

But Mabali's bloodline would not be silenced. Her genes would forge a unique path into the future. Her lineal descendant would become the greatest warrior king of the nineteenth century.

Mabali would never again see her daughter alive, the girl who would become the mother of future kings.

# CHAPTER FOURTEEN

# Heartbreak–Revenge–Freedom

*"The Almighty never abandons an orphan.*
*Always He sends her a friend."*
—L. KÜCHLER

Nobuntu's fate was decreed the day after her mother was taken away.

The nine-year-old believed her beloved mother was gone forever. The separation left her on an emotional roller coaster. How could she move forward? Would the pain in her heart ever diminish? Would the nightmares she had been experiencing since her capture ever cease?

On Nigel's orders, Moses and Daisy returned to the outbuilding. He unshackled the emaciated girl. Having worn a slave collar for so long, her head drooped like a wilting flower.

Free of her restraints, Nobuntu had nothing to say to the other two slaves. But her blank eyes told a story of a deep-rooted grief that had been gnawing at her sanity and invading her mind.

Daisy shrugged her shoulders. She had no words to compensate for the mental and physical torture of another human being. She simply set about washing Nobuntu's face and body with soap and water, then rubbed healing ointment on the child's ankle, wrist, and neck sores. Looking at Nobuntu's lopsided head, Daisy's heart spilled over with grief and sympathy. She gestured toward the iron restraint lying on the dirt floor. "Child," she said tenderly, "given time, your wounds will heal, and you will *never* have to wear this white man's shameful control again."

Nobuntu felt tears stinging her eyes as she recalled a painful memory: "I will make you a necklace of sparkling gems ...." Even though she thought it unlikely, she longed to see her mother, hug her, and tell her how much she loved her. She wanted to tell her that she didn't care if she ever wore a sparking necklace again. But her wrenching gut told her she would never be able to talk to her mother again. She wanted to die. But even more, she wanted to kill the white people who had stripped her of her human rights and taken all that she loved away from her.

Would she get her wish ... as her mother got her wish when the black camel trader died in the desert? Only time would tell!

Flanked by Moses and Daisy, Nobuntu walked down a well-trodden pathway. She began to hear whisperings in her ear: "Be strong, my daughter. Survive this evil place. Learn to read and write, and then tell the world of our people's sufferings."

"Yes, Father," she thought silently.

Before hearing her father's spiritual whisperings, Nobuntu had felt despondent about life. Her father's unworldly presence changed her. She skipped childhood. Her thoughts transformed into those of an adult. Resignation and peace accompanied her new courage. She *would* learn the language and writings of the white man. She *would* secretly document everything.

In the unforgiving hot South African climate, Nobuntu's oversized, heavy woolen dress with dropped shoulders and long sleeves seemed absurd. The Hallworthy slaves' clothing allowance had recently ceased, as had the periodic hand-me-downs, so the slave seamstress had used scraps of blanket cloth to make Nobuntu's outfit. Thankfully, a cotton petticoat prevented the coarse dress from chaffing the girl's leg ulcers. A stained and dingy cloth turban covered part of Nobuntu's shame—hairless sore patches caused by years of exposure to bloodsucking head lice. Daisy would have liked to shave the child's head to make it easier to spot lice, but using the rusty shaving blade today would have ripped her tender scalp. Instead, the maid treated Nobuntu's infested hair with pickling vinegar and coarse salt and then spent hours combing out the lice eggs.

With the hem of her dress dragging through the dirt, a barefoot Nobuntu held Daisy's hand. She had no idea where she was going or what lay in store for her. All she saw was that it was a glorious sunny day, and she was finally free of her shackles. After four years of confinement, the warm sun felt good on her neck.

As best she could, Nobuntu straightened her limp neck so she could look around. She saw wonderful sights and heard amazing sounds, all of which had been denied her during her imprisonment. Birds serenaded from thorn trees; honey bees hovered over exotic plants; the silver leaves of manicured shrubbery shimmered in the sunlight. A smile of recognition came to the girl's full mouth as she observed a dung beetle frantically moving his prized fecal possession from being trampled upon by her feet. Back home, she had marveled at this tiny creature's ability to create a home for its offspring, though the material of construction left something to be desired. Nobuntu sighed. She wished she were a dung beetle trundling homeward.

Nobuntu was renamed "Netty" on Nigel's slave register (a name she refused to accept). She joined other black men, women, and children planting sugar cane seeds at the crack of dawn. The men dug trenches by using ropes to pull wooden plows. The females walked behind, planting seeds by hand.

Nigel thought nothing of using human labor instead of plow horses. He regarded equine creatures to be superior to *apes!*

Hundreds of acres of Hallworthy land, previously wild and untamed, were now dedicated to sugar cultivation and milling. The same land that had once served as the killing fields of its satanic landowner was now being put to an accepted use. That same year, Nigel was diagnosed with chronic rheumatoid arthritis. His condition severely affected his hands and feet, leaving him unable to participate in his favorite pastime—man hunting.

Due to his medical incapacity, Nigel halted the clandestine importation of slaves from the West Coast of Africa, but he kept the indentured servants, many of whom had given birth to what would become his next generation of unfortunate workers. In the years to come, Nigel's son, Peter, and grandson, Alan, would use these ill-fated workers as slave labor for the sugar refinery. Nigel's descendants inherited his lust for murder, especially Lord Alan Hallworthy.

A swollen veil of blood would forever hang over Africa, immortalizing the lost children of the region. Millions of ghostly voices would rise from their graves and scatter worldwide. Their voices would be heard through a great African man, Nelson Mandela, the first president of the Republic of South Africa to be elected under the country's new constitution.

In 1844 the killing fields that had been drenched with slave blood were mercifully overrun with weeds. Nigel's grounds lay as silent as a monastery, quietly honoring the large number of souls whose bodies were entombed on the Devil's property.

Nobuntu's past stirred her to develop a strong will to survive. She moved beyond the shattered fragments of what passed before and turned into a good worker. She was loved by all, especially the younger children of the workers, many of whom had been sired by Nigel and his guests.

One night, when a young female worker returned to the servant shack crying, Nobuntu consoled her and asked, "Why do you weep with such sadness?"

"You are too young to know why my tears of sorrow flow."

"I'm not *that* young!" retorted Nobuntu.

Through her tears, the teenager forced a smile. She knew Nobuntu would one day meet her fate, so she lowered her voice and spoke just above a whisper. "If you can help it, don't go anywhere

near the master's home, and if you see him entering the field, hide
…"

"Why?" Nobuntu interrupted.

After a long sigh, the teenager divulged the dark truth: "I am the new bed warmer. Lots of women and girls here have been bed warmers …"

"What is a bed warmer?"

"Child, you are *young!*"

The teenager felt protective toward this innocent girl, and that prompted her to be honest. She spoke of her own violation—sexual abuse—and how her body had kept Nigel's bed warm, until he threw her out of the room.

Nobuntu clutched at her mouth. She swallowed the bile that had arisen in disgust. When she regained control, she blurted out an idea that had often crossed her mind. "Let's run away!" she urged.

"I wish it were that simple," replied the hurting teenager. "Many have tried, but all of them were caught and whipped nearly to death, or lynched … left hanging on the trees for days."

It was all too much for Nobuntu. She imagined her tender body hanging limply from the aloe tree she admired alongside the shack. The teenager continued. "The Master can do *anything* he likes to us girls. He owns us. We are his property. Fighting back is futile. We have no weapons," she said, taking the girl's hand into hers. "No one cares about us. We are *black apes!*" he tells us.

There was no telling if this man's dark behavior would continue or not!

Tragically, in the British Colony of South Africa, before and after abolition, black men, women, and children continued to be enslaved. No one in power, colonial or republican, cared enough to make a change until the inhumane segregation was abolished by Nelson Mandela.

Nobuntu did not give up her dream of escape, but for now, she pushed it away because she was concerned for those around her.

The field workers' children called her "Ma." At bedtime they crowded around her in a shack where twenty young and not-so-young workers slept. "Tell us a story, Ma!" the children implored.

With the memory of her beloved mother fresh in her mind, Nobuntu smiled broadly and began. "There were two monkeys who climbed down from the sacred tulip tree to help a little bird that had fallen out of its nest …"

When the children were fast asleep, she lay down on her bed thinking of the revered, spiritual tree of her homeland. Although she did not want to admit it, Nobuntu felt the likelihood of her ever again seeing its spiritual splendor was slim. But that didn't stop her from *longing* to return home and tell the tree of her woes—and of her nightmarish fears of becoming a bed-warmer.

That night tears flooded onto Nobuntu's rough straw mattress.

The next day she resolved to no longer relive the past. Certain memories, however, should never be forgotten, and certain sad events were impossible to forget.

As Nobuntu readied herself for work, she remembered her father's words—to document. She knew she must teach herself to read and write. That evening after work, she sought out Daisy.

"I need you to do something for me," Nobuntu said. A shocked Daisy interrupted Nobuntu's request. "I will hang from the nearest tree if I am caught stealing paper and pen for you."

"But Daisy ..."

"Don't say another word, child," Daisy pouted. "I love you, but I'm not going to swing from a tree for you. And that is that!"

Even though Daisy's mind was made up, she gave Nobuntu's request further thought. "How wonderful it would be if she did learn to read and write. She could then teach me and the others who have been denied this right."

In the end it was Moses who "liberated" Nobuntu's requested items. Whenever possible and when time allowed, he tutored her. He marveled at her agility to learn the white man's tongue.

One evening, when Moses was in the shack, Nobuntu needled him into revealing what other heinous deeds, apart from the abuse of young women, went on behind the closed doors of Hallworthy Manor.

"Child, don't ask questions," Moses said. "Questions are dangerous."

Over the course of time, Nobuntu learned the layout of the three-story mansion from Daisy, especially the location of the second floor bedroom. Because of his worsening rheumatoid arthritis, Nigel spent most of his time there with his favorite dog, a German shepherd named Fritz.

Nobuntu became obsessed with plotting a bittersweet revenge

on behalf of her beloved mother, whom she believed died hanging from a tree. The girl was certain her mother would have fought the hands that placed that noose!

She thought often of getting payback for the mixed-blood children who were destined for lives of brutal hardship without pay. And she yearned for revenge for all of the violated "bed warmers."

As time went by, vengeance became more than an obsession to Nobuntu.

A year later Nobuntu turned eleven. She was remarkably mature for her age. Nourishing food had put flesh on her bones, and her breasts were budding toward womanhood. She knew most of the young boys noticed her, but she hoped to avoid Nigel's lecherous gaze. Little did Nobuntu know that the predator *had been* watching her every movement and that he was too close for comfort. Sometimes she could feel *his* eyes upon her.

One fine day Nobuntu did not need to turn around to see whose eyes were boring into her neck. They had crossed paths the first day she was put to work in the field. Mpande, a boy two years her senior, had been her instructor. He had helped her fill her planting quota—forty rows—until she was able to keep up with the rest of the slaves on her own. Apart from talking about farming, they had said little to each other. But recently Nobuntu noticed that at every available moment he would engage her in conversation on matters not related to work.

Today, with his arms behind his back, he sidled up to her. His face was beaming when he said, "This is for you."

Nobuntu stared at a lovely linked-daisy chain. "It's so beautiful," she gushed, and placed the white flower arrangement around her neck.

Mpande flashed a sweet, genuine smile for the person he'd grown to love. He said, "I know it can never replace the one your mother promised you, but at least it will remind you of her."

Mpande's kind sentiment melted Nobuntu's heart and created a magnetic connection. What the besotted young man added was a complete surprise.

"Will you marry me?"

Surprised, she said, "Don't be silly. I am only eleven!"

"But you have the body of a thirteen-year-old, the right age to become the wife of a future Zulu king."

Nobuntu laughed until her insides cramped. But unspoken questions consumed her: "Should she dare love another? Hadn't her mother married young? Hadn't her father, Kofi, fought to gain her thirteen-year-old mother's love?"

Mpande stamped his feet. "You can laugh all you like, Nobuntu of the Bobo tribe, and Netty of the white tribe," he said in an injured tone, "but I will not give up. You'll see. You will become my wife one day."

Even though she spurned his marriage proposal, she wanted to know more about the tall, handsome boy who alleged he had royal blood. Was that true?

It was.

That evening Nobuntu proudly wore her sun-wilted daisy necklace as she sat with Mpande outside the shack. She listened intently as he spoke of the day, when he was just a child, that the slave traders, who were as dark as he, entered his Elangeni kraal in northwest Zululand. He told her how terrified he had been; how many of his people had died fighting for their lives; how his cowardly father, King of the Elangeni, had run away, leaving his wife and four children to fend for themselves; and how he and his mother were chained and marched for days on end to reach the Hallworthy estate.

He talked about how his mother had begged for water to save him when he had fainted. How they became separated.

The last he saw of his mother was when they unshackled her, dragged her screaming to a horse-drawn cart, and threw her into the back. She was gone. Mpande's last memory was of a dust cloud shrouding the woman who had brought him into this sick world.

The day Mabali and Nobuntu arrived at the Manor, they replaced Mpande in the infamous building. It had been his home for two days. When he was released, he was taken to the stables, where he slept and worked with Skinny Tom taking care of Nigel's Arabian horses. Skinny Tom treated him like a son. When the sugar cane fields became operational, Mpande was sent to the fields to work.

Mpande did not know what became of his father. But through a newcomer to the fields, he learned of his mother's sad demise. The new acquisition had the strength of two oxen in the fields, and he loved to gossip.

When Mpande's mother had become too "old" for her employer's taste, she was sold to another slave master, who beat her to death without ramification.

How would these poor, uneducated, enslaved people have reacted if had they learned of the abominable English law decreed in all British colonies? "It is illegal for a white man to have sex with a black woman."

*Time does not pass ... it continues!*

By the time Nobuntu turned thirteen, the wheel of time had changed her. Her shapely, full-breasted body resembled that of a much older girl. She had had her first period, but without the purification rights given to Bobo maidens. Even so, she could not prevent the feelings of sensuality and desire that arose when Mpande's hand clasped hers.

No boy had ever held her hand. It was exhilarating. She had a huge crush. Mpande understood her emotions. He was in love. Every day was magic for them. Nobuntu's desire for Mpande pulsated through her body. But from a distance, someone else was noticing her leap from puberty into maidenhood.

Nigel had acquired a wheelchair equipped with two large wheels and one small. Most afternoons Moses pushed him around his spectacular gardens and then on to the perimeters of the sugar field where Nobuntu worked. He had watched her for two years with debased sexual desire. She was an ape, but she was ripe. She was perfect. She would obey his every whim.

Wrong!

As Nobuntu prattled to herself with her back to Nigel, she failed to notice that her master had advanced or that his eyes were fixed on her. Suddenly, she felt a chill. She sensed his penetrating eyes roving over her body. When she finally looked at the devil, her heart drummed to the beat of fear.

Fortunately, Nigel's visit to the field was brief.

That evening Nobuntu spoke to Mpande in a grave voice about her biggest fear—being raped. In a Zulu warrior stance, Mpande stomped his feet. With a manly voice, he intoned, "I will not let that happen. I will kill him first. We'll leave immediately … run away."

"Yes, please," Nobuntu said with a sigh of relief. "But before we go, there is something I must do."

Mpande's eyes grew wide as he said, "I will help you."

Seven hours later, as planned, the Bobo maiden and her Zulu boyfriend slipped silently from their dwelling places into the darkness.

*Netty* no more, she retrieved the iron collar that had imprisoned her for so long. While hiding it beneath two layers of her clothing, she and Mpande headed for the Manor house under the cover of night. Their shadows merged with the murky air.

They entered the manor house through a downstairs window and made their way to Nigel's bedroom. With beads of sweat running down his forehead, Mpande turned the brass doorknob and jumped back.

Their murder plot was foiled by the fierce barking of a German shepherd and a "Who's there?" shout from Nigel. Mpande and Nobuntu made a hasty retreat. It was only a matter of minutes before Nigel summoned Moses. The runaways were lucky they did not all meet on the stairs.

After the aborted attempt to remove the Devil from his lair, two sets of bare feet raced from the manor house. They seemed to glide on air as they ran toward freedom.

But revenge never left Nobuntu's heart. Would the opportunity arise to finish what she had started?

For a week and a half the young couple carefully concealed themselves as they traveled on foot. When they arrived at Mpande's place of birth—Zululand—they delighted at being alive, happy, and healthy. If Nobuntu's life was to have meaning, she had to begin again without her precious mother. So a week later, standing under a baobab tree, their union as King and Queen of the Elangeni tribe was performed by the village elder. Nine months later, in 1850, Nobuntu gave birth to their first son, Dinuzulu, who would claim his throne after his father died.

Years flew by.

Queen Nobuntu was as happy as she could ever hope to be, but her deeply rooted wounds remained fresh. She had never given up plotting her revenge. She wanted justice for *all* slaves. She did not feel Nigel deserved to breathe the same air as other mortals.

Would she get her wish?

Yes.

One foggy morning in 1858, when Moses opened Nigel's bedroom door to deliver his breakfast tray, he found his master stone-cold dead. What astonished Moses most was the rusty, blood-stained, slave collar lying next to Nigel's stiff body. Moses had no doubt whom it had belonged to.

Not long after Nobuntu's and Mpande's escape, Moses had noticed them entering the infamous outbuilding, which was at the time empty of human suffering.

*Revenge is a dish best served cold!*

The coroner concluded that Nigel had died of natural causes!

Nobuntu waited several years before putting a plan into action. When the time was right, she set the pendulum of the past into inexorable motion.

With heart-pounding anxiety and trepidation, Nobuntu and her husband made their way to the Hallworthy estate under the cloak of darkness. Nobuntu carried a bag of poisoned deer meat strapped to her waist. She had no way of knowing that Fritz the dog had long since passed away.

Using a candle to light their way, they gingerly climbed the stairwell to Nigel's bedroom. As they approached the door, they expected Nigel's companion to alert his master. To their delight there was only stillness.

"Hurry," Nobuntu urged her husband.

Using the element of surprise, Mpande straddled Nigel, placed a pillow over his face, held it down forcibly, and began smothering the hated man. When the flailing of arms and legs stopped, Nobuntu placed an iron collar at the foot of the bed of the dead Lord of Slaves. With tears flowing, Nobuntu softly said, "This is for you, my beloved Amma, and *all* who have suffered at the hands of this evil monster. You and Father can now rest in peace."

Continued whisperings in her ear convinced Nobuntu that her father was *not* alive. She never questioned why she did not hear similar whisperings from her mother, whom she believed had also passed over.

Nobuntu's heart was filled with loathing as she stared into the petechial, hemorrhaged, blood spots in Nigel's rigid, open eyes.

But she also felt tranquility. Revenge was sweet—sweeter than life itself. With injuries and crimes avenged, she felt peace in a heart that had been hurting for too long. Suddenly, her childish laughter returned. She was free.

Wearing the smirk of an avenging angel, Nobuntu, with Mpande at her side, rushed down the stairwell and disappeared into the dawn of new day.

Twenty-five years later, Nobuntu died in childbirth at the age of forty-eight. Her grieving husband died two years later of an unknown illness.

Before Nobuntu passed away, she fulfilled her promise to her father. She documented everything that had happened: her capture in West Africa, her incarceration in the infamous outbuilding, and everything else that had happened before she ran away toward freedom at age thirteen. She did not chronicle her night of revenge. That secret was buried with her in her grave.

Mercifully, Nobuntu did not live to see the cost of their family's achievements to her firstborn son, warrior King Dinuzulu. He was captured by the British in 1890 and exiled to the island of St. Helena, the same island on which another warrior had resided—Napoleon in 1815.

Nobuntu's written records of what happened to her and to other enslaved victims fell into the hands of a renowned South African journalist in the late 1990s. His book, *The Smoldering Fire of the Unforgiving,* would become a bestseller.

How could the woman who had documented such a painful time in history know that her proud Bobo bloodline would, appallingly, live on through the next batch of Hallworthy slaves, this time under the control of Lord Alan Hallworthy, Nigel's grandson?

And how would she feel about another child slave, a white child named Shiya, whose foster mother *did* carry her Bobo blood?

# CHAPTER FIFTEEN

# Mabali, aka Maisie
## -1844-

*"Life only lasts a single day because tomorrow
one may not awake."*
—ANONYMOUS

"This is Maisie, Dr. Flynn," Moses said as he presented the visibly shaking Mabali, who was now named according to Nigel's slave registry.

"She is here to help you with Stanley," Moses added.

Liam did not know whether to laugh or cry.

On his doorstep stood a small, dark-skinned young woman, her eyes downcast, clutching a parasol and wearing a ridiculous outfit.

Liam was taken aback. No lady, young or old, with any pretensions to taste would ever have worn a dress of crimson. But she was no *white* lady!

Mabali's full-skirted, crimson, velvet dress, adorned with green silk and black velvet ribbons, was accentuated by a petticoat hoop that provoked even more mirth in Liam. "If the wind blows, she is going airborne," he muttered under his breath.

What was equally amusing was her head covering: a plain

white bonnet with red and green ribbons dangling on the sides. The bonnet struggled to contain the unkempt, thick, curly hair beneath. "No hairbrush could untangle that," Liam mused. He took control of his amusing thoughts and looked at the real picture. He was positive that Nigel bore a grudge for the events that occurred in his study the day before. This must be his pathetic attempt to show his displeasure—by humiliating a slave.

*Nigel's full fury was yet to come.*

"Welcome, Maisie," Liam said with a warm, welcoming smile. "I'm so happy to have you here to help me with the nursing of the injured boy."

It was a slave name she would *never* acknowledge. She was *Mabali*, the "flower," from West Africa.

His words, wrapped in a strong Irish accent, were lost to her.

Moses intervened, "Her English is poor, Doctor."

"Never mind," he responded. "We will communicate somehow. We will find a way to overcome the language barrier."

Before leaving the doctor's doorstep, Moses dutifully passed on Nigel's parting message: "Lord Hallworthy would like Maisie returned to the estate in four weeks."

Though annoyed by the short notice, Liam was a man of his word. He nodded his acceptance, even though his mind snubbed the idea. In his professional estimation, Stanley's injuries would take at least eight to twelve weeks of caretaking ... if there weren't further lung-related complications.

Moses smiled, tenderly patting Mabali's shoulder. Under different circumstances, he would have liked to get to know her better. By slave rule, he was not allowed to have a wife or girlfriend, so for years he had been lonely and lacking companionship. Moses wished he had not been her escort away from the Hallworthy Estate. But he knew she was better off here than in the hellhole in which she had been imprisoned (and probably would have been for years to come if the doctor had not interceded).

Liam lightly took hold of Mabali's arm and guided her into his house. Mabali, who barely came up to his waist, was in awe. The strange man's home was beautiful, decorated with elegant furnishings she'd never before seen or imagined. She lifted her head to smell nature's perfumes coming from a large vase of cut blooms. What caught her attention most was a large painting of a sad African child about her daughter's age standing in front of a hut. She envisioned her home. It was a world away, but she had never truly left.

The African scene triggered the memory of a recent, pitiful voice: "Amma, Amma, don't leave me."

Mabali's heart jumped to her throat, and tears of anger fell. She screamed in Liam's face. "Where is my daughter? I want my daughter! What has the slave man done with her? Why am I here? I don't want to be here in this bad land. I don't want to wear these stupid clothes! I want to take my daughter home where she belongs!

Naturally, Liam did not understand a word of her tirade, but he guessed that she had unloaded a huge baggage of grief. He knew nothing of her background, except that the trauma of being held against her will played a big part in her outburst.

Compassion overwhelmed him as he circled his arms around her. Mabali pulled away violently. "Do not touch me, white man," she cried, raising the parasol as if it were a spear.

"Oh, my dear," Liam said "What is the matter?"

Her sorrow increased her anger. Mabali pointed at the picture.

Liam's heart went out to the girl whose memory was triggered by the painting, a gift from his solicitor, a dark-skinned man. However, Kadir Yar'Adua was a free man. He was one of very few black men allowed to practice law in this British Colony. His only *white* client was Liam.

Liam considered re-gifting the picture to her when she had a home of her own, but he quickly reverted to a more realistic notion: "You are not thinking clearly, dear fellow. Concentrate on what *is* real!"

"It's all right," Liam soothed her aloud. "You will be safe here. I promise."

He did know how long he could keep that promise. He understood that her tears were words waiting to be spoken.

Liam's gaze lingered on her exquisite black pearl eyes. He hadn't really noticed until now how beautiful she was or how young, which beckoned a question, "How old are you, Maisie?"

Mabali slapped her chest in anger and spat out in her own language, "Maisie, *no*. *Mabali* is my name and I'm twenty-two summers old."

Liam sprang into action—gesticulating counting movements with his fingers: "one, two, three, four ..."

Mabali understood. She grabbed his hand, spread his fingers wide, and counted out twenty-two in her native tongue.

A broad smile broke out on Liam's face. "Given time, we are going to understand each other perfectly."

It did not take her long to become further acquainted with Liam's sign language, as she had previously encountered it with Moses and Daisy.

In the days that followed, Mabali's unbecoming red garment was exchanged for a simple cotton dress and apron. She became a wonderful caretaker and constant companion to the exploited sweep who was healing from a bone fracture and had a twisted spine. The five-year-old's cherub's face, big brown eyes, and unruly hair captured Mabali's heart. He cried when she left his bedside. He delighted when she told him stories. When she was near, he could not take his eyes off her. Neither did his savior's eyes wander far from Mabali.

Liam knew that his developing love for Mabali, the fire burning in his heart, would not end well in this country of hate, if he chose to take his emotions further.

No matter how Liam tried to encourage Mabali to walk freely in his spectacular gardens overflowing with exotic blooms, she refused. He guessed she was fearful of what lay beyond the high walls of Alderbury House.

Despite her self-imposed imprisonment, Liam couldn't have been happier to have her in his life. The greatest improvement to his lonely single lifestyle was enjoying Mabali's company at the dinner table. Afternoon tea with her on the front porch was also delightful. And his heart sang as they wished each other "good-night" before retiring to their separate rooms. Watching Mabali perform her caretaking duties (washing, feeding, and changing Stanley's leg strappings) was icing on the cake. She succeeded at everything she did.

To the unforgiving world around them, colored folk living under the same roof as white folk was the vilest of sins. Nevertheless, Liam had always felt a deep moral obligation to respond to human suffering. In this country of racial hatred, he felt trapped by the unconscionable segregation rules. He never saw *color*, only *fellow* human beings. And he saw Mabali as a sweet, shy woman with whom he would be happy to spend the rest of his life. That is, if she felt the same about him. Was it too soon to feel love? Would the difference in age be a factor?

Teasingly, he told himself, "I'm still young enough at heart to feel the warmth of love again."

But how would he tackle the biggest obstacle to his love? He knew that the odds were stacked high against such a union. If Mabali felt the same as he did, their love would be *illegal*. Strict colonial laws prohibited interracial marriage, cohabitation, and sex, especially with indentured slaves and even with free blacks. Liam would not be able to walk the streets with Mabali without attracting trouble—racial slurs or worse, imprisonment.

Liam refused to dwell on the impossible. But timing was once more of the essence.

It would be a while before the wounds caused by the atrocious British ban on love between people of different colors was healed, and even longer to reconcile the pain caused by the Dutch apartheid ruling that stripped away human dignity.

At a much younger age, Liam had married, albeit briefly. The couple had met at an opera house in Dublin, after being introduced by a medical colleague. Liam fell for the attractive redhead, and a few months later they were married in a Protestant church. He had long forsaken the Catholic faith that his staunch church-going parents believed in. "Look where that got them," he thought.

As far as Liam knew, their marriage was fine—until he was served with divorce papers three months into the relationship. What a surprise! He could have been knocked down by a feather!

Divorce was not easy in those days. What shocked Liam most was that his wife, who supposedly had been visiting her sick mother in England, had cited "conjugal failure due to impotency." Liam, a virile young man, realized that she had not been visiting a sick mother in England, but instead, rekindling an affair with a man whom she had previously been engaged to.

Liam did not fight the outrageous allegations and agreed to the divorce, a costly affair of £10,000 pounds for being "impotent."

Obviously, the wedding oath "till death do us part" would not be fulfilled.

After the decree nisi, Liam had flirted with other women at dinner parties, but the bitten and spurned man had decided to remain single.

Now, his strongest desire was to free Nigel's boy and female slave from having to return to the Hallworthy estate. Could he pull it off? Trust was an issue during these awful times, but he needed to confide in someone.

Liam took a leap of faith and summoned Ajeet and Amrita, who had been in his employ for ages. They were free servants able to come and go as they pleased.

Liam's secret intention stunned both servants. They loved the kind, retired doctor who had treated many of their family members for free.

For a moment Ajeet felt an impulse to laugh, but he respectfully pulled himself together.

"Dr. Liam, it is impossible. What you wish to achieve is not only dangerous, it is suicidal."

Amrita, after a long silence, spoke, but not before taking a long, deep breath. "Does she know you love her?" A troubling thought pervaded Amrita's mind.

"The girl's been here less than two weeks, and he wants to marry her," she thought.

"Not yet," Liam replied.

Ajeet and Amrita also felt affection towards Mabali. With Liam's daily tutoring, her English was improving quickly. While Amrita thought nothing of serving meals to the mixed-race couple, it would have horrified the racists outside Alderbury House. Segregation was part of the world colored servants were born into.

Seated in a chair opposite his solicitor, Liam explained the reason for his visit. His legal adviser tried not to reveal his astonishment.

"Was the man completely witless?" thought the adviser. "Had

he lost his mind and gone stark, raving mad? Had he broken contact with reality?"

"Let me be clear, Dr. Flynn," Kadir Yar'Adua said. "You want to marry a *black* girl who is owned by Lord Nigel Hallworthy. And you want the courts to *free* her from her slave holder?"

"Correct," Liam stated curtly. He was placing his hopes and dreams on this.

The solicitor shook his head. The good doctor had been a client for many years, and the solicitor had undertaken many of Liam's requests—such as drafting a will and defending an unfounded malpractice suit that was dismissed. He had completed servant employment records for Liam, but he had never been asked to take on a suicide mission!

The solicitor admired and respected Dr. Flynn. He regarded him as a true friend. However, it was his legal obligation to advise his client against the course of action he was proposing.

"The Magna Carta of 1215 did recognize that all persons had a basic right to liberty," Liam's solicitor stated. "But, my friend, this does not apply in South Africa because the English courts *favor* slave owners. There are known manumission cases—freeing of slaves by slave owners or giving freedom to devoted servants after long years of service—but I'm afraid this will not happen for a twenty-two-year-old black girl and a black boy owned by someone else."

Liam did not become conscious of his fingernails piercing his palms until they drew blood. "There has to be a loophole, regardless of age, to free a human being from slavery."

If there is, I certainly do not know of it," Kadir responded.

Watching his client's eyes mist with tears brought a lump to the solicitor's throat. He saw a good man who did not see *color* as a barrier to freedom. Liam was trying to save the lives of *his* black people.

"I will do all I can for you to make this happen, but I can't promise you a happy ending."

Liam returned home.

With hope in his heart, Liam conveyed his intention to Amrita, who somehow made Mabali understand. This time Mabali did not pull away from Liam's embrace. She clung to him gratefully and lovingly. Liam surged with happiness when he saw the smile on Mabali's face—a smile that could launch a million stars.

Mabali the slave was being reborn.

A week later, Liam received a letter from his solicitor:

*Dr. Flynn, as I write this letter, a court document is on its way to Lord Hallworthy. I have asked him to provide proof of legal ownership documents for Mabali and Stanley, which he cannot produce. Everyone in the circle of who's-who is aware of Lord Hallworthy's scurrilous practices: capturing and enslaving men, women, and children long after it was legal to do so. It has also come to my attention that Lord Hallworthy has little respect for authority and has bribed judges. So, I reluctantly suspect that the writ served him will most likely be ignored or lead to a retaliatory response. God help us.*

*It was signed "Kadir Yar'Adua, Solicitor."*

*"PS: Please have patience. I will do the best I can for you, Mabali, Stanley, and Mabali's daughter, if she is still alive."*

For three weeks happiness reigned in Liam's household. Everyone was content, waiting for new, *free* beginnings. Liam had gifted Mabali a forgotten right to happiness.

With the glow of love in the air, Mabali took daily walks in the garden with Liam, their hands linked. Her knowledge of the English tongue improved well enough to make her understood by the doctor when they talked. It felt as though they were destined to be together from the moment they met.

The couple spent many evenings by the fireplace with Liam reading aloud. Using a bit of pantomime and a few hand gestures, Mabali was quick to learn.

Liam was a gentleman. He declared they would not be intimate until they were married.

But "death do us part" would apply.

Mabali was in a new frame of mind, looking forward to becoming a wife and substitute mother to young Stanley. But most of all, she delighted at the prospect of being reunited with Nobuntu, whom she missed deeply. The dream of bringing in her daughter to share their happy lives was indescribable.

Against the odds, Stanley was healing well. His lungs were functioning normally, his bones healing properly, and his spirit becoming joyful. One afternoon, with his moon-like face beaming with mischief, he reached over and pinched Mabali's bottom. "Better get used to it if you are to become my mother."

Mabali laughed. Stanley could never take away the ache she felt for her biological child, but he more than compensated by gifting Mabali the rapture of motherhood. She recalled what a fun and happy child Nobuntu was before their capture and how she had struggled to keep the child's bubbly, happy-go-lucky traits alive during captivity.

The serenity in Liam's home came to an abrupt end when a heart-breaking tragedy struck. It began on a Sunday night, the day before Moses was to return Mabali and Stanley to the estate, with what sounded like exploding firecrackers.

It ended as a horrific *murder* scene—*perfect* contract killings.

As dawn approached, the three people in the home—Liam, Mabali, and Stanley—were burning to death. They would never see another sunrise, winter, summer, or spring. Their lives were destroyed in a single night. They were violently robbed of their futures.

Fire was Nigel's choice of weapon, a convenient means of dispensing with the formality of a court appearance. Nigel the serial killer was above the law! Impervious to pity, he sent the world the message: "Do not cross my path!" No one had ever reneged on a deal with Nigel and gotten away with it. In his twisted mind, Liam had gone back on his word.

Lord Nigel Hallworthy was the Devil incarnate.

The inferno, a wall of flames, was unforgettable.

As dawn broke, the sun hid behind the heavy plumes of smoke. It was as if the sun were mourning the dead.

The person who had deliberately set Liam's house ablaze was a professional arsonist. Not only did he know what he was doing, but he understood that arson was tricky to prove. The evidence confirming the actions an arsonist was destroyed in the fire. The opened doors and windows that ventilated Alderbury House enabled the fire to spread rapidly. The flammable substance that had caused the destruction was unknown! But whatever it was—possibly alcohol—fueled the intense heat and burning timbers.

Not far from the catastrophe, Liam's faithful servants, Ajeet and Amrita dressed in their nightwear and satin slippers, dropped to their knees in a carpet of thick ash. They cupped their shaking hands over their mouths. Words failed them. But their horrified expressions said it all.

Standing near the scene, they heard dry timbers crackle—a horrendous noise, like the explosion of many firearms being discharged at once. Yellow and white flames leapt through thick, swirling, black smoke that was twisting and twirling in a fiery dance. With misty eyes and devastated hearts, Liam's servants knew who the ultimate culprit was. Did their employer have foresight of this tragic event? The solicitor, Kadir Yar'Adua, thought so. Liam's instructions had arrived by mail in his office two days ago.

*In the event of my death, I leave everything to my beloved Mabali. Should anything happen to cause both of our deaths, which is likely the case, I wish my estate and savings to go to Ajeet and Amrita. Should we be murdered, I wish to be buried with Mabali in an unmarked grave on the grounds of my property. Should little Stanley meet the same fate, he is to join us.*

Kadir Yar'Adua had a duty to report his suspicions to the proper authorities, which he did. But *no* investigation was ever carried out. He was not surprised. Most of the fire marshals were Masons, as was Nigel and all the other *white folk!*

Kadir was disgusted with the system, but there was little else he could do.

Nigel's influence over life and death had prevailed … for now.

With a heavy heart, Kadir Yar'Adua followed his client's last instructions. Liam, Mabali, and Stanley were buried together at the far end of the Liam's property behind Ajeet and Amrita's cottage.

At the gravesite, Ajeet recited a Hindu prayer for the dead.

"Our salutations, adorations, and prostrations to Dr. Liam, the lovely Mabali, and the child whose African name is Umfunti, who have gone ahead of us. Today we offer our blessings to them who are not visible to our physical eyes but who lived on this earth-plane and who now ascend to a different state of being."

A sobbing Amrita added, "I will miss you all, but you are now *free* of discrimination and *free* to love in the afterworld without punishment."

She and her husband believed in the law of karma, a Buddhist teaching: for every ill one human being inflicts on another, threefold punishment will be visited upon him. This gave them some consolation.

But Amrita would never forget their final agonized screams for help!

Kadir Yar'Adua sighed heavily before he said his final prayer: "Allahu Akbar, O Lord of Two Worlds. Replace their earthly home for a better one, and make their resting place full of light."

Were their prayers heard by divine forces?

The answer hovered overhead, but no one in attendance looked up.

Directly above the mourners, obscured by gray smoke, a dark patch floated over the gravesite. Tears of blood mingled with fallen ash, followed by the whisperings of a departed soul: "I have longed for this day, my darling wife, never to be parted again."

Will this spiritual carrier ever cleanse the rotten blood of Nigel's evil? Will the thousands of previously enslaved souls entombed in unmarked graves across Africa and the globe ever see these crimes against humanity rectified?

Mabali's life was cut short. She would never witness her eleven-year-old daughter's escape, her marriage, or the birth of her royal sons, who would make history. Many of the descendants who carried her bloodline would display her unique eye color. Some would be as small in stature as she was, and others would be as tall as mountains.

Would she know that it was Nobuntu's doing that finally removed the Devil incarnate from the face of the earth? If she did know, she would raise her fist from the grave in a victory salute.

It was long overdue, but Lord Nigel Hallworthy got what he deserved—his permanent removal from all living things!

Sadly, three of Mabali's descendants *would* land on the same rotten soil at the turn of a new century. They would enter the same gateway to hell she and Nobuntu had. One of these descendants would rescue a white child, who would also become a slave—of the worst kind!

Ajeet and Amrita, with the money Liam bequeathed them, left South Africa for good. They travelled to India, the birthplace of their parents.

There, they had three children. They named their first born son Liam, the second boy Stanley, and the third, a girl child, Mabali.

Not a day went by that Amrita did not think of them. She missed them so much.

Ajeet and Amrita lived long lives, and they never forgot that fateful morning in 1844.

# Part Two

## 1927 - 1950

# CHAPTER SIXTEEN

# Anele Dingane

*"Indeed, slave history is nothing more than a*
*tableau of crimes and misfortune."*
—VOLTAIRE

It was February 1927. On this blisteringly hot day in Zulu-land, a tall, slim girl, her body wet with perspiration, emerged through the doorway of her family's hut. Her large, dark eyes, the color of ebony pearls, searched the compound. She huffed. Where were they? Her twin sisters, Thaka and Zhana, age fifteen and measuring less than five feet tall, should have been at the fire pit. It was their responsibility to collect firewood for the cook.

The attached-at-the-hip sisters were nowhere in sight.

Anele, age nine, let out a disgruntled sigh. She wanted to tell them that she was feeling better—that the fever caused by the black widow spider bite had broken. She spotted Mercy, the village cook, scowling with her hands on her hips.

"Mercy," Anele shouted, "have you seen Thaka and Zhana?"

The cook replied snappily, "No, I haven't, and I can't say I'm happy about it. I had to send another girl to collect wood so we can eat tonight."

The mere thought of food prompted Anele's next question.

"What are you making? I'm hungry."

The woman sighed. "That's a good question. I'll make whatever *they* catch. And if I don't get firewood, no one will eat!"

Anele made an "ugh" face. She hoped it wasn't monkey meat again. Of late, this malodorous meal didn't sit well in her delicate stomach. However, she was old enough to understand that the recent drought had devastated most of their crops and livestock. So the daily task of providing food was left to the young men. With their slingshots and spears in hand, they make a three-mile hike to a protected game reserve. When they are lucky, their presence is not detected by a warden. The young poachers target a dainty gazelle and haul it back to the kraal on a reed stretcher.

For the past few days, the warden's patrols had stepped up, so monkey meat was most likely the menu of the day.

Anele headed for the dense shrubbery behind the circle of their mud-and-dung huts. She thought she heard familiar voices coming from behind a tall, concealing clump of dry grass. Anele was puzzled. Why were the twins not out collecting firewood? What were they whispering about? It was very strange, indeed.

Although Anele's curious nature impelled her to barge in and demand answers, instead, she patiently crouched down and strained her ears. Seconds later, she clapped her hand over her mouth. Were her ears tricking her? She strained harder. No, they couldn't be! Were the diminutive sisters, Thaka and Zhana, *really* planning to *leave* home without a word to anyone? How could they? They knew the rules—unmarried girls had to ask permission from their father to leave the village for *any* reason.

Their father, Naboto Dingane, chieftain of the village and a distant relative of King Dinuzulu, Nobuntu's son, was a stickler for tradition. He had made it clear on more than one occasion, "Until you marry, you will obey me in every way, or I'll take a stick to you."

Anele crept closer. She didn't want to miss a word.

"What if the storyteller who visits our village has made up the tale of riches to be had for all colors of skin?" Thaka asked.

Her sister answered, "Didn't you see storyteller's fine clothes? It must be true. But I have to ask you, Zhana, how else are we going to get money to buy cattle to replace our loss if we don't try?"

"Let's do it!" Thaka confirmed excitedly. "We will work hard and bring father lots of money to buy goats, cows, sunflower seeds, millet, and vegetables." She scratched her head and added, "But sister, we don't know the way!"

"I have a rough idea."

"What if we get lost … or worse?" Zhana said with worry in her voice. "We could be eaten by a lion or leopard!"

Anele, her mind racing like a thoroughbred, rushed into their hideout.

"I heard everything," she blurted, her face flushed with excitement. "And I'm coming with you. I can work, too."

Zhana's cheeks were flushed with annoyance. "Don't be so pig-stupid. You're far too young. We've heard from travelers passing through that the *umlungu*—the white-skinned tribe—only hire strong boys and older girls to work in their fields."

Zhana turned and smiled mischievously at her twin. "We might even find husbands."

Identical and inseparable, the gods had not bestowed the twins with comely features likely to excite would-be suitors. They were not pretty or tall and slender like Anele. They were short with mottled facial skin and bellies swollen like watermelons.

Despite their looks, suitors were available, though. But much to their father's annoyance, both girls balked at accepting traditional marriages. The twins were adamant. "We will not marry unless identical twin brothers come along."

*They* were the only twins for miles!

"Little sister," Zhana said, "you cannot go with us. You have to take care of our widowed father. He is much too sick to be left alone."

Chief Naboto, having taken to his bed—likely from a lack of food—was counting on his remaining three daughters. Five of his other daughters had already married and relocated to other villages. His only two sons had died from disease. He depended on the three sisters to care for him: bring him food, empty his urine pot, and fetch beer made from the Marula tree fruit.

Anele's anger spoke volumes. Yes, she loved her father. But why should she be the one to take care of him? Why did she always allow the headstrong twins to ruin her life?

Anele stamped her feet. "There are plenty of single and married women to see to father's needs. There is Matudia. I've seen the way she looks at father."

Zhana, the temperamental one, now made an angry face.

"Our father's private life has nothing to do with us. *You* must stay behind."

"Please, please, please, let me go with you," Anele pleaded.

"No."

Anele's eyes slanted. "I'll go and tell father," she threatened. "Then you'll be beaten and tied up like the goats."

Zhana lunged at Anele. With her hands on Anele's throat, she growled, "I'll see to it that you won't see another day if you dare to tell father."

Thaka, the meeker of the two, came to the rescue. Softly, she said to her angry sister, "If I make her promise, I know she won't tell father."

Anele slumped to the ground. A pool of urine gathered at her feet. Shame, mixed with rage, brought a rush of words. "I hate you, Zhana! I hate you, Thaka," she spat, rubbing her neck. "You're bad. I hope you *never* come back."

It wouldn't be long before Anele would regret those words.

Before daybreak the next morning, with her naked upper body exposed to the rising sun, Anele stealthily followed the twins. After walking for what seemed hours, she slipped on the precarious, rocky path and tumbled down an embankment. Her loud shrieks stopped the twins in their tracks.

Zhana kicked the dirt like a bull ready to charge. "She's in for a beating!" she raged. "That stupid child has followed us!"

"No, sister," Thaka countered adamantly. "I won't let you beat her. I'm going back to see if she's all right."

Anele's grass skirt, wrenched to her ankles, exposed her bare bottom.

Thaka bent down. Her sister's injuries were only minor grazes to her forehead, knees, and elbows. Nothing serious, except for their predicament. What should they do? Take Anele back? Thaka shook her head. Having had no permission to leave the kraal, that would be foolish. Their father would beat them *all*.

What concerned Thaka most was the real reason she did not want to go back—their father's undying hatred for the white race. He had voiced it often. "No child of mine will ever slave for white devils. I would rather starve first."

Naboto's raw hatred was more than justified.

When Naboto was thirty summers old, he led his tribesmen into battle against the Voortrekkers—Dutch colonial settlers. The Zulu call to arms to fight the invaders was answered without question. Every able-bodied man and boy swore to defend his homeland. The Zulu warriors were ambushed near a mangrove swamp, and the skirmish took its toll. They fought courageously, but tragically, their *assegais,* native spears, were no match for the rifles of the usurpers on horseback.

The small band of fighters found themselves hemmed in and trapped. One by one they dropped and were trampled by horses. Naboto was the last man standing, and he was shot in his right leg. He fell sideways. Another bullet struck his upper body. He crashed to the ground, bleeding profusely. Moments later, triumphant Dutchmen shot anyone who twitched. Naboto feigned death. He lay face down on the bloody ground and waited for them to leave. After a period of anguished quiet, Naboto called out, "My brothers, speak to me. Are any of you alive?"

He received no answer.

Naboto called out again.

The breath of silence met his ears.

Was he the only survivor?

The injured Naboto had to think fast. He would join his fallen brothers in death if he did not escape the area. He was about to stand up when he saw them: many pairs of glowing eyes—jungle predators anxious to pounce on a fresh kill. He used his spear as a crutch to help him rise, gritting his teeth through the excruciating pain.

It seemed to take him forever to travel the short distance to the dense undergrowth at one end of the killing field. Thorns and branches attacked his feverish flesh as his eyes scoured the area for a place to rest until daylight. Naboto reasoned that the night scavengers already had enough food. They would not be hungry enough to chase after him.

Naboto found a deep cavity in a decaying tree trunk. He packed his wounds with damp tree moss and hunkered down. Outside his resting place, the din of the scavengers grew louder, and was followed by the night-spitting roar of a dominant lioness summoning her pride.

Naboto hung his head in sadness. The thought of his people being torn apart made him livid. He cried out for revenge. "Ikloba, Dark Spirit of the Invisible Kingdom, strike the *umlungu* from our land with your tongue of fire. Sweep them into the ocean with your breath. Bring disease to all those who have spilled the blood of our brave warriors."

At first light, Naboto repacked his wounds with river mud and headed home.

In the weeks that followed his safe return, Naboto slowly recovered. But nothing could soothe his wounded spirit. Thoughts of the massacre and of being its sole survivor tormented him for the rest of his life. Over the years, Naboto grew bitter. He obsessively hated every white-skinned person—and with good cause.

The afternoon sun beat down like a copper mallet upon the bare heads of the silent sisters as they walked in single file. Lagging behind, Anele was deep in thought. Suddenly, she rushed to the front. She avoided eye contact with the mean twin as she apologized. "I'm sorr*eeee*," she said in a melodic voice. "I'll watch where I'm going so I don't fall again. And if I do trip, you can leave me. I'm sure some animal will find me tasty."

Thaka smiled. Zhana didn't. The unsmiling twin simply urged, "We must keep going before we lose too much daylight."

*Time is of the essence.* But they would wish it wasn't!

It took the sisters five long days to reach the Valley of a Thousand Hills described by the storyteller. They had walked during the day and slept in the boughs of tall Mountain Karee trees at night. Having consumed their meager rations of dried monkey meat, their bodies signaled pangs of hunger and thirst.

It was Thaka who spotted the fast-flowing irrigation ditch paralleling the rows of tall sugar cane plants. "Water, water!" she cried.

They all drank until their stomachs rebelled. Suddenly, their bodies stiffened and their ears cocked. What was that thunderous, fast-approaching noise sounding louder than village drums?

Anele didn't want to know. She flung herself back into the ditch. Flat on her stomach, she clung to the mossy embankment as if her life depended on it.

Nigel's grandson, Lord Alan Hallworthy, age sixteen, rode atop a tall, seventeen-hands-high black stallion. Foamy saliva dripped from the horse's bit. The young man halted his steed within inches of the twins. With his jaw jutting, he yelled in a refined British accent, "Get off my property, *now!* If I catch you stealing sugar cane, I'll shoot you."

The twins screamed at the top of their voices, "God of the Zulu people, help us!"

Anele just cupped her mouth. She thought of her father and the friends she had left behind. They could not help her here. Oh, how she wished she had never heard her sisters whispering in the bush. At this moment, even a monkey stew was more desirable than the unknown.

Kelingo, a relative of Nigel's deceased maid, Daisy, was working nearby in the cane field. He dropped his hoe and made his way over to investigate. When the twins saw the color of his dark skin, their native tongue spewed out of them like burst drainpipes.

Kelingo was their life jacket, or so he thought. "Boss, they are not here to steal. I think they want to work."

Alan gave the girls a dead stare, his lynx eyes hidden behind sunglasses. He began to check them over as if inspecting cattle.

The twins stared up at the sun-bronzed, high-cheekboned blond man who had a deceptively youthful appearance. Lurking behind his striking good looks was a malignant side—inherited, twisted, evil DNA.

The brutal legacy of the Hallworthy line lived on in the new Lord.

*An apple does not fall far from the tree.*

Alan pointed with his riding crop, saying, "Okay. You girls follow me. I'll give you some hoes, and you can begin work."

His mouth opened wide in surprise when Anele's head popped up from the ditch.

Alan said to Kelingo, "I don't want the kid. Look at her. She's stick thin. She wouldn't last a day in the fields."

Kelingo translated his boss's words.

Zhana responded, "Please, my little sister may be thin, but she is as strong as a bull elephant."

Zhana was cut short by a jab in her ribs from a frightened Anele.

"Sister, I want to go home. I'm scared of the white man."

Zhana stressed harshly, "You wanted to come with us, stupid girl!"

Anele stamped her foot and hissed, "If I were older, I'd slap you, Zhana."

"That's never going to happen, puny child," the twin countered.

Alan's laughter sounded like a hyena. The girls didn't know Alan was fluent in their language, and he wasn't going to let on. He said to Kelingo in English, "Tell these ignorant bush girls that I'm in a good mood today. The skinny one can labor at the house, if my mother has work for her. If Mistress Ethel says no, then send her off. I don't want her hanging around being useless. Is that clear?"

"Yes, Boss."

Kelingo went over to Anele and placed a firm grip on her upper arm. "You have to come with me."

"No, I won't," Anele shrieked.

Kelingo tightened his grip.

The twins looked anxiously at their struggling sister. "Where are you taking her?" Zhana asked.

"To the master's house."

Somehow Anele freed herself. She gripped Zhana's hand with such ferocity that the twin cried out, "You're hurting me! Do as you are told for once. You wanted to help. Now's your chance. I should take a stick to you. Go and work in the white man's house so we all can earn money. Remember?"

The tender-hearted Thaka touched Anele's cheek. "Don't worry, little sister. We will see you when our work is done."

Mabali's feisty blood was carried in her descendant's veins. Anele gave Alan a hostile stare, then in a war-like stomp, marched to the horse and boldly spat a glob of phlegm onto Alan's riding boot. She yelled, "Ugly, ugly white ... *umlungu!* You can't make me go where I don't want to go. I won't be separated from my sisters. I will work with them."

Alan's face grew as dark as a summer storm.

"This skinny insect has the nerve to spit and talk to me as an equal?" he roared in Zulu. "How shall I teach her a lesson, Kelingo? Should I whip her? Or blow her head off?"

Before Kelingo could reply, Anele grabbed hold of the dangling rein and began yanking the steed's head down. Then, with a balled fist, she punched the creature on the nose.

The target of her wrath was less than happy.

The Arabian stallion snorted, reared, and bucked, nearly throwing off its rider. Alan, his jugular vein pulsating, quickly tightened his grip on the reins. "Whoa!" he commanded.

Returning his steed to calmness, Alan spat at Anele, "Black bastard! I've a good mind to get down and knock the shit out of you. Or better still, shoot you."

Anele did not need a translation.

"You hurt me, white man," she retorted, "and I'll run back home and fetch my father. He is a Zulu warrior. He will chop you up with his long *assegai*. You'll bleed like a pig from his spear."

As Alan maneuvered his horse, Anele's body was lifted off her feet. All eyes were on the flying girl, who hit the earth with a thud. Back in his grandfather's time, a Shongweni girl similar in age had experienced similar Hallworthy brutality.

Alan, his cobalt-blue eyes glaring murderously, dismounted, and as if he had all the time in the world, he strolled over to the sprawling child. With his abdomen pulled in and his chest expanded, he raised his leather crop over his head and brought it down across her bare shoulders.

Anele's shrieks of agony pierced the humid air. She tried to crawl away, but Alan's riding boot pinned her down. He showered her with blows.

With tears rolling down their cheeks, the twins dropped to their knees in helplessness. The brutal flogging was nothing like what their father doled out for disobedience. It was as if the white boy intended to beat Anele to death.

The whip continued to rain down, sending blood-curdling

screams to the heavens. A flock of nesting sun birds joined in the din and then flew shrieking into the sky.

The gentle twin's heart could not take it. Thaka rushed toward Alan, latched onto his extended arm, and begged, "Please, *umlun-gu-man*, stop! She is only nine summers old, and such a foolish child. She did not mean to harm you or your beast."

Alan's face twisted into a grim scowl. He slapped his blood stained crop against one boot and glared at Thaka with a "how-dare-you-interrupt-me" look.

Thaka, who would not have said "boo" to a goose, snatched this brief interruption to reach down and, with a mighty shove, push Anele out of harm's way. Alan's next strike hit Anele's rescuer full in the face.

Blood poured from Thaka's gashed cheek. Now her screams scattered the birds. Her frantic, high-pitched screeching could be heard for miles.

Kelingo clenched his fists behind his back in helpless fury and focused his eyes on the ground. His facial muscles twitched as if the lash had cut into his own skin. He heard the whip crack, but heard no noise from Thaka. All he heard was the sound of feet pounding the dry ground.

The twins took off, running as fast as their short legs could carry them. To the onlookers, it seemed as if they were running sixty miles an hour toward the outer perimeter of a dense sugar cane field.

Hunger for freedom hurt more than hunger for food.

Kelingo hung his head. He dreaded what would happen next, but it was inevitable. He had witnessed scenes like this before.

Alan galloped after the girls with one finger on the trigger of his rifle. Then, leveling his weapon, he aimed. A thunderous *boom* was followed by repeated *booms*!

A plume of smoke curled from the rifle's muzzle.

Thaka and Zhana lay dead, each one shot in the back of the head execution style.

Anele had never heard gunfire before, yet her instincts told her it was bad. She would have run and met the same fate had it not been for Kelingo.

With his arms stretched wide, blocking his employer's aim, he pushed the girl behind his thin frame.

"Please let her live," he begged Alan. "She is just an ignorant bush girl. If you let me, I'll take her to the house just like you asked."

In a chameleon switch, Alan smiled warmly, as if he had merely been out for an afternoon ride.

"Be a good girl and go with Kelingo. Forget what has happened here and you'll be fine. Work hard for Mother and you'll be rewarded."

He addressed Kelingo. "After you have dropped the *ape* at the house, I want you to get your brother and clean up that mess over there," he said pointing backward.

Kelingo's questioning brows prompted Alan's retort. "I don't care! Bury them. Burn them … whatever."

Alan scratched his chin. "On second thought, fling them down the old water well," he said dryly. "You know where it is, Kelingo."

Without a backward glance, the Devil's new playmate galloped away.

High above the horseman and his racing stallion, a dark cloud streaked with red began to form.

With her shoulders sagging, chin lowered, and dusty feet dragging, Anele walked away from the grisly scene beside Kelingo. The grim words she spoke to her sisters at the kraal played heavily on her mind. *"I hope you never return,"* would torment her for the rest of her life.

In time, Anele would wish she had died along with her sisters.

When the Hallworthy cook heard the side door open, she stopped kneading the bread dough. She stared at the entering pair as if they were two-headed creatures. Cook wiped her hands on her apron before confronting Kelingo.

"Why have you brought this filthy girl in here?"

"I was told to bring her here."

"And who told you?"

"Lord Hallworthy."

Cook squinted. "Tell me what happened."

Scene by bloody scene, the field worker related the heinous events.

Cook sighed. She had known the horrible Hallworthy boy from birth. This was not the first time she had heard of his murderous ways. As the privileged son of a titled family, he got away with all of his crimes. He would *never* face charges. No one *dared* to report him.

Back in the 1840s, a black solicitor named Kadir Yar'Adua had *dared* to confront Alan's grandfather, but he had failed. His legal action had led to the deaths of three innocent people. In those days, slaves were dispensable. They all had expiration dates stamped on them from the day they entered the Devil's domain.

These days were not much different.

At age twenty-one, Peter Hallworthy, who had been living in England, inherited the Hallworthy estate. His maternal grandparents were glad to see the back of him and his new bride, whom they detested. "They deserve each other. Both are sick in the head," Peter's grandmother confided to a family friend, when the couple decided to move to South Africa.

Peter's son, Alan, was an only child, by his mother's choice. After a difficult birth, Lady Ethel vowed never to have another baby.

She kept that promise. She remained celibate until she died.

Ethel Hallworthy had no natural maternal feelings. She rarely saw her son, who stayed on the third floor in the same bedroom Nigel, the boy's grandfather, had occupied. When Alan started displaying dysfunctional behavior at age three, as had his father as a young boy, she washed her hands of him. He was raised by black nannies, many of them during his growing years. His poor caretakers were bitten, scratched, slapped, and kicked. And naturally, the little white boy's words were always believed.

"She hurt me, Mother."

"Nanny pushed me, Mother."

"She looked at my pee-pee, Mother."

But it was his sadistic cruelty to animals that turned even the most hardened of stomachs.

Lady Ethel's toy poodle, its tongue missing, was found floating in the pond.

The family cat, eyes gouged, was found hanging in Alan's closet.

Pet rabbits were dismembered.

*The apple doesn't fall far from the tree.*

Even though Peter defended his son's behavioral problems, his wife had the last word. Alan was sent away to a private, and very expensive, boarding school. He had been there barely a week before his parents were summoned by the school authorities.

It seems the school, too, wanted to wash their hands of this malicious boy.

During his short enrollment at the school, the Hallworthy heir had repeatedly stabbed a white female teacher who had reprimanded him for disruptive behavior in the classroom.

He had stripped a fellow student and locked him in the bathroom.

He had thrown his food in the face of another student.

The school suspected that he was behind the massacre of their chickens. Each one's throat had been cut. In the end, a pound note exchanged hands. No charges or written reports were made. After that, the expelled Alan was home-schooled by a local tutor. The headstrong, disturbed boy refused to turn a tutorial page.

By the age of fourteen, the natural born sadist found his true passion. His father appointed him overseer of the Hallworthy plantation. Empowered and following in his grandfather's evil footsteps, Alan reigned supreme over the *apes* Nigel had bequeathed to his son, Peter.

Alan's sadistic inheritance was playing out this very day.

Cook sighed. How many poor souls were dotting this massive estate in unmarked graves? She looked around to make sure no one else was listening when she said to Kelingo, "He should be dragged through the field and flogged ..." Her eyes narrowing with fury, she ended, "... or worse."

Kelingo bobbed his head in agreement. He spoke with urgency when he said, "I had better return to the fields before *he* takes it upon himself to shoot *me*, as well."

Before Kelingo left, he had something to say to the sad-eyed child.

"I'm sorry that you had to go through all this, being so young and all. You will be safe with Cook here. You can trust her. She is one of us."

The traumatized girl didn't respond. She was floating in a silent, numb world of her own.

Cook's ample bosom rose up and down as she heaved a mighty sigh of resignation and regret. There was nothing she could say or do. There was *nothing* that could make the hellish ordeal the child had undergone any better. But Cook could relate. Like her grandmother, who had labored as the estate's seamstress, Lamella, an indentured servant, had worked at the manor from the age of ten—without pay and against *her* will.

Lamella took Anele by the hand and led her through the servants' entrance to the outside washhouse a few feet away. The fieldstone building had sealed windows and a low, sloped roof. A steady plume of smoke from the crackling fire inside spiraled up through a brick chimney. In the far corner, a huge copper pot boiled on the hearth of the fireplace. The heat in the room was worse than any African summer Anele had ever known.

"This is where you will wash the dishes, pots and pans, and table linens," Cook said in Zulu. "You will also sleep in here until Lady Hallworthy says it's all right for you to share the shack with me. But first, it's time for your bath. You smell worse than the hog I butchered yesterday."

Cook lifted the heavy cauldron, poured the boiling water into the plugged stone sink, and retrieved a bucket of cold water near the doorway. Wordlessly, she removed Anele's sodden, blood-spattered grass skirt, lifted the feather-light child into the sink, and reached for a bar of carbolic soap. After rinsing the suds off, Cook scratched her head. What could she put on the child? "Ah, I have just the thing," she muttered. She went to a large laundry hamper and allowed her hands to rummage through. She extracted a garment. She guessed it would be far too big, but the discarded cotton petticoat that had belonged to Lady Ethel was better than nothing. When she put it on Anele, it hung like a drape past the girl's feet. Under better circumstances, Cook would have laughed. Instead, she nudged the child and pointed. "Sit there on that stool."

Anele did as she was told.

Then, with a wordless don't-you-dare-move-a-muscle glance, Cook said, "I'll be back in a moment."

Cook slid the bolt that locked the wooden door.

On the second floor of the manor house, the kitchen servant found Lady Ethel tending to an array of flowering potted plants. A look of displeasure darkened Ethel's face. She slapped her cook across the face and spat, "How dare you come here without my permission!"

Her cheek smarting, the servant rushed to explain. "Mistress, I'm here because something terrible has happened."

She related the graphic details.

The poker-faced Lady Ethel simply retorted, "Where is the child now?"

"I've locked her in the washhouse, Lady Hallworthy."

"Keep her there until I've had a word with my son."

Ethel beckoned with a wave of her hand. "Follow me."

From a writing desk in an adjacent room, Ethel removed an indentured work contract and backdated it by a month. "Have the child place her mark here and bring it back to me," Lady Ethel ordered. "It will undoubtedly prove that she could not have been anywhere near the fields. I'm not going to be concerned with this *problem*. No one has ever come here inquiring about missing black relatives." Her eyes seemed to bore through Cook. "And if you know what's good for you, don't breathe a word of this to anyone."

The indentured contract that Lamella grasped in her hand stated that Anele would work for the Hallworthy plantation until such time as her owner saw fit to release her. Food and lodging would be provided. Food would be nothing more than table scraps, and lodging meant a cold dirt floor in the washroom.

The aged servant's heart grew heavy as she approached the washroom with the contract. The sound of mournful weeping was more than her tender heart could bear.

"Don't cry, child," she said, taking the girl in her embrace. "I'm going to take care of you. I won't let any more hurt come to you."

Although heartfelt at the time, it would be a promise Cook could not keep.

In the pain-melting warmth of Cook's embrace, Anele's voice murmured softly, "I want to go home to Tswanas."

"Oh, sweet child, you can't."

"You can find the way to my village, old woman."

"Not so much old! And even if I did know where you lived, I couldn't take you."

"Why?"

"Because, child, many have tried and failed." Cook shook her head. "We would end up like your sisters or left hanging on a tree. So let's have no more about running away!"

In order to turn the conversation to a more pleasant subject, Cook said, "You must be hungry. How would you fancy a nice warm bowl of vegetable soup and a glass of fresh goat's milk?"

"No."

"It will do you good to eat, even a little."

"No."

"Child, when did you eat last?"

Anele remained tight-lipped.

Cook sighed as she removed the document from her apron pocket. Guided by Cook's hand, Anele hesitatingly placed her mark on the dotted line. Cook let out another deep sigh, folded the work contract, and put it back into her pocket. She patted Anele on the shoulder. "There are some old sheets in the corner," she indicated. "Lay them on the floor and get some sleep. I'll look in on you later."

Cook left Anele in the sealed room while she busied herself in the kitchen. An extra pair of hands would have been welcome. She was behind schedule for the evening meal. When she finally completed the cooking, washing up, and cleaning, it was past ten o'clock at night. Before departing for her hovel, Cook poured a glass of milk and filled a bowl with vegetable soup—leftovers from what was served earlier.

Cook found Anele curled up in the straw-lined laundry basket. "Ah, poor child," she murmured. She placed the soup and milk nearby, just in case the girl woke up and was hungry enough to swallow her anger and pride.

Cook returned to her workplace at five the next morning, unlocked the washhouse door, stepped in, and scratched her chin. She noted the empty glass standing in the middle of the floor, but she saw no sign of the child. Where was she? She couldn't have gotten out; the windows were sealed and the door was bolted fast. Anele, hiding behind the open door, innocently pounced upon Cook and pinched her generous behind. Cook let out a shriek. She grabbed Anele's shoulder and scolded, "Child, you nearly scared me half to death! It seems you are rested and ready for work. It will take some of that silly energy out of you."

Anele's long workday began inside the washhouse. She started work at five in the morning and slaved in the merciless heat until late at night. Because Lady Ethel had not yet given permission for Anele, a manor prisoner, to join Cook in the servant's shanty, Anele slept on the floor of her workplace.

Anele was no stranger to hard work or harsh conditions. As a young child, she had worked with her sisters and other women of Tswanas in the cornfields. Traipsing to and from the manor's kitchen with heavy trays of dishes, pots, and pans was a challenge for a nine-year-old, but it was the washing and starching of table linens by hand that she hated most. The gooey starch stuck to her fingers, and the smell caused constant sneezing. But Anele was not one to grumble. Hard work helped stem the tide of anger that threatened her relentlessly. Although not a day passed that Anele didn't miss her father, sisters, and village life, she endured the hardships of indenture.

Several months passed. Her life went on.

On a windy fall morning several months later, Anele's mentor and friend, Lamella, set her to work washing the breakfast dishes in the newly installed scullery off the kitchen. Anele was happy she did not have to go outside to the old washhouse. With only a cold-water faucet in the new scullery, cooking and washing water had to be boiled. It was Anele's job to make sure the kettle on the kitchen range was always hot. On this particular day, Cook was rubbing lard over a leg of lamb when, out of the blue, a stabbing pain rippled through her chest and took her breath away. She sat down and waited for the discomfort to subside. She assumed her distress was the result of excessive and prolonged pipe smoking. Smoking was how Lamella chose to momentarily "forget" her circumstances. Every moment she could, she filled her clay pipe with the tobacco she grew outside the shack and enjoyed a smoke.

As soon as Anele stepped through the door after hanging laundry outside, Lamella called her over. "Child, Cook doesn't feel so well. Would you like to help me?"

"What is it you want me to do?" Anele responded helpfully. Even though she loved the old woman who had taken her under her wing, you could see on her sour face that she hated every moment she spent in the whites' world slaving for them.

"Sweet, sweet child," Cook said, "I know that you are not happy to be here, but I am blessed to have you in my life. I'd like you to place the potato pan on the stove and fill it with cold water. When it begins to boil, add a spoon of salt and the washed and peeled sweet potatoes."

Cook gestured with her finger. "There, in the bucket. Can you do that?"

Anele gave an "of course" nod.

The water-filled pot weighed more than Anele. But somehow she found the strength to lift it to the back plate of the coal-burning range and add the potatoes without disturbing the now dozing cook. A few moments later, Anele prodded a potato and frowned. She didn't want to wake Cook, but she was unsure, so she tapped the woman's shoulder. Cook bolted upright. "What is it? How long have I been asleep?"

"Not long. I don't know when they are done."

Cook's eyes twinkled with mirth. "The knife should slip easily through the potato."

Anele rushed over to the stove and stabbed one. "No," she said, "the knife sticks."

Cook clicked her tongue. "Silly girl!" she laughed. "You have a lot of learning to do."

Sometime later Anele tried again. Unable to contain a surge of victory, she shouted, "They're done! They are definitely done!"

Cook's face—as broad, plain, and dark as the bottom of a burnt pie pan—broke into a grin before she said, "I'm coming."

Cook was making her way to Anele, who was waiting at the stove. Suddenly, she heard behind her the swishing sound of taffeta material followed by the strong odor of Lily of the Valley cologne. Lady Ethel strutted like a peacock into the kitchen. Atop her long, shiny skirt was a frilly-white-lace and chiffon blouse decorated with dainty pearl buttons. The garment looked uncomfortably tight, as if it would strangle the large woman should she attempt a deep breath. An oval diamond brooch reflected the colors of her blue and green skirt.

With her mouth agape, Anele stared at the tightly corseted figure whose constricted waistline looked deformed. She did not know whether to laugh at the outrageous attire or be frightened because as soon as the woman entered the kitchen, Cook's cheerful face stiffened.

Lady Ethel looked at Cook and then glared at Anele, who was standing by the stove rigidly holding a wooden spoon pointing upward. Ethel's eyes were large and her expression demonic when she shrieked, "Go to the washhouse, you filthy savage! Since when did I give *you* permission to cook *our* food? God knows *what* is under your filthy fingernails!" Her heavily rouged cheeks reddened even more as she turned on her cook. "You of all people should know better than to let this heathen near my stove!"

In the short period Anele had been at the manor, she had been able to grasp some of the language. Stepping boldly forward with hands defiantly on her hips, she spat back, "Don't you dare shout at Cook! She is sick today. I offered to help her. That's all."

Lady Ethel's eyes took on an evil glint. She marched over to the range, raised the pan to chest level, and, with a mighty swing, flung the contents at Anele. The terrified girl tried to duck, but it was too late. The scalding water struck her with such force it sent her reeling backwards. The back of her head struck a metal bin used for discarded vegetable peelings. The mistress of the house stood over the anguished child as if she were a game trophy.

"That will teach you to be flippant," Lady Ethel ranted. "You will show me respect, girl, or I will fetch my son. He will skin you alive if I told him you had the cheek to talk back to me."

Snapping her mouth shut, Lady Ethel turned on her heels. Her pointed, ankle-laced boots thudded out of the kitchen.

All of the color faded from Anele's face. She placed a hand on her scalded neck. The pain was excruciating. When she saw a piece of pink skin stuck to her palm, she screamed in shock, "Namandla, God of the Zulus, please help me! I'm dying!"

Cook stood in a daze throughout the episode. Her mind tried to unwrap what had just happened. Her senses were awakened by the screams that came from her helper. Cook rushed to the sink, ran cold water, and knelt beside the wailing child. Dipping the corner of a rag into the bowl of water, she gently placed it on the burned flesh. Anele screamed in more pain. The ice-cold water had seeped onto her scalded left nipple. Unaware of how badly injured she was, Anele voiced her main concern. "Cook, that bad woman has blistered my womanhood."

"Whatever do you mean?"

Anele's pain-filled eyes stared down. She pointed, saying, "Look at my breast. How will I be able to give milk to my children when the time comes?" She closed her eyes and then hugged herself.

"Oh, it's all my fault," Cook said. "Take your arms away. Let me have a look."

"No."

Anele rose unsteadily from the floor. Her only thought was to flee from this horrible place. But first she had to stop the pain. She rushed outside. With her eyes darting frantically, she remembered seeing a fishpond not far from the washhouse. She raced toward it, down a steep embankment, and flung herself into the water. Thank goodness it wasn't too deep because she couldn't swim. The cold water chilled Anele's burning flesh, but not her anger. Her hate-filled heart was bursting with a blaze no amount of cold water could extinguish.

Anele would never feel safe again. She must get as far away from this dreadful place as possible. She must! Could she remember the path she took to get here? It seemed so far away now. Her home was in the heartland of the Zulu kingdom and might as well have been at the end of the earth. Without someone to guide her, she knew she could never find her way home.

While tiny goldfish swam around Anele's immersed body, she sobbed into her hands. She tried to make sense of her life so far. She wanted to blame the twins. But deep down, she knew that she alone was to blame. Had she stayed home and not attached herself to her runaway sisters, none of this would have happened.

A large bullfrog hopped onto a lily pad and snatched a hovering insect. It eyed the person invading its feeding ground before it disappeared into the murky water. Anele never saw the amphibian, but she did see the image of her father's face during one of his passionate "I-hate-the-white-skinned" tirades. Anele had never understood his wrath … until now.

Still submerged in the pond, Anele felt an eerie chill creep over her. Her angry heart spoke. "All *umlungu* must be fathered by dark forces."

Demons had inhabited the Hallworthy clan for generations. These entities continued to rule supreme until a descendant who was not guilty of Hallworthy wrongdoings sends them back to the hell they belong in.

Anele was forced to exchange her teenage years for a life of adult slave labor.

# CHAPTER SEVENTEEN

# The Runaway

*"Either be wholly slaves or wholly free."*
—JOHN DRYDEN

The year is 1945. Having slaved all day every day for eighteen years, Anele felt worn out mentally and physically. It became hard to imagine what a pretty young Zulu girl she had once been. The right side of her face carried raised scar tissue from the first-degree burns that were inflicted after Lady Ethel flung boiling water at her when she nine. At age twenty-seven, she had premature white threads streaked throughout her dark hair. Gum disease had taken several of her lower front teeth, and she carried more fleshy pounds on her tall frame than she was comfortable with. She blamed her weight on the excess consumption of table leftovers. She rationalized that she never had money to buy her own food, and starving was not an option.

On Christmas day 1945 Anele could bear it no more. Why had she not run away earlier? She could have. If so, what had stopped her? Fear! Of ending up like the twins, with skeletal remains at the bottom of some disused water well.

Well before sunup, Anele stealthily packed what little she owned. As wary as an alley cat, she sneaked away from the Hallworthy estate. Hacking through thick foliage with a butcher's cleaver she stole from the kitchen, she passed the infamous outbuilding, the hellhole that had incarcerated so many poor wretches. She bowed her head and hummed a Zulu tune about freedom from white oppression. She had no way of knowing that that evil place had imprisoned two of her ancestors, Mabali and Nobuntu, in the 1800s.

Anele was joyful feeling the rising sun on her back, something she rarely felt while incarcerated in the Hallworthy kitchen eleven to fourteen hours a day. She looked heavenward and saw that the sky was suffused with an artist's palette of vibrant colors. It was an awesome sight for a servant who had spent all of her days cooped indoors.

Farther along the trail Anele noticed several creatures also enjoying the sunshine: green salamanders basking, a garden snake wriggling out of its dead skin, a red-and-black bird swooping down on a grasshopper. She delighted in hearing a songbird's joyous trebles.

Before long Anele's legs began to ache. She grimaced. She was used to climbing stairs, but not with a laden basket on her head. She pleaded to the Zulu god Namandla. "Help me make it back home safely and get good medicine for my aches and pains."

To distract herself, she thought of her father. Was he still alive? Had he missed her? What did he look like now? The more she tried to conjure up her father's image, the more her heart ached. There wasn't a day on the Hallworthy property she had not missed him and her village home. But she missed the twins most of all.

How was she going to break the news of their cruel demise to her father? If he *was* still alive, she would have to face it. But for now she hoped that she was heading in the right direction. Suddenly she remembered Kelingo, the black man who had escorted her to the manor all those years ago. "Up there ..." he had said pointing in the direction of the Valley of a Thousand Hills, "... a good way beyond. That's the Kingdom of Zululand, the beating heart of Africa. *Never* forget your true roots, young Anele of the Tswanas tribe. It will help you to survive the dark days to come."

The afternoon sun was as warm and soft as a whisper as it shone on Anele's weary body. The runaway had walked nonstop since sunrise. Fortunately, she had not encountered any police patrols. However, she had been given a "lookover" by a Bantu woman (not from the Hallworthy Estate), who had stared at her in disbelief. Anele frowned, but realized her kitchen uniform—long black dress, white apron, and cap—*was* a dead giveaway.

Anele quickly undressed behind a large boulder. She wrapped stolen floral fabric intended for manor house drapes around her body. The colorful, makeshift outfit that was knotted above her breasts made Anele feel like the African she was, the African she had forgotten to be, until now.

With her manor attire tucked in her food basket, a barefoot Anele plodded onward. Soon, lack of sleep, growling hunger pains, extreme thirst, and excessive heat seemed more than she could handle. But could she risk stopping now? Was she safely away? She hadn't a clue. So she walked on until she dropped.

Surrounding her, as far as the eye could see, were miles of red soil, empty cornfields carpeted with daisies, clusters of large-leafed fig trees, and in the distance, a prominent outcrop. Anele wondered if the outcrop was far enough away for her to rest in its shadows for awhile. Thirst attacked her dry tongue and interrupted her ponderings. A big slurp of beer would go down well, she thought. Should she keep moving until nightfall? Yes. Keep moving. That was the thought that prevailed.

Anele spied what looked like the thatched roof of a traditional Zulu homestead. At last she could rest and even share her food with the residents. But before heading there, she needed a bathroom break. She sunk down in a squatting position and glanced backward towards the winding trail behind her. What she saw caused her to frown. What *was* that swirling haze in the distance? Could it be a funneling sandstorm, something common in these summer months? A prickly feeling ran down the back of her neck. Anele suspected it was horses. Her body froze, but not her inner voice. "Run, woman! Run!"

But Anele couldn't move. It was as if she were mired in quicksand. Her mind raced in desperation, leaping and darting like a scared jackrabbit. Was someone tracking her? Was it the police? Was it Alan? Had he been at home all along and seen her leaving the grounds? No. He would have chased after her. So who were these horseback riders? As far as she knew, no blacks owned horses in these parts. Adrenalin spurred her into action. She gripped with both hands the basket of provisions she had stolen and ran through the deserted cornfield towards the Zulu hut. Would the occupants take pity on her?

*Time was of the essence.*

To Anele's dismay, the abode was empty—abandoned. Just as well, she reasoned. Much too obvious a place to hide. Would the outcrop she saw earlier be a good place?

Her eyes darted from side to side, searching for a hiding place. She hurriedly backtracked, making a beeline for a rocky formation. Panting like a dog, she reached the base of the outcrop. Raising her eyes, she noted a long, deep fissure.

But how on earth could she reach it?

*Where there's a will, there's a way.*

Anele started to climb, gripping the crevices and ledges of the rocky surface. When she reached the narrow opening, she clicked her tongue. "Oh, this is not happening!"

A slim child would have had no problem squeezing in, but could *she* fit in? Neither size nor time was on Anele's side.

Hurriedly, Anele shoved the basket in as far as it would go, untied the knot of her clothing, and threw the makeshift outfit inside. Naked, she slithered in and then wished that she hadn't. The overpowering odor of animal feces assailed her nostrils with such force that she gagged.

"I hope whatever creatures have made this disgusting stench aren't lurking inside their lair," was her immediate thought.

The cavernous interior was not what she had expected. After living in a "closet" for so many years, this was a palace. Clumps of dried bracken clung to the outer ledge of her refuge, partially obscuring the opening. She hoped that would make her hiding place more difficult to detect on casual inspection.

With her heart pounding, Anele crouched and locked her arms around her knees in a nervous embrace. She waited. Without warning, a horse neighed directly above, making her skin prickle with fear. The roof of her hideout began reverberating to the beat of hooves. Anele shrunk back against the cave's rough surface. The color drained from her face, and the hair on her neck stood upright like a pig's bristles. There was no mistaking that malevolent voice. It was Lord Alan Hallworthy, whom she hated with a passion. He would show no mercy. The image of her twin sisters lying dead on the ground intensified her motivation to flee, and fast.

On the flat plateau above, a backhanded gesture from the sour-faced Alan brought the other riders to a halt. His voice boomed out, "The rotten bitch is here somewhere! I'm going to find her. It's only a matter of time; and when I do, I'll break her neck, so help me God!"

Anele could scarcely breathe.

The next voice was also unmistakable. It came from another person Anele hated passionately.

"Why are we searching out here in bush land?" Lady Corrie, Alan's wife, asked. "Wouldn't it make more sense to check out the Durban docks?"

"The tracker found her footprints leading up here."

Corrie insisted, "We should search the docks, not here."

Alan exhaled loudly before uttering a coarse retort. "Woman, are you fucking deaf? Why the hell did you come along? To stick your nose in where it doesn't belong? My affairs are not yours!"

The redhead countered angrily, "Oh, yes, they are! I've had to put up with your nonsense for years. And my dear, I don't want to miss out on the fun. It seems it's the only pleasure I get, seeing you go insane like this."

Alan chewed her up. "Shut up, Corrie! You are a feeble-minded excuse for a woman."

Their eyes locked like horns for the longest moment.

Anele visualized the stubborn jut of Lady Corrie's jaw, lips drawn tight in anger. And from the sharpness of his tone, Anele imagined the ugly contortions etched on Lord Alan's handsome features. Even though Anele couldn't stand Corrie and would have liked to see her strung from a tree, she wondered why Corrie had put up with Alan's despicable behavior for so long. Anele's compassionate moment soon turned into maliciousness. The image of the obese Lady Corrie dangling from a tree brought a bitter smile to Anele's lips.

Corrie was thinking her own thoughts. She knew why she had sold herself to this devil. Now, if she was able, she would sell herself once more to be free of the Devil incarnate.

In the desolation of the valley's wilderness, Alan sat high on his black Arabian horse. He was of two minds: shoot his abominable wife and say it was a hunting accident, or throw her down the same well that served as the slave boneyard.

Corrie's high-pitched voice calling him a bastard interrupted his murderous thoughts.

"Only yesterday I saw you chasing after that young fieldworker." She bit her lip and added, "You know, dear, you would have put yet another child in the family way, just like you did Anele, who was hardly out of puberty."

When Anele was thirteen, she, like many other Hallworthy slaves before her, was marched crestfallen to the midwife's hut almost two miles away. Kabila patted Anele's cheek, handed over a pouch, and instructed, "Child, boil water, then add the herbs I've given you. Drink it when it has cooled. In the morning, your troubles will be over."

The African midwife's foul-smelling, bad-tasting abortion concoction did not work. As the months passed, Anele hid her growing stomach by wearing one of the Lady's front-lacing corsets. Eight months later, Anele, alone in the shack, gave birth to a six-pound baby girl. When she looked tenderly at her precious, light-skinned baby, her heart spoke. "My baby girl fills the big hole in my life. I will be a good mother to her."

Anele named her baby Thaka-Zhana, after her twin sisters, and in those post-birthing moments, she felt content. But that would soon change. Her birthing cries had been heard by a passing field worker who had alerted his boss. Alan immediately mounted his steed and galloped toward the shack.

Alan's face was red with anger as he strode toward Anele's bed, stretched out his arms, and stonily demanded, "You can't keep the child, Anele. Give it to me." Anele tearfully pleaded, "Please don't take my baby. I'll work harder for you, Master. The baby will be no trouble. I'll ask Kabila to mind her during my work hours."

Alan's lips curled back contemptuously. "You know the rules, Anele. Husbands and children are not allowed to live on my property without my permission. Do not make me take the child by force ..."

With his jaw clenched, Alan lunged at Anele. When she clung

harder to her child, he grabbed a piece of wood by the doorway and marched back to the bed. In a demonic voice he snarled, "It looks like you are not giving me many alternatives."

The blow to her head knocked Anele unconscious.

With a satisfactory smile on his face, Alan lifted the baby from Anele's limp arms. He handed the wailing infant over to his own mother, a sharp-tongued, cold-hearted woman who had joined her son near the shack.

"Alan," his mother ordered, "take this black bitch to the hospital. I'll call ahead and make all the necessary arrangements." With that said, the raging windstorm of a woman marched out the shanty.

Anele was none the wiser. She was in a twilight world of unconsciousness. The joy she had experienced evaporated quickly. Anele was thrown into the trunk of a car and unloaded at a "For Blacks Only" hospital about thirty miles from the estate.

After the hospital received a generous donation from Alan, an operation was performed in which Anele's fallopian tubes were cauterized. An hour later, Anele opened her eyes and felt a pain so excruciating that it drew her knees up in a self-protective posture. When she cautiously reached down and realized her abdomen was bandaged, she released a blood-curdling scream.

A dark-skinned surgeon entered the room and told Anele she would never bear another child. A tsunami of sorrow drowned her. She placed her hands on her head and wept.

Two days later, Lord Alan showed up at the hospital to take his *ape* home. When Anele was let out of the vehicle's dungeon in front of her shanty, she grabbed Alan's arm. "Master, where is my baby?" she pleaded tearfully. "You have taken away my woman's parts. You can't take her, too."

As if she were nothing but muck stuck to his boot, Alan replied, "What baby? No baby was born here. That's all there is to it! Be back at work tomorrow morning sharp."

At that moment, Anele longed for death.

Responding to Corrie's statement about Alan chasing yet another young fieldworker, he swatted a fly and laughed. His dry cackle was as humorless as a crow's. "Yeah, I know the one," he bragged. "She shot off like a racehorse, didn't she?"

Corrie steered her mare closer and glared at her husband. "Don't tell me that the European bitch you kept in the cottage can't run like the Zulu girls. Why is *this* plaything so important?"

Alan's face flushed dark red. "Shut your mouth, Corrie," he spat, "or I'll shut it for you."

Corrie whined, "Why are you taking your anger out on me? *I* didn't leave the door open for your precious foreign *thing* to escape."

Alan corrected. "She's Sicilian."

Corrie made an agitated clucking sound before responding, "Sicilian. Italian. Who cares?"

The snarl on Alan's mouth said it all.

Below them, Anele's lips moved silently, "Thank the gods. I'm not the one they're looking for." However, she hoped with all her heart that the young girl known as Maria was long gone, heading homeward, like herself.

Alan leaned across and roughly grabbed the bridle of Corrie's horse. Corrie wrinkled her nose. Alan reeked of whiskey. "If my so-called wife took better care of my *needs*"—his upper lip curled derisively—"I wouldn't need to go elsewhere, would I? You're nothing but a cold fish. The only time I can stand you in my bed is when I'm drunk. If my mother were still alive, I'd kill her for making me marry you. Get out of my sight. Go home. Let me get on with what has to be done."

He raised a fist. "I know who helped Maria escape. It had to be Anele. As God is my witness, she will vanish from the face of the earth when I get back. And I'll just have to find myself another plaything, because as sure as there is a Hell, I won't be coming near you!"

The normally impenetrable Corrie was taken aback, stung by Alan's cruel statements. She gasped and clutched at her throat. But molten anger flooded her veins. How dare he speak to her in that despicable manner! She wanted to crush his head like a soft-boiled egg. Whatever glimmer of affection she might once have nourished had died like the last rays of the sun. She'd had enough. Alan's sick appetite for young girls had gone on far too long. Some were little more than children. Disgusting!

Understanding her power, Corrie said gloatingly, "Husband, dear, as you normally never set foot in the kitchen, I can tell you that Anele has run away, along with my grocery money. So we won't be enjoying a turkey dinner later. Maekela and Isona can't boil an egg, let alone prepare our Christmas meal. And I'm damned if I'm going to start cooking for you!" The sound of victorious laughter echoed across the valley. Corrie wasn't finished. "I spoke to *your* bastard child, Maekela. She saw Anele get up well before dawn. It seems Anele told her to go back to sleep."

"*What?*"

"My dear, do I have to spell it out for you?"

"Why didn't you tell me this earlier, before we set off?"

"Because all you were interested in was finding Maria."

Fuming, Alan exhaled so sharply it lifted the hair of the horse's mane. He stared straight ahead.

Fear rooted Anele's feet. She could not move or breathe.

Lady Corrie also was having difficulty breathing. The long horse ride had exhausted her. She wanted to go home and relax, have a few more martinis, smoke some cigarettes, open presents, and eat an alternative meal that she would most likely be making. Maekela and Isona, Anele's helpers, had few culinary skills. The thought of not having a traditional Christmas meal riled her. She decided to break the icy tension. "Alan, I could kill Anele with my bare hands. She is nothing more than an ungrateful, bloody *wog* thief!"

Alan did not smile, even though he approved Corrie had taken his point of view. He patted his horse's neck and, through tight jaws, threatened, "Not if I get to *her* first. If I find the fat black bitch, I'll put a bullet between her eyes. So help me God, I will."

It was by no means an idle threat. Corrie had seen firsthand what happened to people who crossed paths with her psychopath partner. She, too, was afraid of him at times, and this was one of those times. In a pacifying tone, she said, "My dear, why don't we concentrate on finding Maria before she blabs to whomever will take her seriously. You could end up in jail. Good lord, no. I wouldn't want that to happen!" she ended glibly.

Alan jeered, "Who on God's earth is going to believe anything that crazy bitch says? I'm a Hallworthy, for God's sake. I practically own the Port of Durban—the police, judges, and well over a thousand *golliwogs!*"

Corrie wisely remained silent. It was pointless to argue with the Devil.

As though responding to Alan's anger, white knives of lightning split the sky and were followed by drum rolls of thunder, but it was the dark cloud formation that appeared to be falling from the atmosphere that made them frown. It appeared as if it could swallow them up at any minute.

The next bolt of lightning spooked Corrie's mare. The horse reared and sent Corrie flying from the saddle. Of course, there was no knight in shining armor to pick her up. She dusted the dirt off her riding pants and said, "For Christ sake, Alan! Let's go home. A really bad storm is coming. And there is always tomorrow."

Without another word, Alan twisted in the saddle and ordered his workers, "Turn around. It's time to go home. Follow me."

The posse galloped homeward, abandoning their search. The sound of their retreating hooves was music to Anele's ears. She was safe, at least for now. To cheer herself, she pulled out a bottle of beer. The warm alcohol trickled down her throat like nectar from the gods. Within minutes, she became lightheaded and slouched down in order to take a long, overdue nap. She was near dozing when something seized her arm with the grip of a bird of prey's talons. Anele drew in her breath, tried to scream, but managed only a rasp of shocked terror. A sibilant voice pierced the tomb-like quiet. "*Ees* okay, Big Mama. No more fright because the *bastardo ees* gone."

Anele gulped with relief.

There was certainly no mistaking *this* foreign accent. Anele had taken enough food trays to the old gamekeeper's cottage to know *that* voice well. Had Maria been here all along? Why hadn't she said something? Anele fumbled in the dark and seized Maria's arm, causing her to shriek in broken English, "You make me hurt!"

"I don't care. You are coming with me," Anele ordered.

Out on the ledge, Anele looked into the pained face of the thirteen-year-old foreign-born girl. The woman's heart went out to her. The soiled pink dress Anele had sewn for her was beyond filthy.

"Let me go," Maria screamed, trying to pry Anele's fingers from her forearm.

"No!" Anele said. "You nearly scared me to death!"

Maria whimpered, "I no mean scare you, Big Mama."

"Well, you did!" Anele countered. "My heart almost jumped out of my chest!"

"I no mean …"

Anele didn't let her finish. "Maria, I set you free *yesterday*. You should be long gone by now. I showed you which way to go to the docks."

Maria clutched at Anele's waist. "I run fast from *di diaula* (white devil in Sicilian), Big Mama. He tried to kill my baby and me. The *bastardo*, he beat me bad. I scared, not know way to big ship to take me home to Sicilia. Then I see *diaula* on horse. I run. I hide in hole here."

Anele gasped. "You mean to tell me that you've been here the whole time?"

With her bottom lip quivering, Maria bobbed her head. "Yes. I think I'm lost in this land until I see you coming up the hill. I not know you run away like Maria. My heart knows you're sad like me, no? You, too, run like me from the *diaula*, no?"

Anele knew little about the girl's background, but she recalled it was a spring day, about a year ago, when Maria arrived on the Hallworthy Estate.

The encounter was unforgettable.

Who owns lives that are not their own?

The Hallworthy devils!

# CHAPTER EIGHTEEN

# The Foreign Girl

*"Even in our sleep, pain that cannot forget*
*falls drop by drop upon the heart."*
—AESCHYLUS

On that fateful day nearly nine months ago, Anele was outside hanging laundry when a shabbily dressed foursome arrived at the back door. She saw a stunning teenager flanked by a thin man of about forty; a short woman of similar age; and a handsome, dark-haired young man. Anele couldn't take her eyes off the olive-skinned girl. She was the most beautiful white girl Anele had ever seen. Her waist-length black hair, glistening like polished ebony, was as thick as a horse's mane. Her unadorned cotton dress perfectly matched her emerald eyes.

The older man spoke first. "Signora, where is the *proprietario* of this plantation? We need work."

Anele did not recognize his accent. But she did recognize danger. "Ah, these foreigners," she thought. "They'd be better off starving to death than coming here. The girl is far too lovely. Alan will devour her faster than a fox in a henhouse. Predators know when there is an easy mark." The expression on Anele's face spoke volumes. She cautioned the older man, "Take your pretty daughter and go quickly. There is no work for you here. The refinery owner isn't hiring now."

The clatter of a hoofed animal silenced Anele. She had experienced that sound for the first time as a child, and it was far worse than a loud, unexplained knocking at the door at three o'clock in the morning.

All heads turned as the rider came to a halt. As Alan took in Maria's beauty, Anele's heart froze at his barely concealed lust. With his eyes glued on Maria, Alan said, "What do you want? Are you looking for work?"

Cesare Girdazello nodded eagerly. "Si, sir. Raphaela, my wife," he said while pulling the petite woman up close, "is a hard worker. My son, Paolo," he gestured, "is strong boy. We work hard for you, Signore." He made no mention of his daughter.

Alan removed his sunglasses and looked the family over. "Are you Spaniards?"

"No, Signore. We are from Sicily."

"You're a long way from home. What brings you here? Or shouldn't I ask?"

Cesare explained, "We have bad times from the war. We need a new start in this land."

Alan ignored him and nudged his steed closer to Maria. "You're such a pretty girl. What's your name?"

Maria shrank behind Cesare. He quickly explained, "She doesn't talk, Signore. She has, how you say ..." he tapped at his temple before continuing, "... she has brain sickness. *Ees* no good in the head." There *was* truth in that. Maria was suffering from traumatic amnesia.

"What a shame," Alan said in a voice that could melt butter. "I'm sure I'll be able to find her something to do. Are you and your family prepared to work for food and lodging only?"

Cesare frowned, scratched his chin and responded, "Do you mean … work for *no* money, Signore?"

"Yes," Alan responded icily. "That's exactly what I mean. If you don't like the idea, you can look for work elsewhere. But I assure you, not many white folks are hiring refugees, especially the illegal kind." Alan paused long enough for Cesare and his son to exchange worried glances before he ended smugly, "Which most probably you are. You get my drift?"

The baby-faced Paolo, who didn't look much older than Maria, was worried that Alan would change his mind, so he stepped forward and in good English said, "It is okay, Signore. Your offer of food and a place to sleep will be fine."

While the family conversed in their tongue, Alan grabbed hold of Anele's arm. He pulled her aside and whispered, "Take her to you-know-where. Put her to work. Give her some cleaning cloths. See that she scrubs the place from top to bottom. I'll take her parents and brother over to the stables. They can stay there for the time being."

The "you-know-where" was a place Anele dreaded. To her and many others, the old gamekeeper's abode was a house of horrors—where abominable human atrocities were committed. She knew every inch of that diabolical cottage. In it, she also had suffered untold terror and torture. The depravity still lived in her soul—forever a scar. Alan had "killed" not only her soul, but the souls of countless others, as well. Anele didn't want this to happen to any one else, so she tried to get out of going there.

"But Lord Alan, you heard the man. She's sick in the head, and she doesn't speak English. How will I make her understand?"

"She's not bloody blind!" Alan roared. "Show her what to do, stupid!"

Later that night, locked in the gamekeeper's cottage with no savior at her side, Maria was brutally raped.

The next morning Alan sported a deep scratch on his cheek and an evil smirk on his lips. He handed Anele the key to the cottage and ordered, "Take her some food." He didn't have to tell Anele to keep her mouth shut. His direct glare said it all. Anele felt sick. She yearned to take the butcher's knife she held in her hand and plunge it into Satan's pupil.

A few moments later, she placed a bowl of porridge, a slice of marmalade toast, and a glass of milk on a tray. She arrived at the cottage, removed the key from her pocket, and unlocked the heavy oak door. Her heart wrenched out of her chest when she saw the half-naked Maria tied to the brass bedposts. Anele had been there ... Without a word, she put the tray on the end of the bed, sat next to Maria, and untied her restraints. Even if Maria spoke English, no words could soothe what had been done to her. Wide-eyed with fear, Maria's sharp fingernails sprang up and sunk into Anele's neck. Anele screamed. Her burn wounds were still tender after all these years. Wincing in pain, Anele grabbed Maria's arms, pinned them to her sides, and scolded, "Why did you do that? I'm not your enemy, you stupid girl! I'm the only friend you'll ever have here." She released the struggling girl and tried to hand-feed her. The petrified girl jerked her head away. Her teeth were clenched.

As silently as she had entered the room, Anele left, locking the door behind her. With her head lowered, she muttered, "My spirit no longer lives in the house of yesterday. My soul no longer lives in the house of yesterday."

Back in the kitchen, Anele tried not to think about Maria. But all she saw were the girl's pain-filled eyes. What could a lowly servant do to help? Absolutely nothing! So she went about her work as if nothing had happened ... until she heard a tapping sound. She looked out the window. There was Raphaela Girdazello, standing on a tree stump in order to reach the glass pane. The woman communicated using hand gestures. She was asking after Maria. Anele raised her hand in a "wait-there" sign. She had to think fast. She couldn't take the woman to the cottage. What else could she do? An idea entered her head. "Why not," she told herself.

Anele left the confines of her kitchen and took hold of Raphaela's arm. Without a word between them, Anele led the woman to the front entrance of the manor and knocked sharply. Anele dashed away and hid behind a pillar, leaving Raphaela standing at the door.

"What the bloody hell do you want?" Alan shouted, looking Raphaela over as if she were a blot on the doorstep. "Shouldn't you be working?"

Anele could hear Raphaela's Sicilian tongue going hell for leather, then Alan's reverberating hyena laughter.

"Good Lord, woman!" he said, "I haven't got a clue what you are saying. You'd better learn English fast because I'm sure as hell not going to speak your wop language."

"Maria, I need look at her. Look at her now!" Raphaela stressed, doing her best to get the message across.

His deceitful eyes narrowed. "You can't come in contact with your daughter, not at this point. I noticed some sores on her legs, so I got my doctor to check her. She is contagious. Do you understand what I'm saying? *Contagious!* She has a bad blood infection. I can't have her working alongside you or my other field workers in this condition. You can see her when she is well."

Anele's insides trembled. She could envision his wagging finger. She tilted her head to one side to listen.

"Don't go near the cottage," Alan warned. "Alfred, my overseer, has instructions to shoot."

Anele did not hear Raphaela's response. Perhaps the woman did not understand him, or she understood only too well. After the front door slammed shut, Anele shot back to her workplace.

The next day, Anele was stunned to learn that the Girdazello family had simply vanished without a word. It was a mystery. But it left food for thought. Had Alan silenced them for good?

Later, she tried to explain this to Maria, but her words fell short. Being sick in the head, would she even care? She hadn't shed a tear. But she did point and say in desperation, "Big Mama, you no lock door. I ..." She pointed to her body. "... I run away."

Anele lowered her head and responded truthfully. "Oh, child, if only I could. But *he* would hold me responsible. I don't have to tell you that he is evil, capable of anything."

Now the heavily pregnant Maria was with her in the cave. Two sad runaways abused by the Devil. If Alan found them, he'd blow off *both* their heads. Anele looked at Maria and felt sorrow for the pitiful expectant mother. Her hair was a matted bird's-nest. Her lovely face and eyes were blackened and swollen by brutal blows. Anele blinked before her eyes widened as big as saucers. "Dear God of good Zulu hearts!"

"What is it, Big Mama?"

"Maria, can't you feel it?" She pointed. "That's fresh blood I see trickling down your legs! Does your belly hurt?" She counted on her fingers. "If my memory serves me well, you're at least eight and a half months."

Maria, her mind divided by a fractured wall, chose silence.

Anele didn't think Maria comprehended what was happening to her. Or did she?

Anele sighed in exasperation and revealed, "I was younger than you when I delivered my own baby. Back then I was fearless. But today, I'm not sure I am capable of delivering yours." Anele shook her head and said, "No, it's out of the question. I will have to find a midwife. There has to be someone living around here."

Maria's face creased in pain.

"Do you have hurt in your belly, Maria?"

Maria was silent.

Anele tenderly squeezed the girl's hand. Her voice was motherly. "Don't worry, child. I'm going to get help you."

Maria grabbed Anele's hand and kissed it. "Big Mama, you are a nice lady, but you please not go back to bad sugar place. Don't worry for me. No *bambinos*. Babies are no more."

"Of course I'm worried. You and your baby may die if I don't get help. And no, I'm definitely not going back to the *sugar place*."

"No. Me no die. Me *libero*. How you say? Yes … *free!*"

Anele rubbed her forehead thinking that somehow she had to get the pregnant girl to listen, make her lie down so that she could check the position of the baby's head.

Maria stopped the intended examination. She took hold of Anele's hand and placed it on her swollen abdomen. "See, Black Mama. I *libero*, free. No more *demonio* babies. No *diaula sangue*. The Devil's blood gone from me."

Anele frowned. "Missy Maria Girdazello, I've no idea what you're rambling on about, but you need to be lying down, not standing up. It may lessen the blood loss."

Maria made an angry face. "My name is Maria Picasso Genovese. No say Girdazello name. Not my *familiare*. Those bad people bring me here to this country."

"What are you babbling about, Maria?"

"Paolo, he stole me from Papa and Mama in Sicilia." To blot out the memory, she covered her face with her hands.

Anele had no doubt this young girl was mentally and physically crushed, like she had been at her age. Anele shrugged. She couldn't dwell on the past. She had a more pressing concern: the baby's safe delivery. Anele made eye contact with Maria and asked,

"Maria, how long has your blood been flowing?"

"I don't know!"

Anele knew she was lying. "Lie down," she ordered, "so I can check you."

"No."

Maria began to sob. Her heart held more sorrow than any young heart should. A long and tortuous road had carried her from her home, nestled in the shadows of Mount Etna in Sicily, to the dark shores of Africa. Maria Teresa Picasso Genovese *was* her real name. She was the only daughter of Sofia Maria Picasso, a Spanish-born socialite, and Don Alberto Vincenzo Genovese, a wealthy landowner and a reigning, regional Mafia boss.

Maria needed to get her story out. "Paolo Girdazello stole me from my Papa for big money. My Papa would not pay. Paolo was mad. He sold me to German man. He sent me to bad death camp in Poland. After the war, I not know my name, or where I come from. Paolo, he saw me in the displaced persons camp. He scared that I tell the story, what he did to me. His Mama and Papa, they bring me here to dark land by boat. They are bad, bad people, the Girdazellos. I remember. I remember ..."

Maria's amnesia-frozen mind had unlocked the awful truth, and it had caused the heartbroken girl to sob uncontrollably. Watching it broke Anele's heart. She flung her arms around Maria and said, "Please don't cry."

Anele hugged Maria until her cries subsided to a whimper. Then, using the hem of her floral outfit, Anele dabbed the girl's tear-streaked cheeks. Anele commiserated. "I'm so sorry to hear that you have had so much hurt in your young life, but we have to deal with the now, Maria. Listen to me, please. First babies don't always come out quickly. If I can't find a birthing woman, I'll come straight back and help you myself."

Maria picked at the tip of a mud-caked fingernail and pretended not to have heard. Anele stared at the girl's nails. "Maria, how did your nails get so filthy?"

"Me no say."

Anele let out a frustrated sigh. Did she mean she couldn't or wouldn't say? Anele suggested, "If you like, you can change out of that filthy dress. I've a uniform in my basket for you to put on. I also have some food. Are you hungry?"

Maria's eyes were vacant, her mouth mute.

Anele was worried about leaving the girl alone in the approaching darkness, but what else could she do? She couldn't take her along, not in her condition. Anele informed her, "I'm setting off now, Maria. And with a little luck, I'll have help with me when I return."

"I say again," Maria huffed. "I no need birth woman."

"Yes, you do! What if something goes wrong? The baby could be stuck?"

"I tell you last time, Big Mama, the babies ees *morto*. They are dead!"

"Your baby, *not babies,* is going to come out before the full moon shines tonight."

Maria laughed sinisterly. "Too late. Devil babies have gone. They die. I make sure."

A horrible unease welled in the pit of Anele's stomach. Something wasn't right. She considered continuing on her homeward journey—leaving the befuddled white girl, letting her birth the baby alone. But Anele knew she'd never be able to live with herself if she abandoned this helpless girl. Maria looked dangerously thin. Would her baby be born alive?

Anele had a change of heart. She tilted Maria's drawn face to meet her eyes. "Child, I've decided *not* to leave you alone. But I'm going to need your help. Does the pain come one after the other?"

"Me no say."

"What am I going to do with you?" Anele said. Then in an eating gesture, fingers to her mouth, Anele asked, "Are you hungry, Maria?"

"No want to eat, Big Mama." Maria made a sucking noise with her lips and said, "Drink."

"Would you like some sweet, condensed milk? I stole it from the *bas-e-tar-do's* house."

Maria's pitiful face now lit up like a moonbeam. She loved Anele's pronunciation of the Italian word for bastard. "No. Want water. And Big Mama, pain I tell you *ees* gone for good."

"No, it's not gone for good. The pain is going to get much worse."

Maria shook her head and smirked. Anele sighed. "Okay, Maria. Here's what I'm going to do. I think I saw a rainwater barrel near an abandoned homestead. I'll go get enough for you to drink and to wash the baby when it comes."

Maria puckered her lips in amusement. Her cheeky facial expression reminded Anele of her kitchen helper, Maekela, and laughter overruled her seriousness.

"You cheeky monkey," Anele said. "I bet you understand everything I say. Am I right?"

Maria's broad grin said it all.

"Back to business," Anele thought.

"Come along, little mum. It's time to lie down."

Maria followed Anele deeper into the cave. Anele lit a candle, spread out her uniform on the cold ground, and pointed. Maria sat down on the uniform and pulled the picnic basket closer. It was now a backrest. Anele smiled. She was satisfied that the mum-to-be was comfortable.

"I'm going to go for water. It's not far so I won't be long. Just lie still. I'll be back before you know it," Anele said as she headed toward the exit. With an empty beer bottle in one hand, Anele wiggled out of the crevice and climbed down.

At the bottom of the cave, her mind was besieged with concern. Could she deliver this baby safely? What if it was a breech birth? What if it got stuck? What if Maria had no breast milk? She barely weighed ninety pounds. It seemed unlikely Maria could produce a drop. But there were some lifesavers in the basket—a packet of dried cow's milk and a tin of condensed milk—just in case. About her other worries—well, only time would tell.

Anele was thankful for the hundreds of fireflies flashing like lanterns in the diminishing daylight. She retraced her steps to the abandoned Zulu home and bent down. As she was scooping discolored water into the bottle, she heard an unfamiliar sound. She tilted her head to one side. It sounded like a kitten mewing. After a few seconds, the sound grew louder. Now it struck a note resembling a faint human cry. No. It couldn't be. She carried on with her task. But a loud rustling, followed by a thin wail, forced her to her stop. With a rock in hand, she went to investigate. She nearly jumped out of her skin when a scruffy wild dog sprang on all fours and bared its razor-sharp teeth. Anele dropped her eyes and backed away. Taking this as a sign of submission, the dog simply returned her attention to the cornhusk mound. Anele's taunt muscles relaxed.

Noticing the dog's pregnant belly, she said in a comforting

tone, "It's okay, little mother dog. I'm going. But you should have found a better place to have a litter than out here out in the open." Anele began humming to show the dog she was not afraid. She had only walked a few steps when she heard what she thought was a faint human cry.

*It couldn't be ...!*

Seized with growing fear, Anele grabbed two large stones and hastily retraced her steps. The dog was pawing at something. She walked toward the critter. Nothing could have prepared her for what was to come.

# CHAPTER NINETEEN

# Maria's Abandoned Child

*"It is as natural to die as to be born, and to an infant, perhaps one is as painful as the other."*
—FRANCIS BACON

T he newborn child was barely alive. Her tiny heart thumped fitfully against her rib cage. Her breath came in labored gasps. As life ebbed from the helpless, abandoned baby, droplets of blood from her crudely severed umbilical cord spattered the lifeless body of the twin sister beneath her. For these tiny unwanted humans, discarded like dirty rags, death was inevitable, and perhaps, preferable.

The upper baby's eyelids were shut tight against the dusting of reddish dirt that layered both her ashen face and long, blond eyelashes. The premature girl's bluish lips slowly parted and her lungs sucked hungrily at the oxygen that began to flow after the dog pawed the dirt above her. A few moments later, re-energized, she flailed her arms and legs. Then the traumatized infant wailed until spent. The quiet lasted a few seconds. With her last ounce of strength, she drew her knees into a fetal position, balled her fists under her chin, and became still once more. A heavy shroud of silence cocooned this child of unimaginable misfortune. The baby's struggle for life was rewarded when Anele lifted her from her intended grave. But the slave worker had no clue that another baby lay dead underneath. The second newborn had sunken lower into the pit and was concealed by leaves.

Carrying the abandoned newborn in a blanket on her back, Anele returned home to Tswanas kraal in Zululand, where she joyfully raised the surviving child she named Shiya—the Forsaken One— for five blissful years.

Foster mother and daughter were inseparable until the bogey-man called and snatched their souls.

Shiya would never forget the day her happy childhood was stolen from her forever.

# CHAPTER TWENTY

# Seized and Kidnapped

*"The abduction of a child is a tragedy."*
—JOHN WALSH

Early one day in 1950, Vimbela, Shiya's former wet nurse, was piggybacking the five-year-old toward the river to collect water. Vimbela, a gentle soul who was born with Down syndrome, catered to Shiya's every whim. She loved the child as if she were her own. Vimbela, with her sleeping charge settled on her back, walked quietly beside Anele, who was carrying a bundle of dirty clothes to be washed. Behind them, the tribe was still asleep. It would be some time before sunrise.

Suddenly, the women stopped in their tracks. Vimbela was the first to speak. "What *is* it that makes the ground shake so badly?"

To Anele, the rumbling noise provoked the shudder of past memories. As it grew louder, she said softly, "I don't like the sound of it."

Shiya, awakened by the noise and peering over her caretaker's shoulder, innocently remarked, "Maybe lots of elephants are running away from the jungle?"

It took a split second for Anele to identify the sound. Her mind cried out, *"No! It can't be!"* How could a jeep have gotten through the narrow, single-track, rocky mountain pass up to the kraal?

When blinding lights stabbed through the darkness, Vimbela dove behind a pile of firewood stacked against the fence. Shiya's face struck her nanny's backbone, yet the child seemed to know she should not cry out. She wiped the blood from her top lip with the back of her hand.

The camouflaged vehicle barreled through the fence, snapping it as if it were made of matchsticks. It was still too dark for Anele to make out the faces in the vehicle or of the four horsemen who followed. It was Anele's turn to jump behind the firewood. Hunkered down next to Vimbela and Shiya, Anele's thoughts went wild. "Who are they? Could they be game wardens? What do they want? Had one of the villagers been poaching in the nearby National Game Reserve?"

The jeep careened through garden patches and knocked over a large cauldron hanging in the communal fire pit before it screeched to a halt. With their tails tucked, several dogs yelped and slunk behind the dwellings. The villagers, now awake and startled, were illuminated by headlights as they peered nervously from their doorways. Most had never seen any mode of modern transport or white men riding atop large beasts.

The men dismounted and formed a line, their revolvers at the ready. All eyes turned to the tall man alighting the vehicle with a rifle slung over his right shoulder. From the rear of the jeep, another man appeared. He was a lanky and shabbily dressed black man. A floppy hat obscured his features.

The tall man roared in Zulu, "Where's Anele and the white kid?"

The bogeyman's raucous demand froze Anele's bones. She clamped a hand over her mouth. She knew that razor-sharp voice too well. How did he find her? Zululand was a vast area, over ten thousand square miles. *And kid!* How could Alan Hallworthy possibly know of Maria's child?

Alan aimed his weapon at the person nearest to him, a fifteen-year-old boy. In an intimidating tone he said, "Speak up, *kaffir,* or you're a dead duck." The teenager's eyes were as large as the moon. He was speechless.

Alan's eyes took on a radioactive glow. He beckoned to the black man wearing the floppy hat. "Go get the *kaffir* bitch. You said you knew which hut she was in."

"Yes, *Baas.* Right away, *Baas.* I know exactly which hut Anele and the child sleep in."

Her betrayer's voice floated on the wind … It could not be … but it *was.*

After Chief Naboto of this village died a few years back, Kumdi had hoped to take his place. He had made Anele's life a living hell ever since because he had been overruled in the votes. For the first time in tribal history, a woman, Anele, had been elected tribal chief of Tswanas kraal.

Now she wondered, "How many pieces of silver was this Judas paid for his treachery?"

Granny Matudia, the matriarch of the kraal, rushed toward the sore loser. No one stopped her. She grabbed Kumdi's khaki shirtsleeve, nearly ripping the garment from his body. The ancient woman was angry. "What brings you here with the enemy of our people? You are a piece of dung to do this!"

Kumdi tossed his head haughtily and responded, "It's none of your business, old woman. Let go of me, or I'll tell Lord Hallworthy to shoot you."

With their noses almost touching, Matudia spat in Kumdi's face. In a murderous voice she said, "You ungrateful dung-for-brains boy. I made sure you and your sister left the settlement with full bellies after Chief Anele expelled you from the kraal. Now you repay my kindness by leading the *umlungu* to us." With adrenalin pumping through her veins, she balled a fist and knocked Kumdi over with one blow to his chest.

Alan and his entourage were amused and amazed at the sight of the old woman knocking down a healthy young man.

Alan's laughter danced through the village with the first rays of sunlight.

But there was no mirth coming from the shamefaced Kumdi. He sprung to his feet and shoved Matudia so hard she fell backward. *Thud!* Her head hit the hard dirt. She groaned in pain.

Two women rushed to Matudia and helped her to her feet. Although dazed, she wasn't badly hurt. But her vision was spotty. She didn't see him coming. Kumdi dusted the dirt off his pants and faced off with her.

"Don't you dare touch me ever again, old woman!" Then, he added, smirking with satisfaction, "You know Anele has the stolen child!"

Matudia hissed, "Next time, you won't get up. You've betrayed your own kind. The witch doctor's Dark Ones will come for your miserable black soul."

Alan made an angry guttural cluck. "Enough of this mumbo-jumbo crap," he snorted. He continued, "Kumdi, go and get them *now!*"

With their handguns raised, Alan's deputies followed Kumdi. They entered Anele's house. Within minutes, they exited. Kumdi was shaking his head. "There's no one in here, *Baas.*"

Alan snorted his reply. "They're hiding somewhere. Search all the homes."

Anele urgently whispered in Vimbela's ear, "Please don't ask any questions. We are in terrible danger. Listen to me carefully. Take Shiya and run like the wind to my father's dead rat tree (the biggest baobab tree standing outside the kraal's perimeter). "Can you remember the way?"

Vimbela, her teeth chattering with fear, nodded.

"Climb as high as you can," Anele ordered. "And stay there with Shiya until I come for you both."

A little voice piped up, "*Umama*, why do we …?"

Cutting the child off, Anele commanded, "Be silent, Shiya. You'll be all right if you listen to me. Go with Vimbela and I'll come shortly. I promise."

Their two terrified expressions spoke volumes.

Anele kissed them on their cheeks and said, "Hurry, please. Go now."

Vimbela was shaking like a bush in the grip of a savannah storm as she silently climbed over the mangled fence. Anele waited until they were out of sight. Something made her nose twitch. She tilted her chin and sniffed the air. What was that smell? Could it be the rich aroma of her father's tobacco? Was he here with her? Did she believe in ghosts? Without a doubt! She closed her eyes and said, silently: "Ubaba, I can't see you, but I feel you are here with me. Please, Father, whisper in my ear and tell me what to do."

An incandescent sun climbed higher into the sky, bathing the former Hallworthy servant in soft, yellow light. With her head held high and her body shrouded in her father's spiritual courage, Anele walked toward the unwelcome intruders.

"I am here, Lord Hallworthy."

Alan spun around and swung his rifle. The butt hit Anele square in the head. She fell backward onto the dirt. For a split second it was *déjà vu*.

Alan flicked off a fleck of scalp tissue from his weapon before barking his demand. "Where is my child, *kaffir*? Don't look so dumb. You know damn well what I'm talking about."

Anele feigned innocence. "Lord Alan, I do not know what you mean. What child?"

The rifle's wooden stock slammed down again. A fountain of blood spurted from Anele's nose. "Don't act smart with me, you black bitch," Alan hissed. "You know damn well what I'm talking about. Where is my child? I know she is here somewhere ..."

Thank God, his snarling voice was a blur. But not her inner voice. "Spirits of the Underworld, only you can end my life now. I can't let anything happen to my precious child."

Alan straddled Anele. "Did you think I wouldn't find you?" he scoffed, nudging her mouth with the cold steel muzzle. "Has the cat got your tongue, black bitch? You want to *know* how I found out about you and my kid. Well, I'm going to tell you ..."

"Sorry to interrupt you, Lord Hallworthy," one of the police officers said. "Would you like us to continue searching?"

"Goddammit, yes," he snapped. "Search every inch of the god-forsaken place."

Alan refocused his attention. "Naturally, you don't know this, but Maria, the wop bitch you freed and hoped I'd never find, told me she'd given birth to twins." Alan tapped a finger against his chin. "Now, let me think. Could it be that someone I know helped the wop deliver? She couldn't have done it all by herself! Maybe it was a black bitch named Anele who killed one baby and stole the other?"

Anele's mind snapped to attention: "Maria didn't give birth to twins! She couldn't have! Great God in the Spirit World, in my haste to save Shiya, perhaps I didn't see the other baby? Had the other twin fallen deeper into the compost pit?"

She tried to sit up, but Alan's boot pressed down like a massive concrete block on her rib cage. At that moment she would have sold her soul to the witch doctor's malevolent creatures for the opportunity to shoot him dead so Shiya could be safe forever from his despicable ways. Anele understood that age didn't matter to Alan. Shiya would become another one of his victims.

Many clouds had darkened Anele's life, but this was the worst. Utter helplessness tore at her heart. "I tried, dear God of the white people. I tried to protect Shiya."

Again, Anele struggled to rise. Alan's boot pressed into her rib cage and ensured she did not.

"Don't dare move. I'm not finished," he snapped. "After Maria gave birth, you took the healthy child and ran away with it, didn't you? How do I know this? Ah! I can see by the look on your face that you're dying to know. Am I right?"

Anele's hate-filled eyes glared back at her former slave master.

Alan continued ranting. "Maria thought she could get away from me. Wrong! I found the whore not far from my house bleeding like a butchered pig. I'd have left her to rot if it wasn't for her telling me about my children. I committed Maria to the state mental hospital. If not for her psychiatrist, I would have dismissed her crazy story."

"Bastard! I hope you rot in hell!" Anele cursed.

A rib cracked under the pressure of Alan's boot. Anele grimaced in agony. Alan continued his tirade as if nothing had happened. "At first, I didn't believe any of it because Maria is a lunatic. It was a janitor at the mental hospital." He gestured to Kumdi to come forward. "It was this man who verified Maria's unbelievable story."

The moment was Kumdi's. He grinned, showing a mouthful of rotten, yellow teeth. Alan didn't break a smile. He shouted for all to hear, "Where is the *white* child? One of you better bring her to me, or I'll pick you off like flies."

The tribe remained quiet until the rifle's blast lifted the matriarch off her feet. Granny Matudia was dead before her body thudded to the ground. Paralyzed with fear, no one made a move to help the old lady. But Anele begged him, "Please don't kill any more of my people, Master. They are innocent bushpeople, and they don't understand English. I've no idea why Kumdi would make up such lies. There's no white child here."

The next shot nicked one of Anele's ear lobes.

Frothing at the mouth like a rabid creature, Alan dribbled his words. "You are a lying, runaway bitch. For the last time, where …"

He stopped in mid sentence. Loud gasps directed his eyes in an easterly direction.

There, leaping over obstacles like a gazelle, Shiya raced towards them, clasping a wriggling green snake in one hand. She sprinted past Alan and the other intruders as if they weren't there, and she released the deadly green mamba onto the earth. She stroked her mother's battered face. Her voice was tearful. "Umama, did the *umlungu* man hurt you? Do you want me to get the *imikhuba*? The witch doctor will destroy the bad men."

Anele's physical pain was momentarily forgotten as she wrapped her arms around her precious child and hugged her tightly.

Alan's face showed no sign of jollity. He bent to study his child and was amazed how much she resembled him. She was tall, towering over most children her age. She had his blond hair but not his blue eyes. Hers were green, reflecting Maria's Sicilian heritage. Shiya's nose and mouth were finely chiseled, like those of his mother, Lady Ethel. Yes, she belonged to him, all right, but she would never be a *true* Hallworthy. Definitely not. But she would be his, in more ways than one. As if reading this sick man's mind, Anele pulled Shiya closer and whispered in her ear, "Run, child, run. This man is going to eat you like a crocodile."

Shiya made a comical face. "He's not *ingwenya*, silly Umama. He's not a crocodile. He is *umlungu*, a white man."

Alan smirked. His patience was strained. He snatched Shiya from Anele, threw her over his shoulder, and marched to the jeep. She struggled violently to free herself, crying out, "*Vulela umlungu* (bad white man). Let go of me."

A backhand across her face prompted a flood of tears and tore Anele's heart from her chest. Shiya was flung into the passenger seat.

In a pitiful voice she begged, "Umama, hurry! Get up and save me."

The injured Anele could do nothing but pray aloud. "Watch over this special child. Make this child strong with your spiritual serpent powers, for she will need them against this evil man. He will show her no mercy."

A gunshot *boom* interrupted her prayers. Riding a tidal wave of willpower, Anele forced herself into an upright position. She couldn't see Shiya in the jeep. "Oh, no," she groaned. "The *bastardo* has killed her." She fell back against the hard earth and wept. Then a voice startled her. She looked up. Through tear-filled eyes, she made out the shape of a stooped man standing over her. Twazli softly said, "Shiya isn't dead, Anele. But you will wish she were. I tried to warn you. But if it helps you heal, the *underworld* has heard you."

It was too late for his words.

A second dark shape loomed over her.

Tekenya, Anele's secret lover, said, "It's true. Your Shiya sits in the chair of the tin cart. I want you to know that I shouldn't have listened to the mouths of others when they wanted to stone the white baby you brought with you to the village. My heart now tells me otherwise. Will you forgive me?"

Anele closed her eyes against the sight of him. There was nothing in her heart to forgive. "You should have married me when I asked," he said. "I would have taken you and the child far from here, to Basutoland, where I was born. The *umlungu* would never have found you there."

Tekenya was pushed aside by a white policeman.

"Out of the way, *kaffir*, or you're next!"

Too weak to resist, Tekenya did what he was told. With arms limp at his sides, he watched Anele being hog-tied, dragged across the dirt, and thrown into the back of the jeep. She landed on the limp body of Kumdi. His dead eyes were gazing at the sky. A single gunshot wound to the back of his neck, execution style, marked his demise. Anele felt no bitterness toward Kumdi. Only pity.

"I forgive you, Kumdi. Fly free and seek out my father. He will guide you into the Invisible Kingdom of Spirits."

Alan stuck his head out the window. To one of the uniformed men he smiled and said, "Thanks for your help. I couldn't have done it without you."

"It's been a pleasure to have been of assistance, Lord Hallworthy. And thank *you* for your most generous *donation*. If you ever need our help again, please don't hesitate to call my contact number in Nairobi."

Through his rearview mirror, Alan, with a wry grin on his lips, watched the ex-cons and mercenaries disguised as police officers mount up and ride away. Alan chuckled. He had pulled off the perfect charade. He knew from experience that the tribe would mourn their dead and then resume their bush ways.

Of course, history would repeat itself on this day. Not only was Lord Alan Hallworthy one of the richest men in this part of the world, but he was also a high-ranking Freemason. Like his fore-fathers, he could get away with any crime without investigation: murder, kidnapping, slavery, or sexual abuse.

The jeep sped from the kraal in a cloud of red dust, driving over thorn bushes as if they were small clumps of tall grass. High above, hidden under a canopy of baobab leaves, Vimbela clung to a broad bough. When the flap at the back of the jeep flew open, exposing Anele and Kumdi, she scrambled down. Coughing and choking in the dust of the vehicle's wake, she raced after it. "*Umama*, where are you going?" she screamed. "Come back. It isn't my fault. I did what you told me. Shiya wouldn't listen. She climbed down the dead rat tree and ran. I couldn't catch her. She has the legs of a cheetah …"

Vimbela's explanation was cut short when she tripped over a tree stump. Her temple struck a jagged root, and she lay on the ground unconscious.

A petrified Shiya was held in a vice grip on Alan's lap. She cried out, "Umama, Shiya wants you …"

Alan dug his fingers into her tender flesh, "That black bitch is not your mother. Do you understand? And you can forget that *kaffir* name. From now on, your name is …" Alan scratched his chin's stubble. "Little Shit! Or better still, Little *Wop* Shit!"

A fire rose in the child's tear-swollen eyes. The grizzly bear in her awoke, and she fearlessly attacked him. "The witch doctor is going to kill you for hurting me and my *Umama*. The *Imikhuba* can make his body invisible, you know. He'll cut your throat, and you'll die like the cattle at slaughter time. Then the cook will boil your bones, and I'll eat you."

Alan's chest shook with laughter. But his mirth turned to fury when Shiya sank her teeth into his leg. Alan beat her so badly that the poor child's face looked like it had been put through a meat grinder.

Before the pain sent her into a faint, Shiya threatened, "One day. One day, white man, I will roast you alive, burn your house down, for hurting me and my Umama."

Then she blacked out.

Shiya was "special." She had unexplainable adult qualities. She would be tested time and time again on land owned by the Devil himself.

*Revenge is mine sayeth Shiya …*

Shiya came to learn that unhappiness had no color in a country that judged peoples' worthiness by their skin tone. She didn't know if she was white, yellow, or green. Nor did she realize her pigmentation was as dark as an Arab's, even though she had Alan's blond hair and Maria's green eyes. Her mixed-blood heritage from her Sicilian mother and British father classified her as "colored" by the Afrikaner National Party, which formed when South Africa was granted its independence from Great Britain.

Tragically, Shiya shared the same abominable fate as her mother, and of the many others who had been incarcerated in the infamous outbuilding before her. In the Hallworthy guest cottage, *the essence of time* stood still.

Shiya would not see her beloved foster mother until they were reunited years later.

That reunion would have dire consequences.

# Part Three

1998 - 2011

# CHAPTER TWENTY-ONE

# Solicchiata, Sicily
## -2010-

*"Circumstances are beyond human control,
but our conduct is our own power."*
—BENJAMIN DISRAELI

*"Mama, wake up!"* Alberto, Jr., age twelve, beseeched. The handsome little boy with shiny, black hair and eyes to match placed both hands on his mother's back and shook her hard. "Mama, wake up. It's nine o'clock. I'm going to be late for soccer practice."

Brianna, Shiya's daughter, opened her bloodshot eyes, made an ouch-my-head-hurts grimace, and slurred, "Oh, darling. Mama has a bad headache. Ask Father Risso to take you, or one of the servants. Mama needs to sleep."

With his tanned, oval face looking sad and drawn, Alberto responded, "Mama, he's not a priest anymore. He's my dad. And he's not here. Have you forgotten that he is visiting his sick uncle in Torino?"

Brianna's alcoholic blackouts were impacting her son and everyone else who resided at the Genovese mansion, a cursed place inherited from her grandmother, Maria.

In this picture-perfect, opulent setting nestled in the mountains of Sicily, the demon alcohol was hard at work. The Brianna of late could finish a box of wine by herself, but she didn't drink for pleasure. She drank to drown the past. She was a broken soul who didn't know how to heal herself or release the emptiness left by the sudden death of her mother.

Then there was the surprise of the ghastly Hallworthy revelations her mother, Shiya, had bestowed upon her. Brianna felt defensive about her mother's shocking disclosures. But what really broke her was the futility of knowing she had been unable to save her own daughter, who had been diagnosed at age five with childhood schizophrenia. The power of a mother's love couldn't reverse the condition. Little Shiya was *lost*, hopelessly locked in a hallucinatory world of imaginary animals and people. From age six, Little Shiya had been committed to a residential psychiatric treatment facility in Palermo. It was the final chapter in Brianna's meltdown. And so, alcohol became her dubious savior.

At age thirty-five, Brianna, a once vivacious personality, was unaware that she had diminished capacity due to alcoholism. She displayed no leadership and had no boundaries. The recent disasters that had occurred in her home—a chimney fire, a wine cellar break-in, and a pool drowning of a six-week-old puppy that had strayed from the litter—were insulated from her sodden mind.

She led a champagne lifestyle that was about to change for the worse.

Alberto, Jr., his jaw set and fists balled, stamped from the room, the chunky spikes of his soccer shoes echoing behind him.

Without a care in the world, Brianna succumbed to the balm of slumber.

How had this once pampered child, bright law student, and proud mother of twins slide down this dark, slippery slope toward an early grave?

# CHAPTER TWENTY-TWO

# British Columbia, Canada
# -1998-

*"The heart of another is a dark forest, always,*
*no matter how close it has been to your own."*
—WILLA CARTER

On a fateful day in February 1998, Brianna's life would forever be turned upside down.

Her vehicle tunneled through the dank fog that ushered in Valentine's Day. She was driving on a treacherous, snow-laden highway in the British Columbia interior on a day that would bring nothing close to romantic expectations.

With her hands gripping the wheel in the ten-o'clock and two-o'clock positions, Brianna, age twenty-three, drove with intensity, the skin on her hands stretching tightly over her white knuckles. Worry lines etched themselves into her pretty face. Her eyelids hung heavy with fatigue over her velvet black eyes. Breathtaking winter scenery displayed itself without her giving a glance. She was a law student who had packed six semesters of unrelenting, dedicated academic effort behind her, but all she could think about was the bizarre voice-mail message her mother left yesterday.

"I love you, my precious daughter. See you in heaven."

After the answering machine's beep, Brianna spoke. "Mom, it's me. What the heck is going on? Why the weird message? Please call me right back. By the way, I'm really sorry. I didn't mean to be so rude the last time we spoke."

No response.

Brianna tried wit. "Madam, if you don't pick up, I'm going to come out there and kick your butt."

Still no response.

Yesterday's silence was too much for Brianna's emotional personality. She had thumped her fist on the kitchen counter, sending a coffee spoon flying to the floor. "Damn you, Mother! I have a six-hour criminal law and litigation exam to prepare for this Monday. I could do without this unnecessary melodrama!"

Brianna had angrily flipped shut her cell phone. Why was her mother giving her the cold shoulder?

On the last leg of her journey down the mountain highway, Brianna's thoughts were as gloomy as the dismal weather. With serious trust issues marring their mother-daughter relationship, she had tried to coax from her mother the missing pieces of the jigsaw puzzle that was her life.

Brianna had not even known that her mother's birth name was Shiya. She only knew her as Lynette. Her mother had always remained tight-lipped. Brianna couldn't begin to guess the reasons for her mother's secrecy. As a top law student, Brianna had learned to "read" people's body language, but she couldn't "read" her mother! Prodding her mom was like trying to get blood from a stone.

They had always been incompatible.

Shiya's revelations—taped confessions left for her daughter to find following her departure—were beyond human comprehension. They sent her only child into a downward spiral. Brianna's impulsiveness and her desperation for answers had finally driven her (three months shy of giving birth) to trace her mother's whereabouts to South Africa. In August that same year, they had been reunited in South Africa at the funeral of Anele Dingane, Shiya's foster mother.

That day, the cobwebs of past events were barely cleared from Brianna's mind.

Monsoon-laden rain clouds hung low over Tswanas kraal on the day of Anele's funeral. Six strong tribesmen hoisted the makeshift coffin made from the wood of a gum tree onto their shoulders. With bare feet shuffling, they began the slow walk up the mountainside to the tribe's sacred burial site. Following in the pallbearers' wake, young boys wearing ancestral Zulu attire beat out the age-old obituary for the dead on African drums strapped to their waists.

Brianna couldn't believe how many people were present, but

then she had not known of her mother's incredulous, secret past—a past that belonged to a horror movie—until now.

As if attending a celebrity's burial, the attendees trooped forward.

Sister Bertha was present. Brianna learned that she was a nun who had taught school in Tswanas kraal and later forsaken her vows for a man and an abandoned orphan named Amalonda.

Also present were some relatives of Naomi, a prostitute, who had been murdered by Alan Hallworthy.

Now in their eighties and nineties, a few former Hallworthy indentured slaves were shuffling solemnly in step.

At the rear of the procession marched media representatives from Canada, Great Britain, and South Africa, their digital cameras and video recording devices taking in the event that had made headlines across the world.

Winston Mandekana, who was the first to break the news of the shootings, was there. The day he bagged the story, he used the oldest trick in the book—he lied.

"I was born in Mtunzini, your neighboring village. I am one of you," he had proclaimed to the Tswanas villagers. "You can trust me. The white woman, what is she doing here? How is she connected to the dead woman, Chief Anele Dingane, a descendant of Queen Nobuntu?"

The naïve tribe members gave him the answers he sought.

Mandekana's story became breaking news in London. The headlines in the August 16 edition of the *Mail on Sunday* read:

African Woman Is Murdered
for Saving the Life of
a White Baby in 1945
By Winston Mandekana

Lord Alan Hallworthy, of Hallworthy
Sugar Refineries—a direct descen-
dant of the deceased Lord Nigel
Hallworthy and distant cousin to
Queen Victoria—and his wife, Lady
Corrie Hallworthy, have been named
as persons of interest in this
case.

As the sensational story was breaking, Mandekana's editor urged him to follow up on it, but it was proving to be a problem. The reporter couldn't get near the woman who had survived the tragedy.

The spring sun was high in the sky as Shiya, her head bandaged after a surgery to remove the bullet intended to kill her, and Brianna held hands as they walked solemnly between armed officers. The reporters, who were being held at bay by threats, were not pleased. They had little choice but to tell their stories from a distance by constantly clicking ultra-zoom video and digital cameras.

At the burial site, the incessant hum of mosquitoes offered a soporific backdrop. Shiya was oblivious to the nasty pests feeding on the crowd's exposed flesh. She was still groggy from pain medication and from her overly generous consumption of brandy prior to the funeral. She tried her best to focus on the coffin resting in the dirt hollow below. Reaching into the pocket of her black, full-length dress, she pulled out a folded piece of paper. It was a poem she had written when she had first arrived at the kraal months ago, and the day after she and Anele had returned from the sacred rock outside Tswanas kraal. Sorrow choked Shiya's throat. She swallowed hard before reading aloud what she'd written:

*I will tread the misty stairs, where there is no such word as*
*     time.*
*We can all be together there. I know that we will be just fine.*
*And under stars unfurled, will echo out our laughter.*
*Mother dearest, Umama Anele, we will be as one in this*
*     world,*
*Rejoined in the thereafter. I love you. But I will not grieve.*
*You, my love, will be forever locked in my beating heart.*
*So, until we meet again in the Invisible Kingdom of souls, I*
*     say farewell.*

For those who did not understand her English tongue, Sister Bertha translated. Dark faces beamed with appreciation for Shiya's poignant sentiments.

"Thank you, Sister Bertha," Shiya said when she finished reading.

"My pleas- …"

The nun's mouth opened and shut while many brows arched in alarm. Gasps were heard from the outsiders.

Brianna shrunk behind her mother's back. "I hope it's not dangerous?"

Shiya smiled. She knew the truth.

There, with serpentine undulations, was the most dangerous,

arboreal, feared snake in all of Africa. The fast-moving, bright-green mamba was highly venomous. Its 1.8-meter length slithered toward the burial hole. Reacting quickly, Detective Marquand drew his pistol from its holder, a move that elicited a cry of protest from Shiya. She blocked his aim with her hand.

"Put your gun away," she demanded. "He's not going to harm anyone. He has come to see *me*."

The detective's incredulous expression did not faze her.

The crowd was astonished when Shiya lifted the hissing snake to her chest, bent her head, whispered something, and dropped the snake onto the coffin lid. The deadly mamba slowly slithered downward, coming to rest on the wildflower wreath that adorned the coffin. A stunned Brianna blurted out what many others wanted to, but were too numb to say.

"*Holy shit!*" Brianna exclaimed. "Are you nuts, Mother! It could have bitten you!"

Shiya smirked. "No, it wouldn't have. *We* are one."

"Now you're talking crazy, Mom."

Unnoticed by Brianna was a short, plump, aging woman who was pushing her way through to join them. What the woman said blew Brianna's mind.

"Most beautiful daughter of Anele, *she* has heard your words," Shiya's former nanny uttered. "She will always be with you. See?" She pointed to the snake curled into the flower wreath. "Umama Anele sent you the green snake.

The simple woman's speech was interrupted by an outbreak of loud wailing. All heads turned.

There, standing behind the reporters, was a tall, slim female wearing a heavy veil, a long black dress, and gloves. Sobbing, she was flanked by what could only be described as some "rent-a-thugs"—beefy, foreign-looking bodyguards.

Shiya frowned. "Who on earth is she?" she asked.

Vimbela piped up, "I don't know, but she's not one of us. We don't wear such awful clothes."

Shiya did not want to laugh, but a soft chuckle escaped.

No one seemed to know the woman's identity, so Shiya, with Brianna at her side and police officers following, approached the veiled woman, who immediately turned on her heels. In a flash, Brianna grabbed the woman's thin arm. "Excuse me. I don't want to sound rude, but who are you? Obviously you know Anele or you wouldn't be here."

The woman did not reply. Instead, her long fingers unlatched Brianna's grip. Brianna imagined a piercing glare from behind the woman's concealing headdress.

Shiya joined her daughter and rephrased the question, "Do I know you?"

"I should be in that grave, not her," came the barely audible response.

"What do you mean by that?" Shiya blurted.

"If it wasn't for me, she wouldn't be lying in the cold earth."

Shiya let out a frustrated sigh. "Now you have lost me."

"She not only saved you; she once saved me, as well."

"I don't understand. What are you talking about? Who the *hell* are you?"

"I'm Maria ... Your *real* mother."

This shocking revelation did not register in Shiya's fuzzy brain.

Frowning, she said, "I'm sorry. What did you say?"

"My name is Maria Picasso. I'm your biological mother."

Finally, it hit home. How else would she have known? All of Shiya's nerve endings floated to the surface and created gooseflesh. Then an emotion she had never experienced before gripped her heart. She felt her legs give way.

Maria held her limp daughter in her arms for the first time. Her voice was soft. "I'm taking you home to Sicily. That's where we both belong."

Brianna sprang into action. She untangled Maria's arms, and with a mighty, infuriated shove sent her sailing backward.

"Over my dead body," Brianna hissed. With her blood boiling, she ranted on. "After what I have heard on my mother's recordings, you should thank your lucky stars she didn't send someone to bump you off. What kind of mother abandons her newborn baby to be devoured by wild animals? You are a pathetic piece of shit, and I suggest you get the hell away from here and never try to contact my mother again!"

# CHAPTER TWENTY-THREE

# The Genovese Mansion, Sicily
## -2010-

*"It is not easy for people to rise out of obscurity when they have to face straitened circumstances at home."*
—JUVENAL

O ne day in late August, Brianna did not hear the repeated knocking on her bedroom door. Francesca, Brianna's long-suffering secretary and long-time servant, pushed open the heavy, oak-paneled door and stepped in.

"Señora, please wake up," Francesca said as she shook Brianna's prone body.

It took several shakes before Brianna finally opened her blood-shot eyes.

"What the hell, Francesca!"

"I'm sorry to disturb you, but a courier is at the door. He has a registered parcel that he needs a signature for. It has 'urgent' written in red all over the package."

"Okay," Brianna grumbled. "Give me a minute and I'll be down."

The uniformed DHL courier stared at the dishevelled woman wearing a bright pink housecoat and matching slippers. Her eyes were so puffy she looked as if she hadn't slept in weeks. After the necessary signature, Brianna stared at the box. She noted the sender's name, Miguel Rodriguez, and frowned. She had seen neither hide nor hair of her mother's former attorney since their cantankerous meeting in the Palermo hospital following the birth of her twins. She shook her head vigorously as if denying the memory, but she had no such luck.

Frame by frame, in kaleidoscope colors, Brianna traveled back in time.

After attending Anele's funeral back in Africa, Brianna returned to her home in Sicily and gave birth to twins, a boy and a girl.

During the birth, Brianna had cried out for her mother. But now she felt a warm, maternal glow of love sweep through her as she looked at her babies swaddled in white linen like Egyptian mummies. Pride flowed from every pore. Brianna had never felt anything like it. Her heart was bursting with happiness. She never foresaw what fate held in store for her son and daughter.

In the twilight embrace of a deep sleep, Brianna imagined a willowy female bathed in a radiant blue sphere moving toward her. Shiya's face was somber and her long arms were outstretched. She floated toward the hospital bed as if she were an astronaut in the timelessness of space. What was she saying? In her dream, Brianna strained to hear. "Oh, precious child of mine, what have I done? I've passed on the *cursed* blood."

Brianna bolted upright and tried to relive her dream. She wanted to shout, "Mom, come back."

Dismissing the dream, Brianna glanced adoringly at the infants lying in the hospital crib next to her bed. Her bundles of joy were so different from each other. The dark-skinned Alberto, Jr., slowly stirred as he lazily opened his eyes. They were jet black, as was his mop of thick hair. Shiya, though, was fair skinned with sparkling emerald eyes and tufts of beautiful blond hair. Brianna yawned. A few moments later, a snore escaped from the exhausted mother. But she wasn't to get the rest she deserved.

The nurse stroked her hand. "I'm sorry to wake you. You have visitors, Brianna. Do you wish to see them?"

"Who are they?"

"I don't know."

Brianna could not believe her eyes. She was stunned. "Oh, my God! He is the last person I thought would *dare* show his face," she thought. She had only seen his photograph, but there was no mistaking the aquamarine eyes, sun-bleached hair, and chiseled features of the six-foot plus South African lawyer who had betrayed her mother prior to the Tswanas homicide of Anele and the near fatal shooting of Shiya.

If the pain of her surgery hadn't prevented it, she would have stood up and socked Bryan Durval hard.

Brianna stared at the uninvited visitor.

Holding a bouquet of yellow roses in one hand, the smiling lawyer approached her bed. "This is for you," he said. "Congratulations."

Brianna recalled that not long after Anele's funeral, Detective Pieter Marquand, the homicide officer who investigated the crimes against Shiya and Anele, had declared, "Bryan Durval is nothing more than a deranged animal, and that is putting it lightly."

Now *he* was here.

"You've got *cojones!*" she spat. "What the hell do you want?"

"I have something for you."

Brianna watched as he dug into his khaki safari shorts and pulled out a small velvet box. He handed it to her.

"What is it?"

"Open it and you see for yourself."

Displaying bright flashes of princess pink, two rare diamonds sparkled under the hospital room lights.

Brianna gasped loudly. "Are these for real?"

"Yes. They are rare pink diamonds."

"You mean *blood* diamonds!" Brianna retorted, "I don't bloody want them. Why have you brought them to me?"

Without invitation, Bryan lowered himself onto the hospital chair. Brianna gave him a look that could have brought down presidents, but she decided to hear him out before she asked hospital security to evict him.

"Please, let me explain," he said.

"Oh, please do!" she replied sarcastically.

"They are not *blood* diamonds. No human blood was spilled. They were found at the same river your mother used to play in ..."

Brianna interrupted, "By whom?"

"Sliman," he answered.

"Not the *same* friggin' guy who shot Anele dead and tried to kill my mother!"

Bryan looked down, away from her intense, probing stare. "Yes. Just before he was arrested, he learned that your mother had survived. After she was airlifted to Durban hospital, he came to me and begged me to find out what her condition was."

Brianna's features contorted with rage. "Oh, that's just friggin' ironical! He shoots her and then, with a pricking conscience, wants to know how she's doing? Go on. I'm listening," she ended snappily.

"For the record, Sliman was not the killer. He did not have a weapon. Johannes Abraham de Klerk was the shooter."

Raising his hand to silence another outburst from Brianna, the lawyer continued. "Please hear me out. I am just as anxious to get this over with as you are. You see, old Kelingo, the former Hallworthy field worker was Anele's savior when she was twelve. He gave me the diamonds to pass to your mother as *atonement* for the role he played. The shooter would never have learned of your mother's stay at the kraal had it not been for Kelingo. Why he did what he did, we will never know, but Kelingo was a tribal Zulu who believed that he would never enter the Invisible Kingdom of Souls if he didn't try to make amends."

An acidic response loomed unexpressed on Brianna's lips. "The dog knows what happens to him when he steals food off the kitchen counter."

Bryan continued. "I was saddened to hear that Lynette passed away."

"Sure you are, shitbag!" Brianna blurted.

Bryan shook his head. He wasn't there to be reprimanded. He had come for a specific purpose. "I'm sure Sliman would want you to have them. These diamonds could command prices up to $400,000 per carat, and what you have is 3.14 carats."

A poker-faced Brianna tried not to show her astonishment, but her quivering insides told the real story. She didn't need additional wealth after having been left more money than she could spend in a lifetime from her mother, Shiya, and her grandmother, Maria Picasso, but the prospect of being in possession of pink diamonds was exciting. It was a lovely feeling being filthy rich.

"Okay. I'll accept them. But there is one thing I have to know. Why did you not keep them yourself? No one would have been the wiser."

"I know you are unlikely to accept my explanation, but I'll give it to you anyway. When I met your mother, I was overcome with a feeling that I can only describe as love at first sight."

Brianna's guttural raspberry resonated around the room.

"Oh, I was expecting that," Bryan responded. "But I *did* love Lynette. She was the most fascinating and adorable woman I had ever met. My feelings only soured when she held me and my family for ransom. And, as God is my witness, I had nothing to do with the assassination plot. I swear. Lady Corrie Hallworthy arranged the whole ghastly affair."

Brianna, with tightrope tension pounding in her head, shrugged. Not wishing to hear another word out of this man's mouth, she simply said, "My babies are due to be fed, so I would like you to leave. And hear my words: never darken my life again!"

Bryan slunk from the room like a scolded schoolboy.

Her next visitor would send her to the brink of insanity.

She didn't have to turn to see who had entered the room. The unmistakable odor of his aftershave was an ugly reminder. She glared at Mike, who was making his way toward her. She looked him up and down with contempt.

The Canadian attorney was dressed in an expensive, black Italian suit; crisp white shirt; black tie; mirror-finish shoes; black fedora; and sunglasses. *In a hospital!* His Mafia-like attire appeared ridiculous. But thank the gods, she could happily inform him he was *not* the twins' father. She deeply regretted having had that one-night stand with him, and had convinced herself it would never have happened without her first consuming a large amount of alcohol. Preoccupied by Mike's presence, she didn't at first notice the gray-haired man standing outside the glass doors or Father John Risso. She didn't perceive the priest's astonishment or understand why he couldn't take his eyes off the man in the room or Brianna.

"What brings you here, Mike?" Brianna asked, as if it were an everyday question. "I thought we dealt with all the issues the last time I saw you."

Brianna's gaze traveled to the glass door, and she added, "Do you know who that man is out there with the priest?"

Mike didn't answer right away; his eyes were glued on the twins. But Brianna was one step ahead. "No. They are not yours. Look at their noses. They are definitely my ex-fiancé, Roberto's, children."

"Does he know?" Mike asked in a typical lawyer's trick designed to catch her in a lie.

Setting truth aside, she replied, "Of course," even though she had not had any communication with Roberto for two years, since their breakup in 1998.

Mike then removed his sunglasses and made eye contact with Brianna. She turned away from his intense gaze.

Having attended Roberto's wedding two weeks earlier, Mike knew that there had been no contact between him and Brianna. Her name had not been mentioned at all.

Mike Rodriguez had put the past behind him. He had built a successful law practice in Vancouver, BC, and had begun to pay more attention to his long-suffering wife, who had chosen to turn a blind eye to his infatuation with Brianna.

Mike looked at the young woman in the hospital bed who had stolen his heart. Although he would not admit it, a flame still burned for her. But ... he had to move on, or he would forget the reason he had traveled to Palermo.

"Brianna, I have brought someone here to see you."

"Is it that guy out there?"

Mike turned, beckoning with his hand to the two men who were looking in his direction.

Father John was the first to enter. He rushed to her side and firmly took hold of her hand.

Brianna didn't see it coming as the other man entered the room.

"What the hell!" she cried. "It can't be! You're dead! You fell off a roof! My mom scattered your ashes in El Salvador."

Her biological father, Lionel Martinez, embraced his wild-eyed daughter. In Spanish he said, "My darling daughter, it was your mother who wanted me dead. But I beat her at her own game, and I'm here now."

Brianna's head screamed, "It can't be real. This only happens in movies. No more ... no more ... no ... no ... no ... no ..."

Back in the present, Brianna opened the parcel handed to her by the DHL agent. Taped to the inside of the box was a note:

*5 May 2010*

*Hi, Brianna,*

> *I hope you and your children are well and happy. I would like to take this opportunity to congratulate you on your marriage to John Risso. It came as a big surprise! The reason I'm writing is that in late January of this year, I received an e-mail from Winston Mandekana, who lives in London, England. I don't know if you remember him. He was the crime reporter who exposed the man who killed Anele and shot your mother back in 1998. Mandekana informed me that he had received correspondence from Sister Bertha, a Catholic nun, who asked him if he knew of your whereabouts. He wrote back saying he didn't know where you were living but that he would check it out. Shortly after receiving his e-mail, I telephoned Bertha, no longer a nun, at the number given in her correspondence, and I gathered that she wanted to give to you some items belonging to your mother. So I instructed her to send them to me. They are now duly enclosed.*

> *Take care, and hugs to the twins. If you need anything, you know where to find me. I will never stop loving you, Brianna. How I wish that the twins were mine.*

It was signed with a single initial: "M."

Brianna struggled to unscrew the rusty old tea caddy lid. When it opened, the contents spilled out. Inside were her mother's possessions. Brianna was staggered. One particular piece of jewelry caused her to gulp. She opened the delicate catch on the gold locket.

"Oh, my God!" she gasped.

Inside the locket was the tiny swatch of colored material the five-year-old Shiya had ripped from Anele's skirt that day in 1950 they had been transported to the Hallworthy Estate and brutally separated.

Brianna felt sobered and burdened with remorse. She began to cry. She looked heavenward and said in a soft whisper, "Mama, if you can hear me, I'm so sorry for everything."

To say that Brianna felt embittered after Shiya's death was an understatement. Her rage was an understandable response to hurt and injury. Now she realized she had to make a 180-degree turn if she was going to make it, if she was going to begin to unload the burden that had begun to destroy her character.

Brianna had always been a mixture of lion and lamb, highly spirited, yet extremely vulnerable. But after losing both her mother and grandmother, Brianna had turned into a self-made monster, sentencing herself to a punishing life, finding solace in alcohol. Brianna nodded involuntarily as she accepted this fact. With the pendant clasped in her hand, she spurred herself into action. She lifted the telephone receiver and dialed long distance. A deep voice on the other end answered, "This is Dr. Ungobo."

"Hi. I have no idea what time it is over there, so I hope I'm not waking you. My name is Brianna Risso, and I'm looking for a nun named Sister Bertha. Do you know how I can get in touch with her?"

"Are you a fellow nun?"

"I'm not a nun, but I regard myself as a friend. You see, I met Sister Bertha at Anele's funeral. I don't know if you are familiar with that name, but Anele and my mother were shot in a Zulu kraal back in 1998."

Dr. William Ungobo inhaled deeply. He was well acquainted with the demise of Anele but knew little of Shiya's passing beyond the snippets of information Bertha had relayed to him. The love of his life, Bertha, often spoke about the two ladies, as well as the other women she had loved and lost in Tswanas kraal. However, what this foreign-sounding woman (calling at one o'clock in the morning) wanted was beyond reach and forced William to be the bearer of bad news.

"I'm sorry to inform you, but Bertha is no longer with us. She died last year."

"Oh, I'm so sorry to hear that," Brianna uttered.

To Brianna's surprise, Dr. William added, "Bertha has a daughter. Her name is Amalonda. Would you like to talk to her?"

Brianna was stunned. She blurted, "She has a *daughter*! But she's a nun!"

There was a long pause before William said, "Ah, it is a long story. Wait a minute, please. I'll get Amalonda. She will explain everything to you. It was nice talking to you. Goodbye, Miss Brianna."

Amalonda and Brianna had a long, tearful telephone conversation that ended with a promise.

"As soon as I can, I will come to see you," Brianna said.

Amalonda responded sincerely, "That would be great. I will look forward to meeting you and your twins."

"I can hardly wait to meet you. We have much to talk about!" Brianna ended.

But as the saying goes, "Be careful what you wish for. You might get it!"

Returning to Africa, the Dark Continent that held many emotional wounds for Brianna, would have dire consequences.

# CHAPTER TWENTY-FOUR

# A New Year
## -2011-

*"People need to have the dignity of
risk and the right to fail."*
—NABIL N JAMAL

Brianna's alcoholism had become unsafe and out of control. She was on a suicide path. She was not sure she could take care of herself, let alone her children. She was not currently living at the Genovese mansion, which had become a continuing source of aggravation and bad memories.

In her own way Brianna had provided support, love, and encouragement to her shy, withdrawn daughter, but it wasn't enough. The power of love couldn't make the childhood schizophrenia disappear. Her twelve-year-old child was *lost*.

Brianna's daughter had become hopelessly locked inside herself. She lived at a residential psychiatric facility in Palermo within a hallucinatory world of imaginary animals. It was supposed to have been a short-term program, but it had become long term.

Despite her treatment, Little Shiya continued to demonstrate delusional behavior. She made derogatory and foul statements, confused TV drama and dreams for reality, had difficulty relating to her peers, and failed at times to recognize her mother and friends. In addition, her personal hygiene was declining, and she had extreme mood swings. She also exhibited a strange fascination for spiders, snakes, and shadows. The medical authorities would not release her in this condition.

Brianna recalled the day that Little Shiya, then five years old, was diagnosed with childhood schizophrenia. In absolute denial, Brianna had challenged the attending psychiatrist.

"Are you out of your friggin' mind!" she exploded. "She's *five!* Come on! You must have gotten it wrong!"

But sadly, she was the one who had gotten it wrong!

A mother's knee-jerk defense of her child was a sad occurrence. Little Shiya was lost in a world that no mother could understand.

Father Giovanni (John) Risso, an ordained Catholic priest not much older than Brianna, had accompanied mother and daughter on the visit to the clinic. His religious training suggested a treatment that was contradictory to the conventional medical diagnosis: *Exorcism!* His religious fervor informed him that the child was possessed.

The hereditary Hallworthy demon had found a new host.

But could Father Risso convince Brianna to have the child exorcized? Not a chance in hell! He knew her well!

The priest had been at the hospital when the door of motherhood had opened for Brianna. Now, the door between her and the father of her children was slammed shut. In his opinion, Brianna was suffering through the final stage of a psychological breakdown. Her illusory bliss had had its ups and downs, but how had this beloved child, bright student, and proud mother of twins slide into a dark abyss?

It all began when Brianna learned the truth about the mother she never really knew. Then tragedy after tragedy had struck: the brutal shooting death of Anele, her mother's near-fatal gunshot wound, and her mother's eventual death from a brain tumor shortly after Brianna arrived in Sicily in 1998. Not long after Shiya's death came her grandmother Maria's fatal heart attack.

Another source of anguish was Brianna's marriage to John Risso, the former priest. It appeared their wedded bliss was fading. But worst of all was learning that her beautiful, spirited daughter was schizophrenic! Brianna knew she was not mentally capable of understanding her daughter's mental illness, let alone coping with it. During all of these challenges, Father John had stood by her.

Brianna had met the priest, John Risso, at the Genovese mansion after her mother's death. She was ignorant about priests, how they lived and felt as human beings. But on the day of the funeral, his angelic features, golden hair, and blue eyes—a shade that could make an ocean sing and a sky shine—captivated her. She could gaze into his spellbinding eyes for hours.

Was it "right" to have such passionate feelings for a priest?

She never imagined that John Risso would fall in love with her.

Following the deaths of her mother and grandmother, and after the birth of her twins, Father Risso became a daily visitor. At night they would e-mail or message each other on social media. Feeling more vulnerable and needy than ever before, Brianna felt conflicted. Her feelings for this servant of God were escalating more than morality should allow. But would he be prepared to renounce the vow he had taken before God to remain pure and chaste? Would he become more than a best friend and confidante?

Brianna was not prepared to hear his answers.

One night after the twins were asleep, Father John did not leave the mansion, as was his pattern. He made himself comfortable on the leather loveseat, turned on the television, and addressed Brianna. "Have you seen this one? I saw the preview for it last week. It looked interesting."

Wildlife documentaries and sports channels were favorites of Brianna's and John's, common interests that brought them closer.

"No, thanks. I don't really feel like watching television right now," she responded while pouring herself and John generous glasses of red wine.

John touched her arm. "I have gotten to know you, and I love you, Brianna."

She did not allow her hopes to build because he had often expressed this sentiment to her.

"There is definitely something troubling you," John said. "What's the matter? Do you feel like talking about it? Maybe this will help you relax." He began massaging the small of her back.

Later Brianna recalled her conflicting emotions, wishing she could lift up his frock and run her hands over his muscular abdomen. Despite her grief, she convinced herself that she was only human and longed to be loved again.

On this wintry night the effects of the wine enhanced her senses. Her whole body melted with the warmth of his touch. The force of nature that brought two people together in synchrony could not be denied. This man of the cloth could hold off no longer. He was not shy about his emotions or sexual desires, even while he was clashing with the celibacy ruling of the Catholic Church.

When John gently clasped Brianna's face and pulled it towards his own, something inside her released. A tingling sensation flowed through her body as his lips sensually descended to her neck. She shivered when he said in a warm whisper, "I love you, Brianna."

Although John was inexperienced, his fingers followed the contours of her back, moving softly until his hands found her breasts. She released a moan of ecstasy and then embraced him with a force that pushed him backward. She kissed him with a passion he had never known before. He fumbled clumsily with the buttons of her blouse. Becoming frustrated, he tore at them. Several buttons shot across the room. He awkwardly unhooked her bra, finally exposing her supple breasts.

The sensation of her fingers on his body threatened him with early release, but he fought it. He wanted this rapturous feeling to last forever, even though he was well aware that it was a sinful act.

In the afterglow of their lovemaking, Brianna and John clung to each other tightly.

"I really *do* love you, Brianna."

She felt a tear trickle down her cheek, but she remained silent as a tinge of guilt spiked her conscience. Had she seduced a holy servant of God, or was it the other way around?

Nevertheless, it had been quite a while since someone had professed his adoration and made love to her. What the future held for the "prohibited" couple was anyone's guess.

*Time was not of the essence!*

It took over a year for John Risso to gain Vatican approval to leave his priestly ministry. One week later, the couple married in an Anglican church adorned with Neo-Gothic grandeur—pointed arches, stained glass, and colorful mosaics. They honeymooned on the Island of Malta. On their first married night together, John said, "I'm not going to make a perfect husband or stepfather, as I have little experience in such things, but I will try to make all of you happy."

One year later, the marriage was over. It was John who ended their union. He argued that her excessive drinking was intolerable. She countered that he was the one who insisted her child be exorcised. Eventually, she convinced herself that he had never really left the priesthood. Most of his days were spent praying for his sins!

After a long period of contrite and repentant confessions, John Risso was accepted back into the priesthood and relocated to Rome.

Brianna remained at the Sicilian mansion and tried to fill the empty void left by his departure by taking lover after lover. And everything flowed downhill from there—until she received the DHL parcel from the Canadian lawyer, Mike Rodriguez.

But it wasn't until after the phone call Brianna made to Dr. William and Amalonda in Zambia that Brianna had made up her mind. To fulfill a promise she had made before her mother's death,

Brianna had an urgent mission to tackle. She lifted the telephone receiver and set a scurrilous undertaking in motion. She would come to wish she had not honored her mother's last request!

*Be careful what you wish for; it might come true!*

# CHAPTER TWENTY-FIVE

# Today

*"It is impossible to suffer without
making someone pay for it."*
—FRIEDRICH NIETZSCHE

On a glorious sun-drenched day in March 2011, Brianna—wearing a glamorous, hydrangea-print summer dress accessorized with open-toed, chunky-heeled sandals and a wide-brimmed straw hat sitting atop flowing black hair—gazed upon the burned-out shell of the once majestic Hallworthy mansion, now reduced to silent, ashen ruins. A similar fate had befallen the sugar refinery and the infamous slave outbuilding. Fire officials investigating the scene believed that the cause had been deliberate arson. An explosive blast had torn away the steel girders and concrete slabs of the refinery, as if they were balsa wood. *Somebody* had wanted revenge. It must have been retaliation for the abominable slave history long associated with the property, where, since the early 1800s, the owners played God over the lives of others. Revenge was a very powerful motive.

What was behind the incident was far more cunning. This crime had not been a fly-by-night affair. It was a well-conceived plan to raze a place where the earth remained bloodied with countless dreadful crimes against humanity.

Following Lady Corrie's death, Brianna's mother had inherited the Hallworthy Estate, sugar refinery, and other assets. It was to prove a Pyrrhic inheritance, because Shiya Hallworthy didn't live to see a penny.

Without a doubt, one or more people had unleashed hatred on the estate. The wealthy Hallworthy clan, which had presided over the life and death of so many, had many enemies. However, the fire had protected the arsonist. A thorough and extensive investigation of the cause had been unable to identify the perpetrator or perpetrators.

With a heavy cloud of Chanel N°5 trailing in her wake, Brianna strolled around the circular driveway, its intricate paving stones still intact. She cast her eyes about, observing the bleakness of the gardens that had once surrounded the house.

Gone were the neatly pruned trees, the greenery, and the elegantly sculptured shrubs. All were now brown and dead. Gone were the magnificent marble statues, water fountains, and goldfish ponds of yesteryear. Not one bee hovered busily. Nor did a single bird sing a tune. Brianna's musings were interrupted by her daughter, whom she had removed from the children's psychiatric ward without permission.

"Mama, the brown lady says thank you," Little Shiya announced.

Brianna wanted to dismiss her mentally ill daughter's outburst because it wouldn't be the first time she had conjured up an invisible playmate or person. But her first reaction was curiosity.

Her eyes scanned her daughter's excited face. "What brown lady, darling?"

"Over there," the eleven-year-old gestured with her index finger. "She is naked and wearing an iron collar around her neck."

Brianna sighed exasperatingly and said, "Really, darling! Are you having one of your fits?"

Then a recollection came to her mind. Hadn't she herself spoken to her disembodied mother after the birth of the twins?

Little Shiya's lips drooped in dismay. "I'm not imagining this, Mama. She *is* here, and so many other dark people are surrounding her. But wait, I see a lovely lady who is wearing a beautiful wedding dress. She tells me that I am named after her."

Brianna clamped a hand over her mouth to stifle a loud gasp. This was more than a rational brain could absorb. She turned her head away from her daughter's questioning eyes and walked gingerly over the rubble toward what used to be the main entrance to the house.

Hot on her heels, Shiya caught up. "Mama, don't walk away. I see lots of brown people and this very beautiful lady!"

Before Brianna could open her mouth to respond, Little Shiya's twin brother, Alberto, sidled up to them. "I see that Shiya is off her rocker again, seeing ghosts!" he said. "She needs to go back to the loony bin!"

Brianna grabbed him roughly by the shoulder. "Alberto, please don't mock your sister," she admonished. "She is not like us. She is very special."

Alberto laughed. "Yeah, right!" he said meanly. "You and I know she is as crazy as a shithouse rat."

"Watch your language, or I will wash your mouth out with soap," Brianna reprimanded. "Go and wait in the car."

Brianna adored her children, but of late, Alberto was a handful. She blamed herself for indulging his every demand: "I want this. I want that!" If the boy saw a new PlayStation game advertised on TV, he would manipulatively wrap her around his little finger and possess it before the day was out.

Now, kicking the dirt in a huff, Alberto skulked off toward the rented Land Rover muttering to himself: "Why did *she* have to come with us? I hate her. I wish she was dead! Then I could have Mama all to myself."

The spoiled brat could not have known that his ghastly wish was already in the making.

Back on the driveway, a teary-eyed Shiya turned to her mother. "Why does my brother hate me so? I'm not crazy. He is! He cuts the heads off bugs!"

"Darling," Brianna said, taking her daughter's hand and squeezing it lovingly. "Alberto doesn't hate you. He is a boy who thinks he is a man!"

A broad smile appeared on Shiya's face. In a voice that could have blended with a nursery rhyme, she said, "You believe me, Mama, don't you?"

"Of course," Brianna replied glibly. She did not want to indulge her daughter's fantasy, but the words popped out. "Why don't you ask the lady where she was born?"

With an exuberant sigh of relief, an animated Shiya raised a hand outward, as if offering it to someone. "Beautiful lady in the pretty white dress, my mama wants to know where you were born."

Shiya nodded then faced her mother. "She says she was born right here on this bad land. And the lady also wants me to tell you that she is grateful to you for carrying out her last wish. She says I'm not crazy, but that I'm her very special granddaughter."

Brianna squeezed her eyes shut, hoping that it was all a dream. But the nightmare continued:

"All the brown people want you to know their names. Is that okay, Mama?"

"Sure, why not," Brianna replied in a complacent voice. She kept a poker face as Shiya began naming the dead with perfect pronunciation—a scene straight out of Hollywood:

"Skinny Tom, a coachman; Kholika, the Shongweni girl; Umfunti, also known as Stanley the chimney sweeper; Moses, a butler; Daisy, a maid whose real name is Deliwe; Mabali and Nobuntu, captured slaves from West Africa; Nobuntu the little girl is wearing a pretty crocodile-print dress; Mpande, Nobuntu's Zulu husband; Anele, Zhana, and Thaka of Tswanas kraal; Kelingo, a field worker; Lamella, the cook; Maekela and Isona, kitchen helpers; Naomi, a prostitute, but not out of choice." Little Shiya paused. "Oh, and way too many black boys to name who tell me they were hunted down like animals. But there is a pretty lady standing next to you, Mama. Her name is Shiya, like mine. She says she is *your* mother and *my* grandmother."

Brianna's heart jumped to her throat. She leaned against a driveway wall for support. Naturally, she hadn't seen anyone, but she had experienced an overwhelming feeling of presence.

"Mama, what's the matter?" Shiya asked. "Have I said something bad?"

"No, darling," Brianna said, hugging her daughter closely. "When we get back to the hotel, I'm going to tell you the real truth about the pretty lady you see. In the meantime, please tell these poor dead people that although there will never be true justice for them, I hope they will forgive me for not having this dreadful place burned down sooner."

"Tell them yourself, Mama. They surround you with love and gratitude in their hearts."

Impromptu words flowed from Brianna. "You are all free now. Please go to your Kingdom of Light. Your enslaved bodies were tormented, but your pure souls have been freed for all eternity."

Out of the blue, a strong Santa Ana-like wind came out of nowhere and rustled dead foliage around the mother and daughter. Debris twirled into the air, raising fine clouds of debris. Then it was gone. Complete calm descended over the desolate ground. It seemed as though the brutal history—the man-hunting killing fields and sadistic enslavement of so many people was swept clean away. But the African God of Wind could not cast forth one soul who would wander this place forever—Shiya, aka Lynette Hallworthy-Martinez.

This was verified by little Shiya when she announced, "Mama, all the brown people are gone, but my grandmother remains. She wants to tell you something."

Brianna shook her head.

After a few minutes of inaudible whisperings, Shiya shared the conversation. "Grandma says she wants you to sell her pink diamonds, her gold jewelry, this property, and Maria's mansion in Sicily. With the proceeds you must build schools, orphanages, hospitals, and homes for the elderly African people so that poverty will never again lead them to enslavement. The brutal history of this continent must never be repeated."

"Mother," Brianna said, looking at her feet. "I fulfilled your last wish without question, to have this evil place burned to the ground, and I will do my best to comply with your new wishes. I owe that much to you because I failed you when you were alive, but I promise I won't fail you again. I love you."

"I know you do, Mama. And I love you, too," little Shiya piped up, not thinking that her mother was referring to the presence of the disembodied spirit.

The family's time at the infamous site was over. A new chapter was waiting to be written now.

Brianna smiled at her special daughter.

"Let's go back to the hotel, have something to eat, and get packed for our trip to see Amalonda."

As mother and daughter approached the Land Rover holding hands, they spotted an enormous cloud of dust heading their way. A vehicle was rushing at top speed toward them. Brianna frowned. Before she could make sense of the arrival, the doors of an SUV were flung open. Two heavyset African men brandishing military-style automatics and large knife holders strapped to army belts charged at them. The shorter of the two commanded, "Get on the ground! Get on the ground!"

Pure terror sent mother and daughter to the dirt. Every hair on her bodies stood up. Brianna's mind screamed, "Oh, my God! Is this really happening? Who the hell are they? What do they want?"

With fearful thoughts racing through her head, a trembling

Little Shiya spoke softly. "Who are they, Mama? What do they want?"

"I don't know, darling. Please keep very still and don't say another word."

From the open window of the Land Rover, Alberto witnessed the unimaginable scene and quickly ducked behind the passenger seat. He tried desperately to conceal himself with a travel blanket.

Face down on the ground, Brianna felt like a little bug about to be trampled. This wasn't how she had pictured her death.

The pungent, skunk-like odor of marijuana was overwhelming.

Brianna wasn't sure how to piece her disturbed thoughts together, but her brain numbed when one of the attackers put a knife to her throat. The carbon steel blade dug painfully into her neck as he ordered her to cooperate. "Don't scream, or I'll slice your vocal cords," he threatened.

Brianna was panic frozen, until she found a shaky voice. "I have money and credit cards, but please don't hurt my children! All they have is me!"

As an awful thought crossed her mind, fear gripped more tightly: *Carjackers!*

She couldn't let them take the rental with her son in it, so she hurriedly added. "I have diamonds and gold jewelry in my hotel room."

It seemed like a forever silence before the knife brandishing attacker stated, "We did your bidding, white bitch. We burned the place down. Where is the rest of our money?"

"Oh, my God! Is that what this is about?" Brianna thought.

She had not made the connection until now because her previous communications with the arsonists had been by telephone. When the knife retracted, Brianna rolled over and sat upright. She could barely contain her fear, but in a calm, programmed voice, she made herself heard. "I paid you a half million U.S. dollars, wired into an account of your choice. That was the deal."

Pacing, clearly agitated, her angry attacker spat, "You rich white bitches are all the same. We want a million U.S. dollars now, or we will kill you and your kid!"

He did not know of the other child hiding in the rental vehicle.

An impulsive Brianna, fighting fire with fire, snapped, "Are you out of your friggin' minds! I don't carry *that* amount in my back pocket! The only way I can get my hands on that kind of money is through a bank, and don't think for one moment that it will be that easy to transfer cash from my foreign account without any questions."

The brothers, probably in substance abuse distress, began ranting and raving in their native tongue. The shorter of the two stuck his hand in his pocket and removed a rolled marijuana cigarette. They shared the smoke. It seemed to bring calm, albeit temporarily.

"My brother will drive you to the bank," the taller of the two said. "And the price has gone up. We want two million in cash."

Brianna inhaled sharply. It was a ridiculous demand. How would she get away with withdrawing such a large amount without bank scrutiny? Nevertheless, in order to become her own hostage negotiator, she had to tread lightly. It was beyond stressful, but she had to regain composure and calm the unpredictable duo.

"I will do as you say, whatever you want, but please don't harm my *children!*"

The shorter of the two scratched his head. Then he glanced over to the Land Rover.

A terrorized Alberto, clasping on to the travel blanket, was dragged from the car, screaming.

In order to survive this nightmarish ordeal, Brianna begged, "Please, please don't harm my son. I will do anything you ask!"

The taller of the two kicked Brianna in the small of her back. "Shut up, bitch, while I think!"

Brianna's knees drew up. The pain was unbearable, but she uttered not a sound.

Plastic zip-ties bound the hands, wrists, and legs of the mother and her children. Their mouths were sealed shut with duct tape. Alberto and Shiya were carried like bags of sugar to a dense clump of evergreen bushes where they would be concealed. Even though the estate was isolated from suburban life, many hunters had been known to roam these parts in search of game.

Back to back, the siblings' wild eyes spoke of their terror. One of the arsonist brothers stayed with the children as their guard. "Don't move a muscle until your mother returns with our money."

Pale and robotic, Brianna couldn't believe this was happening. She turned the ignition key and drove away with a gun cocked and pointed at her heart.

Brianna headed for the City of Durban, approximately fifty minutes away.

Her hands, moist with sweat, gripped the steering wheel tightly. In survival mode, her thoughts tumbled: "Should she crash the car? But what if it didn't kill him? What if they both perished? Her motherly instincts kicked in. If she died, how would anyone know about Shiya and Alberto's captivity? Should she open the driver's door and jump out? What if a passing vehicle on the three-lane highway drove over her? No. She did not want her children to grow up without her! The only realistic option remaining was the bank. But would she be able to attract attention and alert the staff to her hostage-for-ransom plight? And then what? Would her kidnapper have time to call his brother?"

As if reading her mind, her kidnapper raised his eyes to meet hers. "Don't even think of getting smart with me, lady, or I will call my brother on his cell phone. He will cut your kids' throats and disembowel them." An evil chortle followed. "And believe me, he is good at it ... lots of practice gutting pigs on a farm."

Brianna suppressed the bile that was threatening to regurgitate and responded meekly. "Trust me. I will not do anything to harm my children. Okay?"

Brianna and her captor arrived at the National Bank.

She was ordered to park the vehicle close to the main entrance. The hard-faced man handed her a canvas carryall. "The money goes in here," he said. "I will accompany you into the bank, and if you make a peep to anyone, your kids will die. Tell the cashier that you have made a cash deal on a house you want to buy from me."

What the kidnapper did next blew her mind. He undressed and discarded his military jacket and trousers. Underneath he was wearing a good quality suit and crisp white shirt. He pulled out a tie and knotted it neatly.

Brianna looked at him with disgust. She wanted to get this awful charade over with, return to her children, get on the next flight home, and never return to this godforsaken country.

Inside the air-conditioned bank, Brianna presented the teller with the withdrawal slip for the sum of one million dollars. Before entering the bank, she had reasoned with her abductor that the higher amount demanded would, for sure, attract attention. Brianna was knowledgeable about bank policies regarding large cash withdrawals. It was too risky, she had said. He had reluctantly agreed.

"I will need to see three pieces of ID, please" the bank teller requested in a polite but official voice that showed no concern with the large withdrawal amount.

Brianna handed over her passport, driver's license, and a credit card bearing her photo ID.

"One moment, please," responded the teller.

Holding her breath, Brianna watched the young woman make her way over to an older white man sitting at a desk. With heads lowered, they spoke in low voices. The manager got up from his desk and walked over to Brianna and the poker-faced man beside her.

"Good afternoon, Mrs. Risso. My name is Paul Vanguard, the manager of this bank. You have requested an extremely large sum. I must ask you for a satisfactory explanation as to the purpose of this withdrawal. I am afraid it is bank policy."

Brianna wanted to yell at him: "Is it also bank policy to allow children to be murdered! It is a matter of life and death, idiot." Instead, with a racing heart, she responded articulately. "I understand your need to comply with banking policy ethics, but it is *my* money. You see, I want to buy a seafront residence through the realtor here," she indicated her companion, who smiled and nodded in acceptance of the lie. "Are you going to give me *my* money from *my* account, or should I take my business somewhere else?"

A fine piece of acting because it worked!

Brianna drummed her fingers impatiently as she waited for the money to be counted. Brianna couldn't help but visualize her frightened, trussed-up children held by a "loose cannon" pig butcher.

For the first time in a long while, Brianna prayed under her breath. "Please, God, let this transaction take place safely. Make them hurry so I can save my children. And I promise You, I will never drink again."

Brianna and her hijacker, who was clasping the heavy bag, finally emerged from the bank and climbed into the Land Rover.

The relieved woman drove out of the bank parking lot with a parking ticket flapping under one windshield wiper.

Not a word was said between the two occupants of the car. Thanks to small mercies, the grinning man did not mention the diamonds and jewelry offered earlier. He was too busy counting the bundles of banded $100 bills. It made Brianna sick to her stomach. Nothing would have delighted her more than to grab the automatic resting at his feet and shoot the bastard dead.

Her angry foot hit the gas pedal. She was doing well over the urban speed limit of 60km/h. When she hit the freeway, the speedometer flickered between 130km/h and 140km/h, way beyond the 120km/h limit.

Fortuitously, she did not spot one police cruiser. Had she been pulled over, the open bag of cash, a loaded weapon, a hunting knife, and the smell of marijuana would have led to more than a speeding ticket. Brianna gave herself a mental slap for speeding. She couldn't trust luck. She slowed down the vehicle.

An hour later, a dust cloud enveloped the Land Rover as it jerked to a halt on the Hallworthy Estate.

Brianna didn't wait for instructions. She jumped out of the driver's seat and ran toward her children, who were groaning under their mouth restraints. She gently removed the tape.

"It's okay, my darlings. Mama is here. It's all over," she said tearfully.

She faced the children's keeper and, in a stern voice, said, "Your brother has the money. He is waiting for you. Cut the ties off my children so we can leave."

A sharp blade easily sliced through the zip-ties, and the children fell into their mother's arms. As they clung to each other, the hostage-taker sauntered away—as if nothing unusual had happened. He joined his brother, who was loading the bag of cash into their SUV. A sigh of relief escaped her lips as she watched the cloud of dust circling behind the departing vehicle.

"Let's get the hell out of here," she said, helping her weeping children to their feet. "I'm so sorry for what has happened to you. I will never let anyone hurt my children ever again. We are going home to Sicily as soon as I can get a flight."

Alberto was the first to speak. "Call the police now, Mama."

"I can't," she lied. "They took my cell phone, but I will call them when we get to the nearest phone."

She ordered the children into their rental car, locked the doors, and, with a shaking hand, frantically turned on the ignition. The Land Rover's engine sputtered. She removed the key and tried again, digging deeper into the switch. The engine wouldn't start. It was as dead as a doornail. Had the high speeds caused the problem? The empty fuel tank indicator answered her question. Panicked, Brianna could have kicked herself. She had been so preoccupied with her car racing that she ignored the warning light reminder.

"Oh, God, not now," she cried. *This can't be happening!*

To her horror, she saw their assailants in the rearview mirror, driving toward the disabled Land Rover.

Frantically, Brianna turned the ignition key. "Please, please start!" she cried.

Then all hell broke loose. It sounded like a war zone.

Staccato rattling shattered the still air as hails of bullets thudded into the vehicle. Windows shattered and holes appeared in the door panels.

The merciless harbingers of death and betrayal laughed their heads off.

"Well, that solves the problem," one of them coldly announced to his partner-in-crime as they drove off, leaving the bullet-ridden Land Rover behind.

Their three bodies, awash with blood, were found later that day by a passing hunter.

"10111 (911), what's your emergency?"

"Please send an ambulance and the police, and quickly, to the old Hallworthy place on Plantation Road," a voice urged. "There are two children covered in blood, too much blood loss to sustain life, shot to death." He paused as if to catch his breath. "There is a woman, probably their mother, barely alive. She has been shot several times. I've found a very weak pulse. Please hurry."

The operator immediately cautioned, "Do not move the injured woman or disturb the crime scene. What is your name, sir?"

"My name is Dr. Peter Siegel. I'm afraid I had to remove the woman from the car in order to perform CPR on a flat surface."

"Please stay on the line, Dr. Siegel," the emergency operator requested.

A few moments later, she confirmed. "The ambulance and the police are on their way."

An unconscious Brianna took the journey with her deceased children to Addington Hospital, the same hospital in which her mother had a bullet surgically removed from her head.

There, the children were taken to the mortuary and Brianna to the operating room.

Above the hospital roof, a strange cloud formation shaped like angel's wings suddenly turned dark. Raindrops, like crystal tears, fell upon the poor victims of this senseless violence.

The Hallworthy demons had failed to claim the last of their bloodline. Brianna was desperately clinging to life on the operating table. Would she want to survive without her children? Would the guilt of surviving the massacre break her?

Certainly, the final sounds from Alberto and Shiya's small mouths would have been a desperate cry for *her* help!

Six hours later, Brianna opened her eyes in the recovery room. Disorientated, she tried to make sense of her surroundings. "Where am I?" she mumbled. "Why is my head hurting?

Visible to the human eye, a radiant figure in full form approached Brianna's bedside. The disembodied spirit, arms outstretched, mouthed, "I've come to take you home, my beautiful daughter."

*–The End–*

# Afterword

*Diabolical slavery still thrives*
*after the 150th anniversary*
*of the Emancipation Proclamation*

On September 22, 1862, in the United States of America, President Abraham Lincoln set the date of *freedom* for his country's three million slaves. The opening statement of the Declaration of Independence of 1776 reads:

*"We believe these truths to be self-evident: that all men are created*
*equal with the right to life, liberty, and the pursuit of happiness."*

In 1865, almost 100 years after the Declaration of Independence, the Thirteenth Amendment extended this sentiment to "Negroes."

To this day, involuntary servitude is outlawed, and yet, *it still exists!* **Why?**

"In its many dark forms, slavery did not die when America abolished it in the 1800s and Great Britain in 1834," says Lucia

Mann, author of *Beside an Ocean of Sorrow*, *Rented Silence*, *Africa's Unfinished Symphony*, and *A Veil of Blood Hangs over Africa*, the final book in the series. Mann's books are historical, African-set novels that explore British Colonial slavery in South Africa and the victims who survived the institutional brutality before and after abolishment.

According to the United Nations, there are more than 37 million slaves worldwide, a number that represents more than twice the number of those who were enslaved over the 400 years that transatlantic slavers trafficked humans to work in the Americas. ***Why?***

"Today, many slaves are forced into prostitution while others are used as unpaid laborers to manufacture goods bought in the United States, Canada, and globally," Mann says. "It's almost impossible to buy clothes or goods anymore without inadvertently supporting the slave trade." ***Why?***

Human trafficking has become the second fastest growing criminal industry worldwide behind drug trafficking, according to the U.S. Department of Justice. It's a $32 billion industry, and half of those trafficked are children. Half of the billions spent come from industrialized nations, according to the National Human Trafficking Resource Center. ***Why?***

# Fifty-five ghastly, sobering, little-known facts about modern day slavery/human trafficking

1.  Approximately seventy-five to eighty percent of human trafficking is for sex.

2.  Researchers note that sex trafficking plays a major role in the spread of HIV.

3.  There are more human slaves in the world today than ever before in history.

4.  There are an estimated 27 million adults and 13 million children around the world who are victims of human trafficking.

5.  Human trafficking not only involves sex and labor, but also organ harvesting.

6.  Human traffickers often use a Sudanese phrase "use a slave to catch slaves," meaning traffickers send "broken-in girls" to recruit younger girls into the sex trade. Sex traffickers often train girls themselves, raping them and teaching them sex acts.

7.  Eighty percent of North Koreans who escape into China are women. Nine out of ten of those women become victims of human trafficking, often for sex. If the women complain, they are deported back to North Korea, where they are thrown into gulags or executed.

8.  An estimated 30,000 victims of sex trafficking die each year from abuse, disease, torture, and neglect. Eighty percent of those sold into sexual slavery are under twenty-four years old, and some are as young as six.

9.  Ludwig "Tarzan" Fainberg, a convicted trafficker, said, "You can buy a woman for $10,000 and make your money back in a week if she is pretty and young. Then everything else is profit."

10. A human trafficker can earn twenty times what he or she paid for a girl. Provided the girl was not physically brutalized to the point of ruining her beauty, the pimp can sell her again for a greater price because he has already trained her and broken her spirit. This saves the future buyers the hassle. A 2003 study in the Netherlands found that, on average, a single sex slave earned her pimp at least $250,000 a year.

11. Although human trafficking is often a hidden crime and accurate statistics are difficult to obtain, researchers estimate that more than 80 percent of trafficking victims are female. Over fifty percent of human trafficking victims are children.

12. The end of the Cold War has resulted in the growth of regional conflicts and the decline of borders. Many rebel groups turn to human trafficking to fund military actions and garner soldiers.

13. According to a 2009 Washington Times article, the Taliban buys children as young as seven years old to act as suicide bombers. The price for a child suicide bomber ranges between $7,000 to $14,000.

14. UNICEF estimates that 300,000 children younger than 18 are currently trafficked to serve in armed conflicts worldwide.

15. Human traffickers are increasingly trafficking pregnant women for their newborns. Babies are sold on the black market, where the profit is divided between the traffickers, doctors, solicitors, border officials, and others. The mother is usually paid less than what is promised her, citing the cost of travel and the creation of false documents. A mother might receive as little as a few hundred dollars for her baby.

16. More than 30 percent of all trafficking cases in 2007 to 2008 involved children sold into the sex industry.

17. Western presence in Kosovo, such as NATO troops and civilians, has fueled the rapid growth of sex trafficking and forced prostitution. Amnesty International has reported that NATO soldiers, UN police, and Western aid workers "operated with near impunity in exploiting the victims of the sex traffickers."

18. Lady Gaga's *Bad Romance* video is about human trafficking. In the video, Gaga is trafficked by a Russian bathhouse into sex slavery.

19. Human trafficking is the only part of transnational crime in which women are significantly represented—as victims, as perpetrators, and as activists fighting this crime.

20. Global warming and severe natural disasters have left millions homeless and impoverished, which has created desperate people who are easily exploited by human traffickers.

21. Over 71 percent of trafficked children show suicidal tendencies.

22. After sex, the most common form of human trafficking is forced labor. Researchers argue that as the economic crisis deepens, the number of people trafficked for forced labor will increase.

23. Most human trafficking in the United States occurs in New York, California, and Florida.

24. According to United Nations Children's Fund (UNICEF), over the past 30 years, over 30 million children have been sexually exploited through human trafficking.

25. Several countries rank high as source countries for human trafficking, including Belarus, the Republic of Moldova, the Russian Federation, Ukraine, Albania, Bulgaria, Lithuania, Romania, China, Thailand, and Nigeria.

26. Belgium, Germany, Greece, Israel, Italy, Japan, the Netherlands, Thailand, Turkey, and the U.S. are ranked very high as destination countries of trafficked victims.

27. Women are trafficked to the U.S. largely to work in the sex industry (including strip clubs, peep and touch shows, massage parlors that offer sexual services, and prostitution). They are also trafficked to work in sweatshops, domestic servitude, and agricultural work.

28. Sex traffickers use a variety of ways to "condition" their victims, including subjecting them to starvation, rape, gang rape, physical abuse, beating, confinement, threats of violence toward the victim and victim's family, forced drug use, and shame.

29. Family members will often sell children and other family members into slavery; the younger the victim, the more money the trafficker receives. For example, a ten-year-old named Gita was sold into a brothel by her aunt. The now twenty-two-year-old recalls that when she refused to work, the older girls held her down and stuck a piece of cloth in her mouth so no one would hear her scream as she was raped by a customer. She later contracted HIV.

30. Human trafficking is one of the fastest growing criminal enterprises because it holds relatively low risk and high profit potential. Criminal organizations are increasingly attracted to human trafficking because, unlike drugs, humans can be sold repeatedly.

31. Human trafficking is estimated to surpass the drug trade in less than five years. Journalist Victor Malarek reports that it is primarily men who are driving human trafficking, specifically trafficking for sex.

32. Victims of human trafficking suffer devastating physical and psychological harm. However, due to language barriers, lack of knowledge about available services, and the frequency with which traffickers move victims, human trafficking victims and their perpetrators are difficult to catch.

33. In approximately 54 percent of human trafficking cases, the recruiter is a stranger, and in 46 percent of the cases, the recruiters know the victim. Fifty-two percent of human trafficking recruiters are men, 42 percent are women, and 6 percent are both men and women.

34. Human trafficking around the globe is estimated to generate a profit of anywhere from $9 billion to $31.6 billion. Half of these profits are made in industrialized countries.

35. Some human traffickers recruit handicapped young girls, such as those suffering from Down syndrome, into the sex industry.

36. According to the FBI, a large human-trafficking organization in California in 2008 not only physically threatened and beat girls as young as twelve to work as prostitutes, they also regularly threatened them with witchcraft.

37. Human trafficking is a global phenomenon that is fueled by poverty and gender discrimination.

38. Human traffickers often work with corrupt government officials to obtain travel documents and seize passports.

39. Women and girls from racial minorities in the U.S. are disproportionately recruited by sex traffickers in the U.S.

40. *The Sunday Telegraph* in the U.K. reports that hundreds of children as young as six are brought to the U.K. as slaves each year.

41. Japan is considered the largest market for Asian women trafficked for sex.

42. Airports are often used by human traffickers to hold "slave auctions," where women and children are sold into prostitution.

43. Due to globalization, every continent in the world has been involved in human trafficking, including a country as small as Iceland.

44. Many times, if a sex slave is arrested, she is imprisoned while her trafficker is able to buy his way out of trouble.

45. Today, slaves are cheaper than they have ever been in history. The population explosion has created a great supply of workers, and globalization has created people who are vulnerable and easily enslaved.

46. Human trafficking and smuggling are similar but not interchangeable. Smuggling is transportation based. Trafficking is exploitation based.

47. Sex traffickers often recruit children because not only are children more unsuspecting and vulnerable than adults, but there is a high market demand for young victims. Traffickers target victims on the telephone, on the Internet, through friends, at the mall, and in after-school programs.

48. Human trafficking has been reported in all fifty states, Washington, D.C., and in some U.S. territories.

49. The FBI estimates that over 100,000 children and young women are trafficked in America today. They range in age from nine to nineteen, with the average age being eleven. Many victims are not just runaways or abandoned, but are from "good" families who are coerced by clever traffickers.

50. Brazil and Thailand are generally considered to have the worst child sex trafficking records.

51. The AIDS epidemic in Africa has left many children orphaned, making them especially vulnerable to human trafficking.

52. Nearly 7,000 Nepali girls as young as nine years old are sold every year into India's red-light district—or 200,000 in the last decade. Ten thousand children between the ages of six and fourteen are in Sri Lanka brothels.

53. Human trafficking victims face physical risks, such as drug and alcohol addiction, STDs, sterility, miscarriages, forced abortions, and vaginal and anal trauma, among others. Psychological effects include clinical depression, personality and dissociative disorders, suicidal tendencies, PTSD, and Complex PTSD.

54. The largest human trafficking case in recent U.S. history occurred in Hawaii in 2010. Global Horizons Manpower, Inc., a labor-recruiting company, bought 400 immigrants in 2004 from Thailand to work on farms in Hawaii. They were lured with false promises of high-paying farm work, but instead their passports were taken away and they were held in forced servitude until they were rescued in 2010.

55. According to the U.S. State Department, human trafficking is one of the greatest human rights challenges of this century, both in the United States and around the world.

# Millions of Modern Day Slaves Need Our Advocacy

If we fail to address this plague of crimes against humanity, we'll never be able to bring an end to the unconscionable, heinous trade in human flesh.

### WHAT CAN WE DO IF WE SUSPECT A CASE OF HUMAN TRAFFICKING?

- **Catholic Sisters congregations:** (888) 373-7888.

- **Victims hotline and online tips reporting:** The *Modern Day Slavery Reporting Center*, created by Mann, is a Web site that makes it easy for third parties to report suspicious activity by clicking "File a Report." This section allows visitors to volunteer information. www.ReportModernDaySlavery.org

- **Federal Bureau of Investigation, report human trafficking:** (888) 428-7581. This number can be used 9 A.M. to 5 P.M. EST to report concerns to the FBI. They also offer plenty of information about human trafficking on their Web site.

- **Various easy-to-find anti-trafficking organizations:** Type in "human trafficking" on any online search engine, and several sites will appear promoting various methods of combating modern slavery. The important part, Mann says, is to follow through on an interest to help.

*"Although I have a firsthand account of dealing with national prejudice and human slavery, many other people are compelled to help victims of human trafficking because freedom is a universal desire,"* Mann says. *"Any individual can make a difference in someone's life. That is the motive behind my books. I want victims to know that, like me, their tragedy can become their triumph."*

TOGETHER LET US TIRELESSLY
PURSUE THE FIVE A'S:

- **Awareness**
- **Acknowledgement**
- **Action**
- **Abolition**
- **Accountability**

WE ARE MAKING A DIFFERENCE!

www.LuciaMann.com

*Help Report Modern Day Slavery*
**www.ReportModernDaySlavery.org**

# About Lucia Mann

Lucia Mann, humanitarian and activist, was born in British colonial South Africa in the wake of World War II. She now resides in Fauquier, British Columbia, Canada. She retired from freelance journalism in 1998, and wrote her books to give voice to those who have suffered and are suffering brutalities and captivity.

Visit www.LuciaMann.com and
www.ReportModernDaySlavery.org for more
information on how you can help alleviate
the scourge of modern-day slavery.